Devoured BY EDEN

INTERNATIONAL BESTSELLING AUTHOR

JADE MAY

DEVOURED BY

BY

EDEN

MEMBERS ONLY

ISBN: 978-1-7635917-5-2

Formatting and Chapter Art: Design by Kage
Cover Art: Design by Kage
Editing: Spice Me Up Editing and Penny Carroll
Proofreading: Stacey's Bookcorner Editing

To those living with invisible chronic illness:
I see your strength, even when the world doesn't.
Your resilience is not quiet. It's fierce.
You carry pain no one else can feel and still keep showing up.
This one's for you.
You are powerful. You are seen.
You are badass.

Author's Note

Dear reader,

Thank you so much for choosing my book to read. I hope you enjoy it.

Devoured by Eden is the third book in the *Eden* series, a collection of interconnected standalones. Please be aware that it contains mature and graphic scenes, along with language that is suitable for those who are 18+. It also contains scenes that may be triggering to some readers. These include: chronic illness, medical emergencies and procedures, depictions of blood and gore, death and grief, life-threatening situations, and elements of BDSM including daddy kink and cockwarming.

Much love,
Jade xx

CHAPTER ONE

Chloe

Present, 7 a.m.

If I puke one more time before rounds, I might have to call it a personal best. I'm so fucking tired I could cry. This is bone-deep, knees-buckling, "I might pass out on the bathroom floor" exhaustion. The kind that makes your brain lag like a buffering video and wonder if you can pause... *everything* for a second to catch up.

The stench of bile wafts up from the porcelain bowl. I lean over the toilet, spitting out the last of the acid that burned its way up my throat. My whole body shakes and shivers.

Grabbing a fistful of paper, I swipe my mouth and flush before I gag again. With my forearms bracing on the seat, I squeeze my eyes shut, trying to breathe through it.

In. Out. Three deep breaths.

I push to standing, legs wobbling, head spinning—and all I can think is: *of course it happens today.* Murphy's law is such a bitch. And for what? One stupid slice of pizza. Probably that pineapple. I bet it was the fucking pineapple.

I stagger to the sink, splash cold water on my face, and scrub my hands, the sting sharp against my skin. It's a fleeting relief before the next wave of nausea hits. Pressing a wet palm to the back of my neck, I count down the seconds until the dizziness fades.

My hand dives into my pocket, finds the anti-nausea pills by touch. I toss back two and swallow them with a palmful of tap water. When I look in the mirror, bloodshot eyes, blotchy skin, and smudged mascara stare back at me. If someone walked in right now, they'd probably guess I'd been partying for a week—not puking up in a hospital toilet on my first day at work.

"Confident. Capable. In control," I tell my reflection—my mantra since last night. "You've got this."

I yank my ponytail tighter, like I'm strapping on armor, square my shoulders, and push open the bathroom door.

St. Vincent's ER reeks of bleach, antiseptic, and poor life choices. IV drip machines beep in rhythm with heart monitors in a sad hospital remix, complete with moans and cries in the background. It's chaos, sure, but weirdly choreographed. Everyone's dancing to a disaster they've practiced a hundred times.

Two people in green scrubs like mine linger near the entrance. The guy's gripping his notepad, wide-eyed and blinking, as if he just realized med school didn't cover this part. The girl next to him? Cool as ice. Her self-assurance either comes from knowing her shit—or being completely delusional. Hard to tell yet.

"Hey, you guys interns?" I ask, making my way toward them.

"Yeah," the guy replies, stepping forward. "Jaxon. But you can call me Jax."

I shake his hand. "Chloe."

Jesus, he looks *young*. I mean, *barely legal* young. I know I've got the baby-face curse too—great for Eden, not so much here—but Jax? He could have easily wandered straight out of a Disney Channel audition and into his dad's scrubs. Total baby-deer energy: wide eyes, fragile frame, one stern voice away from snapping in half. I want to swaddle him in a weighted blanket and tell him everything's going to be okay.

"Nice to meet you," he adds, cheeks flaring red. Even his ears blush. It's kind of cute.

The woman next to him rolls her eyes.

"Dr. Sienna Rhodes," she announces crisply, smile razor-sharp. "And you can call me Dr. Rhodes."

She gives me the once-over, slow and deliberate. Her lip twitches, and I catch that glint in her eye: *challenge accepted.*

Awesome. Nothing says female empowerment like being eye-fucked by Regina George in scrubs.

"Napoleon Dynamite and I were starting to think you'd bailed. Come on," she says, already striding off.

"I told you not to call me that," Jax mutters.

I bite my lip hard. The resemblance is... uncanny. All he's missing is the perm and a VOTE FOR PEDRO badge.

"Relax, it's a term of endearment," Sienna chirps, walking backward, hands up in faux innocence. "We're friends, right?"

"Sure." He sighs and shoots me a look—half pleading, half disbelief.

I shrug. *Welcome to the jungle, Bambi.*

We approach the ER central station, and I barely register the man perched on the edge of the desk, flipping through a chart with his back to us. Staff are already gathering, pulled toward him as if the department pivots on his presence.

Then he turns.

And my feet freeze. Someone's yanked the plug on my motor cortex.

I blink once. Twice. *Nope. Still there.* That jawline. That mouth. That stupidly broad back I've definitely clawed at. And that gruff American voice—casually chatting to a nurse as if it hasn't whispered filth against my neck.

No.

Fucking.

Way.

The man who's had his lips on every inch of me is now standing under hospital-grade fluorescents, flipping through charts like he's in charge of something other than my orgasms.

At *my* hospital.

"Oh shit," I whisper under my breath.

"You coming?" Jax glances back at me.

I nod and somehow move, praying my legs won't betray me by collapsing mid-stride. The bile makes a dramatic comeback, burning up my throat, demanding an encore performance.

Z looks up. His gaze sweeps across the group, then hits me. Dead on.

For a split second, his eyes widen. Then narrow, fast, shutting down.

To everyone else, it's nothing. Just a blink.

To me? It's a siren. Neon red, screaming *ABORT MISSION* in the middle of the ER.

I know that look.

Recognition.

And worse—dismissal.

"Good morning, good morning. I'm Dr. Zachery Bennett, but feel free to call me Dr. Zac."

His tone is smooth, professional, a far cry from the dirty groans whispered in the dark. I roll my lips inward, trying not to smile when I hear his full name.

"This morning we've got some new faces joining us. Let's start with our Resident Medical Officer, Dr. Hannah Ellis. She's joining us for a second rotation in our department."

A brunette with glasses gives a stiff wave. "Hey! Glad to be back," she says, shoving her hands into the pockets of her white coat.

Zac glances at the clipboard in his hand, then nods toward Jax. "Dr. Jaxon Wells, I presume? Intern, second rotation."

"Oh, um—hi," Jax says. "Nice to meet you all."

Zac's eyes land on me again.

"Dr. Chloe Monroe," I say. "Intern. First rotation."

His eyes linger a second longer than they did with Jax, then move on to Sienna.

Cool, cool. Definitely not sweating through my scrubs.

"Dr. Sienna Rhodes," she says with a smile you wear when you've already decided you're the main character. "Intern. Fourth rotation."

He returns her textbook-professional smile. "Welcome to the Chop Shop," Zac announces, spreading his arms. "Where miracles happen—and we try not to kill anyone before lunch."

It's almost funny how polished he looks in those scrubs and white coat when I know *exactly* how he sounds when he's coming undone.

A nurse leans over from the nearby desk, a red phone wedged between her ear and shoulder. "We got two traumas coming from the helipad. ETA ten minutes."

"Copy that," Zac replies, then gestures toward her. "That's Olivia, our head nurse. She's your boss, your savior, and the person most likely to ruin your life if you screw up. Do what she says—immediately."

Of course the scariest person in the room isn't the guy who's seen me naked; it's the nurse with resting murder face.

Olivia lifts an unimpressed brow, still on the phone.

"Our beds are jammed. Patients are waiting for admissions upstairs, so we're running tight. Be fast, be smart, and don't let anyone die while waiting to be seen. Triage order only."

He gestures toward two other doctors. "Your senior registrars—Dr. Addison Clarke and Dr. Patrick Kensington. You report to them. They report to me."

Hierarchy established. Alpha energy radiating. And now I know who to avoid when shit hits the fan.

"Questions?" he asks, scanning our faces.

Silence.

"Alrighty then. Let's do this."

The six of us trail behind Zac to the first patient. Notepad out. Pen ready.

Dr. Clarke grabs the chart and reads it aloud. "David Morgan. Forty-nine. Head wound after falling from a ladder. Ten stitches."

Zac nods. "Morning, David. How are you feeling?"

"I'm fine," David grumbles. "When can I go home?"

Zac turns to the interns. "Excellent question. Who can tell me why he's still in my ER?"

Before I even think, the words are out of my mouth—muscle memory kicking in like I'm back in finals week, running on caffeine and blind panic.

"What caused Mr. Morgan to fall off the ladder in the first place?" I counter.

Zac's head tilts. His eyes find mine, and for half a second, everything else in the room blurs.

"Well done, Dr. Monroe. That's the right question." He turns back to the group. "David wasn't pushed. Didn't slip. He blacked out and doesn't remember a thing. So, two-point question: what tests are we waiting on before he can be discharged?"

I don't hesitate. "Head CT to rule out intracranial trauma, ECG for arrhythmia, and a full blood panel—electrolytes, glucose, cardiac enzymes."

He stills for a beat, then lifts his gaze to mine again—and just like that, my heart's in its own arrhythmia, and I realize I haven't blinked in what seems like a lifetime.

"Correct."

He turns to the patient. "David, Dr. Monroe will follow up on your labs and make sure we get you out of here soon."

David nods. "Thanks, Doc. Appreciate it."

Zac brushes past me, close enough that I catch a hit of his cologne. My lungs finally remember how to work, and I breathe out. Totally *not* flustered.

"What a suck-up," Sienna mutters as she breezes by.

Wow. That didn't take long.

I already know what she is: queen bee in a lab coat. The type who needs to be the smartest, loudest, and hottest in the room. And I've met her kind before. Hell, I've sat next to her in every science class since puberty. Glitter pens, perfect grades, backhanded compliments. The works.

She wants drama. A sparring partner. Someone to rattle.

Too bad. She can have her little power trip. I'm here to work, learn, and not get steamrolled in the process. Let her swing. I won't flinch.

We move on to the next patient, and it's the same routine. Dr. Kingston walks us through the case—eighteen-year-old woman, drug overdose. Although, I'd hardly call her an adult. She's tiny, all bones and hospital gown, with two terrified parents clinging to each other.

Zac draws the curtain closed behind us after we step out. "Any questions so far?"

Before anyone can answer, Zac's pager goes off. He checks it, brows knitting. "Helipad trauma is now five minutes away."

The way he says it, there's no doubt he's already a dozen steps ahead.

"Kensington, Ellis—you're with me."

The three of them disappear down the hallway without another word.

"Everyone else—start clearing beds," Dr. Clarke instructs, turning to us. "Coordinate with Olivia. Present your cases to senior doctors only before ordering any tests or treatment. Clear?"

We all nod in sync.

Sienna lets out a dramatic groan. "Ugh. I wanted that one. Chopper trauma's where the action is."

Dr. Clarke gives her a sharp look. "Let's not be eager about human suffering, Dr. Rhodes. You'll get your chance."

And just like that, she stalks off, leaving us to sink or swim, no lifeline in sight.

"I refuse to be the IV bitch," Sienna spits under her breath.

I smirk. "Could be worse. You could be the tea-and-toast doctor."

She fake shudders. "Don't even joke about that."

Our conversation fades as we approach the central station.

"Hey Olivia," I say. "Do you have the list of near-discharges?"

"Yep." She hands each of us a couple of charts. "Labs are back on these. If they're clear, they can go. The rest are quick-fix cases. Come on, I'll show you the front."

We follow her through double doors and... *Holy shit.*

The room is bursting at the seams. Every chair is taken. People line the walls. Some are sitting on the floor, heads between their knees. The air is thick with sweat, and that heavy, low-grade panic that never quite leaves a place like this.

Hopelessness clings to everything—skin, fabric, breath.

My stomach tightens. I press a hand low over my abdomen and breathe through it.

Fuck off. Not now. Please, not now.

"This is Triage check-in," Olivia explains. "A nurse gives them a once-over. If they're not dying, they get vitals and labs, then wait."

"For how long?" Jax asks, voice jumping half an octave.

"Two to four hours, if they're lucky. Six to eight is standard."

"Is it always this busy?" I keep my voice steady as the pain in my gut flares.

She snorts. "Nah. It gets worse."

Of course it does.

We push back through the doors into the ER.

"Call me if you need me. Otherwise, fast and efficient, like Dr. Zac said."

"See you on the flip side, losers," Sienna calls over her shoulder, strutting off into a bay.

I roll my eyes and turn to Jax. "Good luck."

"Yeah," he says. "You too."

I open the chart and head to bed fifteen. Please let this be a sprained ankle. Or an ingrown toenail. Something low stakes. This is my first real patient. Not a mannequin or a peer playing Dying Woman Number Three in Sim Lab. A real, actual, live human.

I whisper my new mantra again, "Confident. Capable. In control," and pull the curtain aside.

The man sitting—well, *hovering*—on the edge of the bed is sweating through his hoodie and flinching with every minor movement. Mid-twenties, beard patchy, hair slicked back. He's two seconds from making a run for it. His expression is equal parts panic and embarrassment.

I look down at the chart and bite my lip. The dumbest thing this guy has ever done is going to be officially on his medical records.

He glances up, sees me, and pales. "Oh God. You're the doctor?"

"Intern," I correct. "But I've been trained and supervised. Dr. Clarke will review everything with me. What brings you in today, Mr..." I check the chart again. "Lachlan Young?"

I already know what's wrong. But protocol is protocol. The patient has to explain in their own words why they came to the ER. Still... I can't pretend I'm not a *little* gleeful about making him say it. There's something oddly satisfying about watching a grown man try to wrap medical terminology around an objectively terrible decision.

He hesitates. A long, awkward pause stretches between us, filled only by the faint beep of a monitor in the next bay and the sound of him shifting against the crinkly paper on the bed.

"Well..." He clears his throat. "I, uh. I had a bit of an accident."

"Mm-hmm," I say, nodding solemnly. "What kind of accident?"

His eyes dart to the curtain, then back to me. "It involved a speaker."

I bite the inside of my cheek. "A... speaker?"

He rubs his temple. "Like a Bluetooth speaker. A Beats Pill or whatever. Long. Red. Slimline. You know the kind."

I do. I own one. I haven't used it in forever; it's probably sitting on a shelf somewhere, covered in dust.

The corners of my mouth twitch.

"I see." I jot something down on the clipboard, mostly to give my hands something to do besides applauding him for the commitment. "And how exactly did the speaker come to be... involved?"

He exhales loudly before rushing out, "I slipped. In the shower."

Sure. Let's go with that.

I keep my face locked in neutral professional mode. "You were using it in the shower?"

Lachlan blinks. "The acoustics are amazing."

"Okay. And the speaker is currently...?"

He jabs a thumb toward his lower back. "Still... inside."

Right.

I glance at the notes scribbled in triage: *Patient presents with abdominal discomfort and suspected foreign body retention. Reports onset during solo use of personal electronics in shower.*

I inhale through my nose. "Any bleeding? Pain?"

"No bleeding. Pain? Yeah, like someone shoved Excalibur where the sun doesn't shine."

"Okay," I say, slipping on gloves. "Let's do a quick exam and get an X-ray. We'll need to see where and how deep it is before attempting a retrieval."

He turns a lovely shade of fuchsia. "Do I... have to drop my pants?"

"I'm afraid that's standard protocol for ass-speaker situations."

He groans. "I thought I wouldn't have to bend over for a doctor until I was, like, seventy."

"Honestly? You're not the worst we've had. I once heard about a guy with a pool cue."

He doesn't need to know it's my first day or that he's my first patient.

His brows lift. "Seriously?"

I grin. "Deadly. You're practically vanilla."

He lets out a strained chuckle. "That's... weirdly comforting."

Job done.

I walk him through the process, then help him onto his side. His knees draw up, and I angle the overhead light. There's no visible trauma, no protrusion, which is both good and bad.

"Okay, I'm going to do a gentle rectal exam to confirm placement."

"You say gentle, but I feel like this is going to be the worst moment of my year."

"Trust me," I mutter, "same."

The exam is awkward but quick. I note where the speaker seems to be lodged and how far up. Definitely not something we can pull out without imaging—and possibly some sedation.

"All done. You handled it like a champ."

He exhales. "So... what now?"

"We get an X-ray and let Dr. Clarke review it. Depending on how cooperative your Beats buddy is, we'll decide if it's a manual retrieval or if we need surgical assistance."

He groans again, flopping back onto the pillow.

"My cousin dared me. Said it wouldn't fit."

Finally, the truth.

"And you thought your rectum was the place to prove a point?"

Twenty minutes later, the X-ray's back. And yes—there it is. Clear as day. The *entire* speaker lodged like a rogue submarine halfway up his colon.

Dr. Clarke glances at the image. "Bet that's not what they meant by surround sound," she deadpans.

I snort.

"All right," she says. "You're up. He's stable, the object's smooth, and he's not in acute distress. Prep for retrieval. But if it doesn't budge in two attempts, we call GI."

"Yes, Dr. Clarke."

I'm both thrilled and horrified that she trusts me enough to take the lead. My hands are steady as I glove up again and explain the process to Lachlan. He's game—resigned but cooperative.

"You sure you've done this before?" he asks.

"I've practiced on mannequins. And one very brave med-school tutor who now walks with a limp."

He doesn't laugh. *Tough crowd.*

With Clarke supervising, I use a little gentle traction and a *lot* of lube, sliding in. I coax the speaker down, centimeter by centimeter, until finally—blessedly—it slips free with a soft, wet *pop.*

I hold it up in gloved hands like I'm presenting Simba at Pride Rock.

"Boom," I whisper. "We've got audio."

Clarke clears her throat and murmurs, just loud enough for me to hear, "Clean him up, observe for another hour, and advise him against repeat performances."

I nod, grinning under my mask. "Yes, ma'am."

Lachlan looks up from the bed, pale but grateful. "So... do I owe you dinner or something?"

I smile. "Only if you promise to never look at a speaker in that way again."

"Deal."

I walk away on a high. First patient of the day, and I didn't screw up—or puke. Small victories. But the second I step into the main corridor, the buzz starts to fade, replaced by the familiar, dull ache in my stomach. The meds are already losing their magic.

And then there's Zac.

I still can't wrap my head around it. Of all the hospitals, of all the rotations I could've drawn, I somehow landed *here*. Working under the man who knows what my "O" face looks like. My stomach churns, less rollercoaster, more slow-motion car crash.

Today was always going to be brutal. First day. First rotation. First time pretending I know what I'm doing. But now I've got *him*—towering, confident, and extremely off-limits—walking these halls like it's no big deal.

I turn the corner, cheeks burning, and immediately stop short at what's either a spilled protein shake or a very unapologetic puddle of vomit outside the supply closet.

A janitor glances up from his mop bucket. "Watch it, newbie."

"Thanks," I mumble, sidestepping in time to save my sneakers.

Whoever's up there listening: please. I'm begging you. Don't let me puke, pass out, or completely crash and burn in front of Zac.

I'm already one for three. And my pride?

She's not built for this shit.

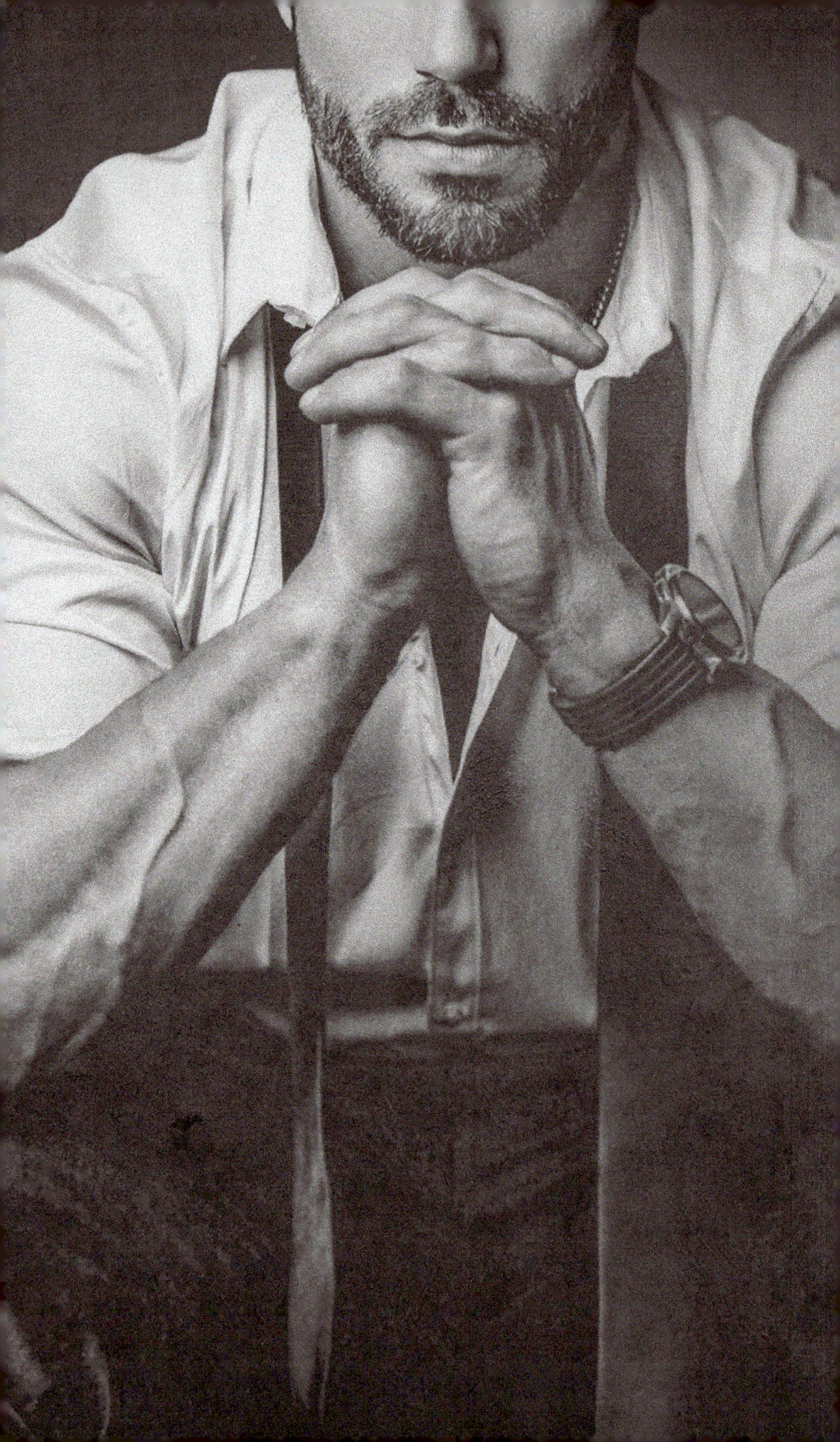

CHAPTER TWO

Past

I'm already counting the seconds until I can exhale. My back's tight, shoulders aching from hours spent hunched over patients. And even here—in the hidden world of Eden—I can still hear the echo of sirens in my skull. It rattles behind my ears, woven into my pulse. Always ready. Always listening.

"Another drink, sir?"

A goddess kneels before me, posture perfect, tray steady. Her eyes stay low, but I can feel her attention. I lift the empty glass and set it gently on her tray.

"I'm good, thank you."

She rises with practiced grace and disappears toward the bar. I want another drink—desperately—but rules are rules. Even at Eden, I'm always on call. My phone's locked in a drawer outside, but I can't switch off the part of me that listens for the beep. The doctor who can't afford to be caught off guard. Madame Anna has strict instructions. If my phone rings, she must find me.

I close my eyes and breathe. *Let it all fall away.*

That's why I keep coming back. Because Eden gives me the one thing the ER never can: silence without consequences. No crashing monitors or begging hands. No families breaking in two while I try to glue together the pieces. Here, everything is measured and controlled. Power offered or taken, and always by choice.

I need this. The control. The quiet beneath it. Because without somewhere like this—a safe space where I set the rules, where no one dies and nothing precious slips through my hands—I'd come apart. Rip at the seams until there's nothing. Eden holds me together. It's the only place I can let go without breaking something sacred. And at least here, I'm not going home to an empty house, dragging shadows behind me like chains. Not tonight.

When I open my eyes, the goddesses are kneeling on the stage. Ten women, each with their head bowed, energy coiled tight. I roll the token in my palm. Number Three. The metal disc is smooth against my skin, warmed by my grip.

The crowd quietens as a woman with long platinum-blonde hair announces from the corner, "Gentlemen, it's time to make your selection."

It doesn't matter who I pick. They all offer the same thing—relief. A place to disappear. A warm body to crawl inside and forget the noise. To bleed out the ache in silence and to fuck the ghosts for a little while. To quiet them. The goddesses give me the illusion of peace. Of forgetting *her*.

I stand and move toward the stage, eyes sweeping the line. And then I stop. Honey-blonde hair falls in loose waves around her face, the ends grazing the top of her breasts. Her chin is tucked, her posture straight, but her energy... it's different.

"Come with me," I instruct, extending my hand.

Her fingers are warm, delicate in my grip. She keeps her head dipped as I lead her from the stage and down the hallway to Room Three.

The door shuts with a soft click behind us, and the silence is instant. Only the sound of my own breath and the soft scuffle of movement fills the air.

When I turn around, she's already stretched out on the bed. She settles in, completely owning the space, one leg bent, head propped on her hand, and those dark, curious eyes watching me. She's built for sin. Long limbs, supple curves, cream-like skin glowing in the low light. Every inch of her is that impossible combination of softness and strength.

I stay standing. Watching. Letting the want tighten in my chest until it stings. She studies me just as intently. We're circling each other in silence.

Every curve of her body is built to tempt. But it's her tits that undo me—high, perfect, begging to be touched. I want them in chains. In clamps. In diamonds. I want to bite them, bruise them, watch them swell under my mouth. Leave her marked, every inch of her skin telling a story only we know.

Fuck.

"You gonna stand and stare all night?" she drawls, lips curved. "Or am I getting that drink?"

The question startles me. My brows lift. "What?"

"Water," she replies, sitting up with a shrug. "Please."

I cross to the minibar and hand her a bottle. She drinks, the line of her throat flexing with each swallow. Dragging in a breath through my nose, I remain still.

She sets the bottle down on the bedside table, eyes fixed on me. "So. What are you looking for tonight?"

I say nothing.

She tries again, head tilting. "Something rough? Or slow? Any kinks you want to try?"

Still, nothing.

She shifts onto her knees, expression unreadable. "Okay… not into talking?"

A pause.

"Correct."

"You need quiet?" she asks gently. "I can do quiet."

I nod once.

She holds my gaze for a long moment, then sits back on her heels and waits. The quiet stretches between us. I don't fill it. And neither does she.

Crossing the room, I lower myself into the chair facing the bed. My body sinks into the leather, my chest easing slightly for the first time today. This is what I needed. Someone willing. Someone *here*, while everything else fades away.

I let my gaze drift over her, from her parted lips to her thighs. She's letting me take her in, and I'm greedy enough to do it at my own pace.

She doesn't fidget or blink. She waits.

Goddamn. This woman understands energy. Tension. She's not just performing—she's listening. Reading the room. Reading *me*.

Casey's voice echoes in my head. Laughter, quick and bright. Then, pain. Endless nights of it.

I clench my jaw.

This girl in front of me isn't anything like Casey. And that's the whole fucking point.

But now she's watching me with something close to softness. There's no pity or concern in her eyes. Only... patience.

It almost makes me flinch.

I rub the tension from my chest and try to bury the ache. This is about control. About holding it, not losing it.

She speaks again, her voice low. "Can I offer you something else?"

I blink out of it. "What did you have in mind?"

"The fantasy," she explains. "The one you came here for."

My pulse kicks.

She shifts again, slow and fluid, hips moving with the grace of a snow leopard. She crawls to the edge of the bed, close enough now that I can smell her—faint perfume with a tang of honey.

She's younger than I expected. But there's nothing immature about her. She *owns* the air in the room.

"You sure you don't want to talk?" she asks, barely above a whisper.

"Yes," I rasp.

She dips her chin. "Then let me speak your language."

Reclining slowly, she allows her knees to fall open.

"Wider," I say.

Her thighs part, slow and sure, revealing her glossy lips.

"Now, show me that pretty pussy," I order, voice rough.

She smiles faintly. "Yes, Daddy."

That title shouldn't land the way it does. But it hits—hot and deep—because it's not a joke. She says it like a truth.

Like she's already *mine*.

She obeys, still watching me, her face open, mouth slightly parted. She's offering something real—herself, without any pretense. Her vulnerability is as naked as her body. And fuck, it's more powerful than anything else she could've done.

She bares herself—pale thighs, flushed folds, swollen and shiny. She's drenched. And she hasn't even touched herself yet.

Slipping one hand down her belly, her stomach flexes, the anticipation tightening her muscles. She strokes down her slit, the soft drag of her fingers creating a frictionless tease. Her hips lift slightly into her hand—automatic and greedy.

Beautiful.

Her breath becomes ragged.

I watch, locked in place. Every subtle twitch of her hips is choreographed by instinct and pure sensation.

A groan catches in my throat.

"Touch your clit," I order.

Her fingers obey, like they've been waiting for permission. She presses lightly at first, gasping at the contact, followed by slow and tight circles. Her lips fall open. Her eyes flutter shut.

"Eyes on me, little one."

They snap open again. Obedient.

When she rubs harder, the sound is slick and obscene in the silence. I shift in the chair, cock straining against my pants, but I don't touch myself.

She starts to pant—short, rhythmic gasps that match the movement of her fingers. Her back arches, and her thighs tense. She's not faking it. She's building.

"Not yet," I say.

Whimpering, her hand stills. Her whole body twitches, straining against herself.

"You're so fucking pretty like this," I tell her. "You know that?"

"Yes, Daddy."

I drag in a breath. That word again. Soft and reverent. Her version of worship.

I've never leaned into the whole daddy kink—not really. But from her, it feels right. Familiar in a way it has no business being. Almost like she's been calling me that for years. It slides beneath my skin and burrows deep, settling into the part of my soul that's been hungry for more and never knew what it was missing.

My cock throbs at the thought of her saying it again—moaning it—while she rides me into the early hours of the morning.

"Two fingers," I order. "Inside."

She presses them in slowly, jaw dropping open at the stretch. I can see the resistance in her muscles, how her cunt grips tight and pulls them deeper. Her face crumples in pleasure.

"Good girl," I whisper. "Now fuck yourself. Slow. Give me a show."

She moves her fingers, working herself open with careful precision. The air between us grows hotter, heavier, saturated with need. My whole body is wired. My skin buzzes.

"More," I instruct.

She thrusts deeper until her knuckles disappear and her palm hits her folds. Her breath chokes.

I move forward in the chair, bracing my elbows on my thighs, and fight the urge to grab her hand and suck her fingers clean.

"You want me to touch you?" I tease.

"Yes," she mewls.

"You want me to taste you?"

"God—yes," she gasps.

I lean in slightly. "Too bad."

She lets out a strangled, frustrated sound. A laugh breaks through it, breathless and wrecked. She loves this—loves the *not-quite-there.*

"You're going to come like this," I demand. "Touch your clit while you fuck yourself."

Obeying, both her hands working in sync—one driving deep, the other circling fast and wild. Her thighs tremble, her skin flushed up to her chest. Her eyes don't leave mine. She wants me to see every bit of it.

Her moans turn frantic.

"Wait."

She stops. Shaking. Sweat beads across her hairline.

"Smack it," I order, voice low. "On your pussy. One slap."

She whimpers but does it anyway. Her hand strikes her folds with a wet *snap.* Her body jolts. Her cunt clenches around her fingers, her breath hits the ceiling.

"Again."

She follows through with tears pricking her eyes.

"Attagirl," I whisper. "Now finish."

Not holding back, she rides her hand hard, the slick slap of her fingers moving faster and faster until her body pulls taut.

"That's it," I praise. "Come for me."

A cry splits the air. High and cracked, ripping out of her.

Her legs go taut, her hips bucking off the mattress. Her body clenches and jerks as the orgasm hits in waves. It rolls through her, shattering whatever control she had left, leaving her gasping.

I reach down and unbuckle my belt with shaking hands. My cock is heavy, red, and soaked at the tip. Wrapping my hand around it, I stroke once, twice.

I could take her right here, right now. Bury myself in her, lose myself in that slick heat, and never come back up. But if I touch her, I won't stop. I'll lose whatever restraint I'm clinging on to. And I can't. This must stay simple.

It's the only rule I haven't broken.

It's just seconds before I let go. I groan, long and low, spilling across her swollen pussy. Without hesitation, she scoops it up, rubs it into herself like it's a sacred gift.

And it is. Because this feels holy. And I'm already half destroyed by it.

Breathing slowly, her body is still, limp against the mattress, pussy smeared with me. Her skin glows, damp with sweat and sex, and her eyes flutter shut before she opens them again and meets my gaze.

She looks... unguarded. And that's what undoes me. Because I wasn't supposed to see *her*. I wasn't supposed to *feel* anything. I was supposed to come, thank her, and leave.

Instead, my chest is tight. My throat closes. A feeling coils beneath my ribs—guilt or need dressed up like desire. I can't tell. I don't want to name it. But it's there. Lodged between my sternum and spine like a blade that won't come out. And I feel the ache every time I drag in a breath.

She sits up on her elbows, thighs still parted, my come slick against her pussy. Her expression is unreadable—quiet and present.

"Are you okay?" she asks gently.

The sincerity in her voice makes me flinch.

She sits up; her hand reaches toward me, fingers curled in hesitation.

"Don't," I whisper.

She freezes with her hand suspended between us. Then slowly, she draws it back, resting it beside her.

"I just wanted to make sure you were all right," she says softly. She's not pushing or demanding. But offering something I've forgotten how to take.

I look at her—*really* look. Flushed and messy and absolutely fucking gorgeous, but none of that is what's getting to me.

It's her calm. Her stillness.

The way she isn't reaching for more, even though I *know* she could. She could ask me anything. She could smile in that smug way girls do when they think they've cracked you. But she doesn't. She allows me my silence.

That's somehow worse.

My fingers shake as I tuck myself into my pants. I run a hand through my hair, sharp and hard enough to sting.

"I can't stay," I rasp.

There's a pause. Then she says, "Okay." With no judgement or disappointment.

Just... *okay*.

I can't breathe. Can't see straight.

Because I want to stay. I want to crawl onto that bed, bury my face between her thighs, and lose hours with her. I want to talk to her. I want her to touch me and mean it. And I can't remember the last time I wanted any of that with someone. But if I do that... I won't come back as someone Casey would recognize. Hell, I'm not even sure I'd recognize myself.

That thought unravels me from the inside. My wife's voice crashes through me again, cruelly vivid.

I feel like I don't know you anymore, Zac. I want to feel like I matter.

I back away.

It feels wrong. My own pulse is too loud.

She watches me go, not moving, with those eyes, steady and warm.

"See you next time?" she asks, softer than silk.

I don't even need to think. "Next time."

Because I know I'll come back.

I leave her there, already etched into my memory.

After all these years of coming to Eden—after all the times I've kept the lines clean and my rules clear—why her? Why now?

For the first time in a long time, I know exactly what I want.

Exactly what I'll come back for.

I know one thing with absolute certainty: I'm fucked.

And I haven't even touched her.

Chapter Three

Chloe

"So, how did this happen?" I ask as I flush the scratches on her chest with saline and blot with gauze.

"We were doing a TikTok dance, and then Mikala went crazy and started clawing at me. Crazy bitch."

I pause mid-dab, glancing up from the angry red wounds. "Wait. Your friend did this?"

"Mikala's my cat."

"You were dancing with your cat? Before eight in the morning?" My voice could sand wood.

"You haven't seen the tabby TikTok challenge?"

"No," I reply. "Can't say I have." I barely have time to scratch my own ass, let alone doom-scroll through viral cat videos.

"Everyone's doing it. I don't know why she freaked out."

I can take a guess. Maybe forcing a cat into human nonsense for likes isn't Mikala's idea of a good time. But sure, blame the cat.

"Well, the good news is these scratches—while deep—don't need stitches. I'll put on some Steri-Strips to hold them together. After a couple of weeks and some scar cream, they'll heal up fine." I toss the bloodied gauze and empty saline tube in the trash. "The laceration on your head's more significant, but we can use glue instead of stitches."

"Really?"

"Yep. Head wounds bleed like horror movies, but it's not as serious as it looks."

"Thank God," she sighs.

"I'll be back with the dressing and glue, then you'll be good to go."

I peel off my gloves and make my way to the central station. I need a minute. I'm still shaky from a night of barfing and I'm only one hour into a twelve-hour shift. I drop into a chair at one of the desks, start charting, and glance around to make sure no one's watching. I crack open my water bottle, dump in a packet of electrolytes I swiped from the staff first-aid kit and take a cautious sip. Pure heaven. My throat is raw, but I don't dare gulp—it'd just be round two of vomit city. No way I'm risking it all coming up again.

Olivia materializes beside me. "How's the Chop Shop treating you so far?"

"Can't complain. One hour down, eleven to go." I manage a smile. "Why do you guys call it that, anyway?"

"Because it starts to feel like an assembly line. Quick fix, next patient, don't look back."

Figures.

"You're doing good, kid. Keep it up."

"Thanks." I take another small sip, letting it sit on my tongue before I swallow. I finish my notes and log everything in the system.

"Dr. Monroe, how's it going?" Dr. Clarke appears, clipboard in hand.

"Perfect timing. I was about to come find you."

"What've you got?"

I hand her the chart. "Twenty-two-year-old female. Three scratches on the chest, one on the forehead—cat attack during a TikTok challenge."

Her raised brow says it all. She signs off and hands it back. "Good work. Keep moving."

"On it."

I'm halfway down the hall, trolley stacked and ready to finish TikTok Chick's glue-up, when Dr. Clarke calls out.

"Dr. Monroe. Hold up a sec." She strides toward me, patient chart under an arm, tugging off a pair of gloves. "I'm getting pulled into a trauma. Bay four's yours." She passes me the clipboard mid-stride, barely breaking pace. "DIY piercing gone wrong. Low priority. You won't need me."

I flip the chart open.

Patient: Renee Dawson. Age: 16. Chief complaint: Facial bleeding, possible infection.

"Piercing?" I ask, already hearing the teenage drama in my head.

"Lip, I think. Safety pin," Clarke says, already making her way to the trauma room. "Simple stuff. Clean it, patch it, talk her down if she's spiraling. You can handle it."

"Right." Because nothing says simple like a teenager with self-inflicted facial trauma.

I reroute to bay four and gently push the curtain aside.

Inside is a teenage girl with a thick black hoodie pulled over her head and sleeves down to her knuckles. She's hunched forward, hands in her lap, and a strategically placed tissue taped to her bottom lip. I catch a glint of metal beneath it—and the faint, unmistakable tang of... vodka?

"Hey! I'm Dr. Monroe," I say brightly, pulling up a stool beside her. "Mind if I take a look?"

She lets out a sigh and shrugs, as if it physically pains her to respond.

I lift the tissue and blink.

"Okay. So... looks like you attempted to pierce your lip."

"Successfully," she corrects, glaring at me from behind a curtain of eyeliner and adolescent rage. "I got it through."

I nod, lips twitching. "Fair enough. Although the word 'successfully' usually implies bloodless, sterile, and ideally done with something other than a safety pin."

"I sterilized my lip. With vodka."

Naturally.

"And the safety pin?"

"Boiled it. For like... a minute."

I hum. "Got it. More doctors should know you can swap medical-grade sterilization for a splash of Grey Goose and some light poaching."

She scowls. "It wasn't Grey Goose. I'm not bougie."

"Well, Renee, can I ask what inspired the... body modification?"

She hesitates. "Wednesday Addams."

Honestly, she pulls it off.

I glance at the thick black eyeliner, combat boots, and black nail polish chipped just enough to say, "I'm too cool to care." It's a whole aesthetic.

"She's iconic," I agree. "But I think even Wednesday would spring for a piercing gun."

She shrugs again, lower lip trembling—not from pain, I realize, but something closer to shame.

I keep my voice light. "All right. Let's take a proper look. You mind?"

She lets me tilt her chin up, her jaw stubborn but not resisting. This close, the damage is obvious. The safety pin is half-in, half-out of her lower lip, which is badly swollen around the puncture site. There's already faint purpling and probably the start of a nasty infection.

"Does it hurt?"

She rolls her eyes. "Duh."

I chuckle. "Just checking. I've heard of people walking in with an entire screwdriver embedded in their thigh saying they're fine. Pain's subjective."

That earns me a small, unwilling twitch at the corner of her mouth. Progress.

I clean the area gently, keeping my movements slow and clinical. She flinches but doesn't pull away.

"I'll need to remove the pin, clean the site more thoroughly, and prescribe a short course of antibiotics."

"Will it scar?"

"If you pick at it? Yes. If you let it heal and follow instructions? Probably not."

She scoffs, visibly deflating. "My mom's gonna kill me."

"Maybe," I reply, glancing at her. "But I'm guessing this isn't really about your lip."

Renee doesn't answer right away. Her fingers twist in her sleeves. "She never lets me do anything, y'know?"

I hold for a second.

"I do know," I tell her softly. "The world feels really big at sixteen. And sometimes the only thing that's yours is your body. So you claim it. With piercings. Tattoos. Hair dye. Whatever makes you feel like you belong to yourself."

She looks at me sharply, teenage suspicion still there, but tempered by curiosity. Teen girls can sniff out condescension faster than a bloodhound.

"But here's the thing," I add. "Taking ownership shouldn't come with an infection."

This time, I earn a small snort. "Noted."

"I need to take the pin out," I say, finding her eyes. "I can numb the area with cream, but that'll take twenty minutes to kick in."

She shifts, already looking restless.

"I'm guessing you've been here a while and want to get out faster than that. So I can take it out now—quick and clean. It'll sting, but nothing like it did going in. Your call."

"Take it out." She's firm.

I nod. "All right. On the count of three. One, two—" I pop it out before we hit three.

"Shit. Ouch," she hisses through her teeth.

"Yep. But no screaming, well done. You're one tough chick." I grab some gauze, swab the wound, and apply a tiny dressing with antibiotic cream.

"Done," I inform her. "Now you just have to tell your mom."

"She's going to freak."

"Probably." I'd be pretty pissed if my kid ended up in the ER with a DIY safety pin piercing and a potentially serious infection.

Renee grabs her hoodie sleeve, biting the edge of it. "Thanks."

"No problem. But next time you want to channel your inner goth queen, maybe stick to eyeliner."

"Or like... a fake piercing?"

I grin. "Fake piercings are underappreciated. All the edge, none of the MRSA."

"What's that?"

"Stands for methicillin-resistant Staphylococcus aureus—it's a type of bacteria that's resistant to antibiotics, which you can get from unsanitary DIY body piercings."

"Gross."

"Yep."

I write her script, note the wound care instructions, and watch as she slides off the bed with a little more confidence.

As the curtain swings shut behind her, I blow out a breath and glance at the clock. Still early. Still surviving.

I head out into the corridor to retrieve my abandoned trolley—just in time to spot Zac peeling off a gown as he exits Trauma One. He pulls off a pair of goggles, that serious doctor face locked in place, jaw tight, eyes scanning.

My stomach does that stupid swoop again.

I duck my head and head straight for bay two, gripping the trolley tight. Maybe if I move fast enough, he won't see me.

"Sorry for the delay. Here's a sample of silicone scar cream," I tell my patient as I slip back behind the curtain. "You can pick it up at any pharmacy. After a couple of weeks, start using it on your chest."

"Thanks." She grabs it and inspects the tube.

I snap on fresh gloves and clean the laceration on her forehead, squeezing out the glue and pressing the skin together.

The curtain rustles. We both glance up—and there he is. My pulse spikes so fast it's a miracle my hands don't shake.

"Goddamn," TikTok Chick whispers, and I bite back a laugh.

Same, girl. Same.

"Dr. Monroe," Zac says. "A moment, please?"

"Of course." My hands remain steady, even if my heart isn't. "Almost done here."

Without another word, he slips back through the curtain, and I exhale.

"Shit. Can I come? I want a moment with him too," she jokes.

I laugh softly. "You're all set. See the nurse on your way out, okay?"

"Thanks, Doc." She grabs her purse, flashing me a grin.

I smile back—then step out of the curtain and nearly walk straight into him.

Shit.

He's still here, lurking like a very attractive gargoyle, just outside the bay. Arms crossed. Stance wide. Carved from stone.

Jesus. Green scrubs should not look that good.

His expression gives nothing away, but his eyes lock onto mine and don't let go. I feel it like a burn, crawling under my skin. My mouth goes dry. My fingers twitch to fidget, to smooth down my coat or adjust my stethoscope, but I don't. I hold my ground.

He flicks his head to the side. "Follow me."

It's not a question. It never is with him.

My legs are like jelly as I head down the hallway behind him, but I refuse to let him see it. If I faint now, he'll think I'm not cut out for this.

He holds the door open to the empty staff lounge. "After you."

I walk in, tearing off my gloves and tossing them in the bin. I slap some sanitizer on my hands, purely to have something to do.

The door clicks shut behind us, sealing us into something I'm not ready for. I keep my eyes on my hands, rubbing them together, too aware of him, and how it feels to be this close, alone together. It's stupid. We've seen each other naked. We've touched, kissed, crossed lines most people never even get close to. And yet, this feels like the real risk.

He's just standing there—feet planted, arms still folded.

I let my eyes do what they've wanted to since this morning. I drink him in. His thigh muscles are straining those scrub pants, which are fighting for their life, and those arms? They're practically auditioning for a Marvel movie. But it's his hair—dark, just enough gray at the temples to make him look distinguished as hell. I know exactly how many of those grays there are, too. I've counted them like a bedtime ritual.

And the best part? He's not just hot. He's apparently brilliant, too. And that right there is what does me in. He could be the prettiest man alive, but if he's as dumb as a brick, I'd be drier than the Sahara. But this one? Seems he's got the brains to back it up. It's almost unfair. My ovaries don't stand a chance.

He clears his throat. "*Doctor* Chloe Monroe."

"*Doctor* Zachery Bennett," I echo, a smirk on my lips.

"Did you know?"

I shake my head. "No. You?"

He huffs a laugh. "No. But... a pleasant surprise, nonetheless." His mouth curves into a smile that's all crinkled eyes and crow's feet, and my insides flutter. He's older. Smarter. But if I let myself think about it, I'll liquefy right here.

"I can't believe you're here, little one." His voice drops, and that name crawls up my spine like a sin.

There it is.

The name. The voice.

My body remembers faster than my brain. It doesn't belong here, yet it fits too perfectly to deny. I should say something professional, draw a line in the sand—but the words won't come.

"Same, Z," I breathe. "Or should I say... Zaddy?"

It slips out before I can stop it. Zac freezes, then completely breaks, shoulders shaking with laughter as he chokes, "You did not just call me that." I'm gone too, laughing so hard I nearly have tears in my eyes. It's one thing to say it in the dark at Eden. But here? Under fluorescent lights, it's absurd. And yet, perfect.

It suits him. Maybe too well.

Hell, I might need to upgrade it—*Dr. Zaddy* has a certain ring to it.

He sobers up and lets out a long breath, raking a hand through his hair. "And that's exactly why you can't be here. Why you can't be working in my ER."

Just like that, the laughter dissolves into a full-body chill. My stomach dips, the free-fall catching me off guard.

My smile vanishes. "What? Oh no. No, you don't." I cross my arms, pushing my tits up, and his gaze flicks down for a half-second before snapping back to mine.

He clenches his jaw like he's punishing himself. Good. Let him squirm.

"Our time at Eden has nothing to do with this. We're consenting adults. We can keep them separate."

"Look—"

"I worked my ass off to be here. I've earned this. You're not taking it from me." My voice is steady, but my mind is a panicked mess. "I'm not looking for special treatment."

"Good," he says quietly. "Because I don't give it." A muscle tics in his cheek, as he studies me, calculating and quiet.

I step closer. "Then it's settled," I reply, determined.

Is this where he tells me to go? To leave?

I won't let him. Not when I've fought hard to be here.

He doesn't move. Doesn't blink. His eyes pin me in place like a scalpel to flesh.

"You think you can handle it?" he murmurs, voice rough. "Handle *me*?" His words drop into the air as a challenge.

My lips twitch. "I'm not some wide-eyed newbie. I'm young, yeah. But I'm not fragile. I won't break if you push me."

His mouth curves slightly. "No," he says softly. "You won't."

There's a pause between us—longer than it should be. A stare too loaded to be professional.

We stand there, in the quiet of the staff lounge, the tension between us so dense it vibrates in the air. Finally he shifts an inch closer, enough that I feel the heat radiating off him.

"Come find me when you're ready to present your next case," he instructs, both a command and a promise.

I swallow. "Yes, Doctor."

He nods once, eyes lingering before he steps back and opens the door. And just like that, the moment ends—he's gone, but the air he leaves behind tastes like a dare.

And I'm too stubborn to back down.

Chapter Four

Chloe

Past

The Eden dressing room always smells faintly of perfume, body oil, and a touch of disinfectant. The holy trinity of sex work, basically.

I shimmy into my long black silk gown and adjust the straps in the mirror. The fabric falls just right, hugging my body but allowing enough room to move freely. Beneath it, I'm wearing a thong for extra coverage. It's tiny—barely there—but still technically against house rules. I don't make a habit of breaking rules—but this one? Worth it. And it's not like anyone will know.

Beside me, Hailee's perched in front of the vanity, sweeping highlighter across her collarbone.

"You on bar tonight or Le Jardin?" Hailee asks. "I forget what rotation you're on."

"Bar. Is it busy out there?"

"Packed. Vibes are high tonight for some reason." She caps the highlighter and leans toward me, brushing a stray piece of lint from my dress. In here, details matter. Smoothing the silk and perfecting the winged liner are the little ways in which we prepare to become someone else for a few hours.

Hailee eyes me sideways. "You seen Blaire yet?"

"No. Why?"

"She's in a mood."

"When is she not?"

She snorts under her breath. "I heard she complained to Madame Anna about Le Jardin last weekend. Apparently you stole her client."

I scoff. "I didn't steal anyone. He chose me in the lineup. I'd never spoken to the man before last Saturday."

"You know how she is."

The dressing room door swings open, and speak of the devil—Blaire struts in, wearing the same silk gown as the rest of us.

She clocks me in the mirror, lips curling. That faux-polite smile cuts her face in two.

"Chloe. Didn't know you were working tonight." Her smooth tone is laced with artificial sweetness.

I press a diamond stud into my earlobe. "Why? Worried I'm going to steal your client again?"

Her smile stays fixed, but her nostrils flare enough to betray the sting.

She eyes me from head to toe. "How's school going? Still pretending to be a med student while you play fantasy Barbie at night?"

"Still projecting?" I reply sweetly. "Your insecurity's showing."

Hailee raises both brows and mutters, "I need popcorn."

Blaire's gaze sharpens, but she turns away, heading for her locker. I've won this round, but the thing about Blaire is, she never forgets. This little spark will turn into a blaze later, probably in front of Madame Anna.

I grin at that. Madame Anna knows me well; she'll see through the bullshit. She trusts me.

I lean toward Hailee, whispering, "She's got that high school prom-queen energy. You know, peaked at seventeen and is still pissed the rest of us grew up."

She grins. "You're not wrong."

I take one last look in the mirror and fluff up my hair.

"Ready?" Hailee asks.

"Always." I exhale. "And if I'm not, I fake it better than most."

She nudges me on the way out. "If Blaire tries anything, I'll throat-punch her. Discreetly."

"I appreciate the solidarity."

We step out of the dressing room and into Eden—velvet curtains, moody jazz pouring from hidden speakers. It's just another night of making someone's fantasy come true. But for me, Eden isn't only a fantasy factory—it's the place that gave me something I was starving for. A place to put theory into practice, to learn what my body wanted and how far I could take it.

I step behind the bar, my gaze tracing the chandeliers overhead, the claret furnishings and plush couches. There's always an air of anticipation in here; some nights it's more intense than others. And tonight? Hailee is right... it's electric.

I found Eden when I was nineteen—too young for this world, but too stubborn to stay away. Would I want my own daughter here at nineteen? Hell no. But for me, back then, it was a lifeline.

Madame Anna never took girls my age. But I was determined. Eden doesn't just need pretty faces—it needs goddesses who can carry someone's secrets like gospel. Who can shoulder the weight of the emotional baggage clients unload without flinching. I wasn't naive, but I was inexperienced. A virgin, untouched, but my head was stuffed full of theories. I could rattle off every kink like a dictionary, but I'd never lived any of it.

I snicker, remembering the day I demanded an interview. Madame Anna shut me down at first—too young, she said. But I didn't budge. By the time I walked out of her office, I had the job. She's never regretted it, and neither have I.

"Hey, can you cover me for a sec?" Violet bustles up with her tray balanced precariously. "I need a bathroom break."

"Sure thing. Who am I serving?"

She glances across the crowded room. "Gray suit, black tie, white hair—back corner. And the three on the couch... oh, and the built guy by the stage."

"Got it."

"Thanks." She tucks her hair behind her ear, exhaling. "I already put the orders in."

"No rush," I reply, grabbing her tray from the bar and loading up the drinks. "I'll take these out."

I move through the crowd, balancing the tray on my palm. Eden's busy, but it's controlled chaos.

I drop off a beer to the silver-haired gentleman, kneeling with my head down until he dismisses me. Then to the guy near the stage, and finally, I make my way back to the bar.

Some nights, clients keep you kneeling, wanting to chat for hours while your legs go numb. But tonight, no one's in the mood to talk.

And that's when I see him.

He's here.

He's *back*.

I almost walk right past him, but I stop dead, a bright smile stretching across my face.

"You're back," I breathe.

"I am," he says, his American accent threading through the words. He's more relaxed tonight, a small smile curving his lips that's simply... devastating.

"Would you like a drink, sir?" My eyes drop, but this time, I almost don't want to. I want to keep staring into those warm brown eyes flecked with honey and see everything they're not saying.

"A CC and dry, please."

"Coming right up." I smile as I head for the bar, grabbing drinks for the men camped out on the couch and waiting for his. I risk a glance over my shoulder—he's watching. My smile widens. He winks.

Jesus. This man is lethal.

I reach the group of guys sprawled across the couch and sink to my knees, offering drinks one by one. They're too engrossed in some debate to notice me. It's a relief. Some nights, the quiet is a gift. A chance to disappear inside my head for a bit without small talk, just me and my thoughts.

Several minutes drag on. Still no dismissal. They're too wrapped up in their Dubai sheik story to notice me, kneeling like a prop.

I shift my weight, hoping to catch their eye—no dice. I glance sideways. Daddy's watching, and he's definitely amused. His fingers brush his mouth, hiding a grin. A soft laugh escapes me, and that's all it takes. One of the guys finally notices.

"Sorry, sweetheart. You can go."

Thank fuck.

I rise quickly and head over to him. He's watching me with that half-lidded stare, and my heart jumps.

He looks sinfully good tonight. Reclined in his chair, legs spread, rolled-up shirt sleeves. I swallow hard.

"Sorry about the wait," I say, kneeling beside him. He picks up his drink and I place the tray on a table nearby.

"Another minute and I was coming to get it myself," he says with a grin. He spreads his legs wider and motions between them with his chin. "Come closer. I want you here—between my legs."

My breath snags, but I crawl forward, face inches from his lap. The scent of him—soap, cologne, and spice—wraps around me. My whole body softens. My skin tingles.

"Look at me," he murmurs.

I lift my head. "That's better," he praises gently. "I need these beautiful eyes on me. No more looking at the floor."

I nod, a soft smile parting my lips. Every detail—every line, every crinkle around his eyes—feels like something I should commit to memory. Like my mind's a camera, and he's the only frame that matters.

He pauses, then says, "I know it's against the rules, but I have to ask."

Of course.

Every client has some version of "how did you end up here?" or "why do you do this?" It's their way of soothing their conscience. So they can feel okay about using us to chase their fantasies. Some of them want to save us. Some of them just want permission.

"Let me guess," I reply, lips curling. "You're going to ask why I'm here. Or if I like what I do."

He winces, chuckling. "Guilty."

"It's fine," I tell him, waving him off. "My answer's predictable, too."

He raises an eyebrow. "Student, paying off school?"

"Ding, ding, ding."

His laugh is a low rumble and my pussy perks up at the sound. She likes that sound. A lot. His groin is so near, I have a sudden urge to close the gap and nuzzle him like a needy bitch in heat, breathing his scent in.

"I'm the cliché." I shrug. "Didn't want to leech off my parents. Needed something that worked around my classes and paid enough to live on. Eden ticked all the boxes."

My gaze drops back to his lap—fuck, I can't help it. I lean in, pressing my face to his groin, inhaling. The scent of him fills my head. A soft sigh escapes me. This is what I needed.

He doesn't stop me; instead, his hand slides to the back of my head, fingers firm and warm, and I come undone. My skin lights up. It's a jolt of pure, electric want. He's anchoring me to him, and I don't want him to let go.

I nestle into the thick ridge of him, cheek pressed against the heat straining through his pants. There's something grounding about it—comfort and filth braided tightly together; I can't tell where one ends and the other begins. The scent of him curls into my lungs, and I want to sink deeper, disappear into him. My thong is soaked, slick with need, clinging to me like a second skin. My clit throbs in perfect time with the rhythm of his fingers stroking possessively through my hair.

He tilts his hips forward—enough to nudge his cock against my jaw. "I like how you feel. The weight of you against me," he mutters.

My lips part without meaning to.

He exhales softly, the sound threaded with approval. "That's it. Open for me."

I tip my head up, eyes meeting his. There's a pause—charged and breathless—before he reaches for his glass.

"Mouth," he orders.

He takes a slow sip, then leans down, his gaze never leaving mine.

I open.

He spits the CC and dry into me. I swallow without flinching, my eyes locked on his.

He smiles. "You're dangerous."

"Why's that?" I whisper, lips tingling.

Shifting in his chair, his voice comes low, almost thoughtful.

"Because you'd let me keep you..." he says it like a realization he's savoring. "Warm. Wet. And stretched open around me."

My breath hitches. The throb between my legs is already answering for me.

"I would," I exhale. And I mean it—every inch of me means it.

His fingers skim down my arm, light as breath.

"You'd look perfect with me resting on your tongue."

Heat floods my cheeks, but I don't look away.

"You want to know what I think about?" he asks, softer now.

I nod slowly, anticipation curling tight in my belly.

He brushes a finger along the edge of my mouth, his eyes burning into mine.

"I think about fucking you full," he murmurs. "Then tasting it—*us*—on my tongue. Spitting it back into your mouth and watching you swallow what's mine."

The air leaves my lungs in a rush. A sharp, hot shiver sparks low in my spine and shoots outward, wildfire-fast.

He doesn't gloat. He watches me, quiet and waiting. Like he lit the match and now he's watching it burn.

And it does. *I* do. I'm razed to the fucking ground.

He lifts me easily, settling me on his lap. "I want you up here, where I can see you." His eyes linger on my face, taking inventory, memorizing every detail.

"What can I call you?" he asks. "Goddess is too long."

"You can shorten it to G."

"What about Gigi? It's sweet—like you."

"And what should I call you?" I purr.

"Call me Z."

"Oh, that's too perfect." I giggle. "My very own Zaddy."

The way he laughs, head thrown back, is better than any orgasm.

But then he sobers up, fingers trailing up my thigh, slipping under the slit of my dress. When he finds my thong, he raises an eyebrow.

"Take it off, Gigi," he whispers, voice hot against my ear. "Discreetly. And spread those beautiful thighs."

I lift my hips just enough to shimmy my thong down. After I hand it to him, he brings it to his nose, inhales deep—eyes never leaving mine. Then, slow as sin, he sucks the gusset into his mouth.

Everything inside me clenches.

He tucks the thong into his pocket, then slides his hand up my thigh, fingers trailing higher until they find the heat of my core.

The first stroke of his fingers against my folds is a shock—ice against fire. My skin prickles and my heart pounds, thudding so hard I feel it in my fingertips. When he spreads my wetness up to my clit, it's like my whole body tunes to a single note of need.

"Beautiful."

I shiver at the word, fighting the instinct to close my eyes. But he's watching. "Eyes on me," he reminds me. He pushes two fingers inside, his thumb a constant pressure against my clit. My nerves light up; he's rewiring my body from the inside out.

"I need more," I whisper. My hips ache to move, ride his hand until I shatter, but I can't—I'm pinned in place, and he's making me feel every slow, torturous stroke.

He curls his fingers, hitting that sweet, rough patch inside me. I hook one arm around his shoulder for balance, breath ragged. Our foreheads touch. Our lips are so close.

"Come for me, little one," he whispers. "Squeeze my fingers, soak me."

The orgasm is a lightning bolt—brief and bright. My muscles clamp around him, my breath shuddering out in a low moan.

"That's it," he praises tenderly. "Good girl."

He slides his hand out, wiping my wetness into the ruined thong he's pulled from his pocket. When he's done, he dangles it from one finger.

"Open my pants. Jerk me off into your thong."

A thrill races through me. I pop the button of his slacks, slip my hand in, wrapping the wet scrap around his thick length. It's hot and silky and so fucking heavy in my hand. I stroke him slowly, then faster, every drag making him groan.

"Make me come, Gigi."

I squeeze tighter, moving faster. His eyes lock on mine—dark and hungry. A moment later, he tenses and spills into the gusset of my thong. The fabric's not big enough to hold it all—some of it leaks out, hot and sticky over my fingers.

"Fuck," he breathes, head tipped back.

I pull out my hand, the thong coated with both of us.

"Put it back on," he says.

My eyes widen. "Really?"

"Put your thong back on."

I don't question him again. I untangle the gooey mess and hook it over my feet, sliding it up my legs under my dress. It smears stickiness on my thighs, and I place it snugly against my pussy. I sit on his lap, the wet heat of us pressed against my folds.

"Christ," he groans, shaking his head.

My lips twist, wicked heat pulsing low in my belly. He's completely gone for it.

"Yeah, I know," I purr. "Keep worshipping, Zaddy." The words feel reckless on my tongue—but tonight, I'm not playing safe.

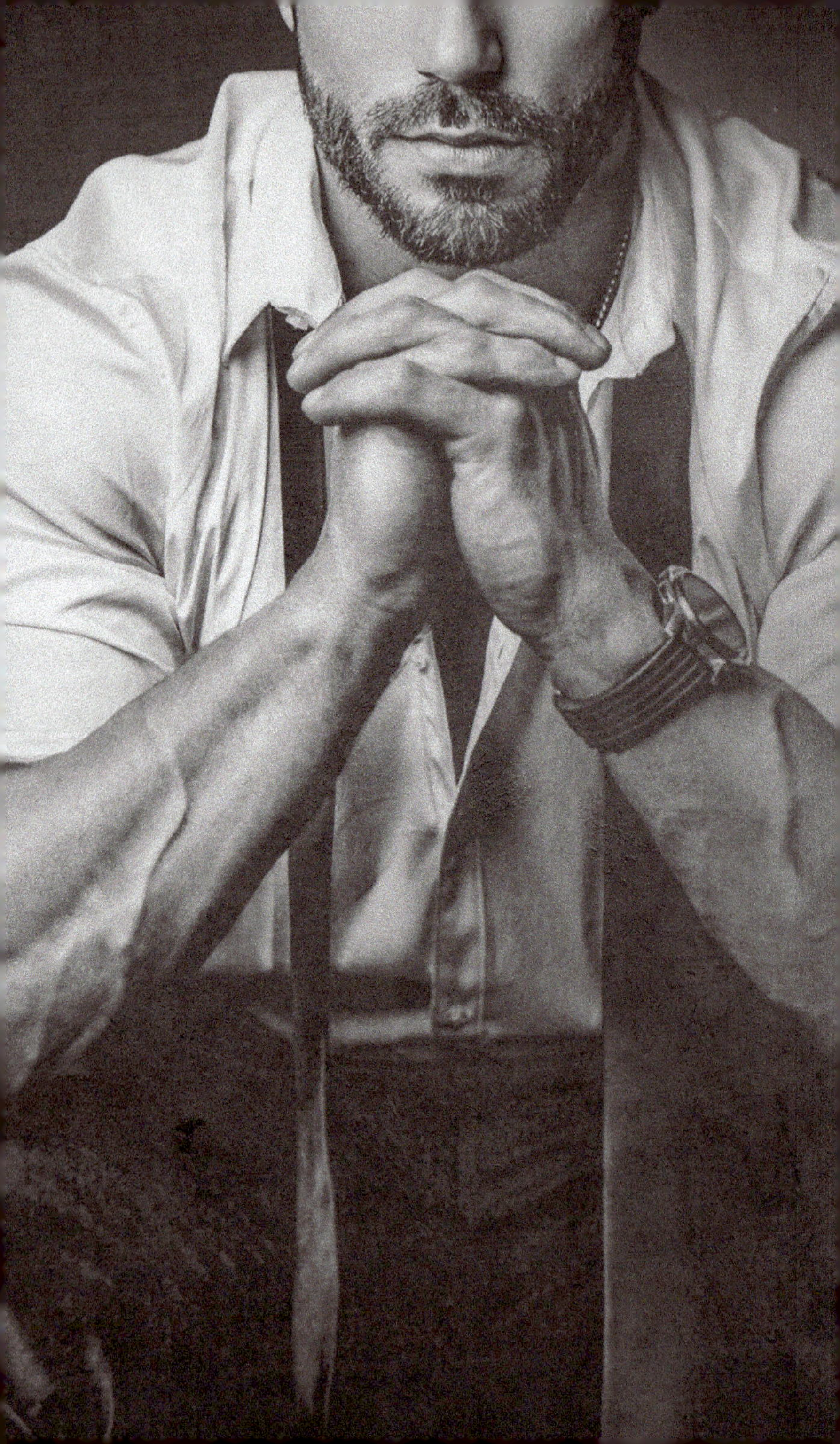

Chapter Five

Zac

Present, 9 a.m.

Chloe shouldn't be here.

My world has tilted, and fuck, I wasn't ready for it. I can't focus with her around. I'm the biggest piece of shit admitting that, but she's a distraction I can't afford. Worse, she looks like hell—sheet-white, sweat slicking her forehead. She kept swallowing, her throat working over and over.

She's not fine.

And I hate that I notice. Hate it more that I care. Because I'm not supposed to. I'm supposed to be objective. In charge. The kind of doctor who doesn't let his judgment become clouded by a woman he once had on her knees. A woman who now works *under* me.

Fuck.

Has she been sick for long?

I should pull her aside. Call her out. It's my job.

But I don't trust myself to ask it like I'm supposed to—with clinical distance, with the detachment this role requires. Because there's no neutral ground with her.

And the moment I open that door—the one between professional and personal—I'm crossing a line I won't be able to walk back.

That door doesn't just creak open. It blows off its hinges. And I need to stay on my side of the line.

For now.

"HELP ME!"

The scream slices through the ward, and I snap back, adrenaline surging, and sprint down the corridor toward bay ten.

Clarke and Kingston materialize at my side.

What the fuck?

A parrot—green and red, the size of a small chicken—sits on an elderly woman's shoulder, flapping its wings, about to launch into battle. It squawks again, ear-splittingly loud.

"HELP ME!"

"Can you get it to stop?" I ask the woman, yelling over the top of it.

She shrugs helplessly. "Sonny's been saying that since I called the ambulance. He won't stop."

I pinch the bridge of my nose, then glance at the others. "I got this," I mutter.

Clarke and Kingston shuffle out, and Olivia slides in beside me.

"What the actual fuck?" I hiss under my breath.

"A sixty-year-old woman and her emotional support parrot," she deadpans.

I mouth, *A parrot?*

She nods. "Emotional support, apparently."

"Yeah, I got that the first time you said it." I don't mean for it to sound sharp, but Olivia takes it in stride; she always does.

Sonny—the demon bird—spins on the woman's shoulder and flaps hard enough that I have to duck to avoid getting winged in the eye.

"He's sensitive to energy," the woman offers cheerfully. "He senses distress."

"You think?" I reply stiffly.

"He doesn't like men," she adds.

"Smart bird," Olivia comments.

Sonny lets out another shriek, "HELP ME!"

I tip my head back and sigh. "Olivia, figure out how to shut that thing up before I sedate *it*."

"Got any bright ideas, Doc? I'm not Doctor Doolittle."

Closing my eyes, I shake my head. "Just get her seen and discharged as fast as possible. Hand her off to Rhodes."

"On it." Olivia disappears, and I turn back to the woman.

"Mrs. Carlisle," I read off the chart. "I'm Dr. Zac. We'll get you taken care of and out of here ASAP. If you can do your best to keep... Sonny calm, we'd appreciate it." I press my hands together, dip my head, and back out of the curtain.

"HELP ME!" the bird shrieks again, and I swear it's a direct shot to my nerves.

Chloe walks by, her brows pinched.

"A parrot," I say, answering the question she didn't even ask.

"What?" she replies.

"Never mind." I sigh, shaking my head again.

Fuck. Now I'm explaining myself to interns.

Olivia yells out from Central, "Car crash en route—two victims, ETA one minute."

I turn, adrenaline surging through my veins once more. "Dr. Rhodes, Dr. Wells—trauma incoming. You're with me."

They drop what they're doing and join me at the ambulance bay.

"Finally, some action," Rhodes mumbles behind me as we suit up in PPE.

I fix her with a stare. "Need I remind you, Dr. Rhodes, these are real people in pain, not just practice for your résumé."

"Of course, Doctor," she says, contrite. But I've seen enough interns like her—full of bravado after one good rotation, convinced they're gods. Wells is harder to read, but he seems solid. Chloe's still an enigma, professionally. But I know personally, she's got that rare mix of empathy, intelligence, and steel. The kind of doctor you'd want in your corner.

The ambulance doors swing open, and the paramedics spill out with two stretchers. A pregnant woman, unconscious, and her eight-year-old son, wide-eyed and silent.

Clarke joins me. "What've we got?"

"Take the kid. We'll handle the mother." I steer the gurney into Trauma Two.

"BP's low, O2's tanking," a nurse rattles off.

"She needs intubation." I lift my chin at Rhodes. "You're up."

"Really?" She grins as if she's just been handed front-row seats to the Super Bowl, rather than a pregnant woman whose life hangs in the balance.

"Let's go, show me what you got."

She slides the scope down the woman's throat, hesitating briefly.

"Easy now, watch out for the vocal cords."

She gets it in on her second attempt, attaches the bag, and starts to pump.

"O2 improving—up to ninety," the nurse states.

"Good," I reply.

"That was freaking awesome!" Rhodes exclaims in an excited rush.

I ignore her. "Wells, diagnosis?"

The kid's fresh-faced, curly hair flops into his eyes, but he's sharp. "Internal bleeding?"

"From where?"

"Leg's busted, but no external hemorrhaging," he says.

I nod again. A nurse moves the ultrasound probe over the mother's stomach, frowning.

"Heartbeat's strong," she says. Relief blooms in my chest, but it's short-lived.

"Fetus looks small, though," she adds, sliding the probe lower.

Rhodes leans in, brow furrowed. "Placental insufficiency?"

"No," Wells offers, hesitant. "Maybe she's earlier along than she looks?"

"Let me." I take the probe from the nurse, but my gut knows. Something's wrong. The measurements are off. Way off.

I move it around and measure. "Baby's about fifteen to twenty weeks."

"How is that possible? She looks almost full-term," Rhodes asks, blinking.

"Exactly." I shift the angle. Adjust the pressure. There. I freeze the image and flip the screen toward them. "What does that tell you?"

Wells' eyes widen. "That's *not* the baby."

"No, it's a mass. And it's ruptured."

There's a sharp intake of breath. A beat of silence.

"That's the source of the bleed. Call Dr. Rosenberg—she needs emergency surgery."

Everyone moves like clockwork around me, falling into the rhythm of the trauma room.

"This is so cool," Rhodes breathes out in wonder.

"Stay with the patient until Rosenberg takes over," I tell her. "Your job's to keep her and her unborn baby alive until she hits the OR."

"You rang?" Right on cue, Rosenberg pushes through the double doors, and that's my signal to step out as the nurses and interns give him the rundown.

I head next door to check on the kid.

"He's good—just a few broken ribs, no head injury," Clark reports.

"Keep me posted," I say, and head back into the chaos.

"HELP ME!" the parrot shrieks again.

I groan. "Fuck's sake! Olivia, why is the damn bird still here?"

She sighs. "Waiting on Rhodes to finish with the car crash patient, remember?"

"Shit. Put Ellis on it."

"Fine, but stop barking at me, old man."

"I'm not old—I'm... seasoned."

"Yeah? Well, you're starting to look like jerky, boss," she says with a grin.

Despite the banter, I know I'd be lost without her. Olivia keeps this place running like a finely tuned orchestra—every note, every instrument, in perfect sync. Without her, the whole operation would fall into pandemonium. She's been here longer than I have and knows every inch of this department and everyone in it. She's the best multitasker and manager I've ever seen—a conductor keeping us all in harmony. In a place where one slip could cost a life, she's the steady hand we all rely on.

"I'm taking a piss," I mutter.

"Have fun with that," she calls after me.

I'm almost to the staff bathroom when I catch a flash of movement—Chloe, slipping into the women's, trying not to be seen.

The hair on the back of my neck stands up, so I follow.

The second I push the door open, I hear it—ragged breathing, then the unmistakable sound of her knees hitting tile, followed by violent retching.

"Shit," I whisper, stepping inside, instinct overriding protocol.

I drop beside her just as her body folds forward, caught in another heave. The smell hits me—sour bile and sweat. This isn't the first time today. Her whole frame trembles. I gather her hair, my other hand pressing to her forehead.

She flinches at my touch.

"Hey," I say, gentler now. "It's just me."

She sags a little but keeps her eyes shut, panting.

I wait until the worst of it passes, then quietly ask, "When did it start?"

She swallows hard. "Last night. I ate pizza. I'm fine."

"The fuck you are," I growl, checking her pulse. It's racing. She's dehydrated—pale, sunken-eyed, and clammy.

She wipes her mouth with toilet paper, flushes, then takes my hand and lets me pull her up.

I should send her home. I *have* to. Because she isn't just a patient. And that's the fucking problem.

"Don't. Please don't do this," she says, her eyes begging.

"This is my ER. You're under my watch." I keep my tone low, even, but inside I'm raging.

"Please. Don't bench me. It's my first day—I can't leave after two hours. They'll think I'm weak. I *can* do this. I'm used to it."

"You're sick, Chloe. One slip-up, one mistake—it's someone's life."

"I won't fuck up," she insists. "You have my word. I've got this. Please."

Fucking hell.

I need to send her home. That's the right call. For her wellbeing, for her patients, for everyone in this department. She's shaking, barely staying upright—and still, I hesitate.

Because the second I say it, I know she'll walk out of here thinking she failed.

And I refuse to be the one who knocks her down.

I rake a hand down my face. Close my eyes. Breathe.

This is a bad call. I know it. But I also know she won't last another hour out there without something to hold her up.

My voice is rough when the words finally come out.

"Fine." I rub my eyes again. "But my way. No arguments."

She nods, relief and gratitude flashing across her face—and just like that, I've crossed another line I won't be able to uncross.

Jesus, this day...

"Meet me in Trauma Four," I instruct. "I'll put in a cannula and draw blood. Once the results are back, you're going upstairs to my office for a bag of saline and rest. When you're feeling better, you can come back. If anyone notices, I'll tell them you're doing a special assignment for me. Got it?"

"Thank you," she whispers.

I fold my arms. "So much for not giving you special treatment." It's a dickish thing to say, especially when she's not well, but anyone else would be gone already. This is why she can't be here—because I'm in so deep I can't see daylight.

"Let's go."

I don't wait for her—she follows because she has no choice. In Trauma Four, I motion to the bed.

"Sit," I order.

"You don't have to—"

"I know," I cut her off. "Sit."

I prep the supplies, tie the tourniquet, and focus on the back of her hand. My fingers find the vein and I still for a moment, bracing myself.

"You're not pregnant, are you?" I don't dare look at her. If she is, it's mine. God knows I've pumped her with enough of my cum to fill a milk carton. It wouldn't be hard to imagine that one of my sperm found its destination.

"No," she replies, quiet and sure.

I release my breath and slip the needle in, draw the blood, then insert the cannula before taping it off.

"No patients alone until I get the results," I tell her.

"Got it."

I meet her eyes for a heartbeat, and I see the fight in them, but also the exhaustion. She's pushing herself. Hard.

I leave her there and drop the tubes at Central, telling them it's urgent.

How am I supposed to keep on pretending that I'm not already in too deep with this woman?

I'm the one in charge. I'm the one who's supposed to protect her, or remove her, or do whatever it takes to keep this place safe.

But when it comes to Chloe Monroe, I don't trust myself to do the right thing.

I already haven't.

And something tells me, next time I screw this up, it's going to blow up in my face.

This fucking day.

Chapter Six

Chloe

Past

I don't know where to put myself. I try reclining on the couch, hair flicked dramatically over the armrest—it feels like a porn parody. I flop onto the bed, trying out a few poses, but everything feels forced. I've never been nervous with a client.

When the door finally opens, I'm standing awkwardly near the bed, naked and feeling far too self-conscious for my own good.

Z steps into the room, his dark eyes drifting down my body before meeting mine.

Oh, good lord.

He's traded his sharp suits for sweats and a plain black T-shirt. His hair is tousled from the wind, his stubble flecked with silver. He looks so much better like this—undone and effortless.

I didn't know if I should be in lingerie or a silky robe—something that says, "fantasy," even though tonight feels... different. Le Jardin only happens on Saturdays, but tonight? It's mid-week, a one-on-one booked by Madame Anna herself. Ten thousand dollars extra for an evening with Z. I'd be a fool to say no.

The idea of Z has been living rent-free in my head for weeks. All I can think about is the weight of him on my tongue, and the ache to hold him in my mouth. Whenever I'm working, my eyes stray to the door, hoping he'll walk in. A dangerous little crush, and a reminder that getting attached to a client is the fastest way to lose yourself in this job. Or to lose your job.

I assumed he had forgotten all about me as I haven't seen him since. But here he is, looking like every dark, sleepless fantasy I've had.

"Couldn't stay away, huh?" I tease.

"Why would I?" he counters, closing the distance between us. His hands settle lightly on my arms as he leans in and presses a kiss to my forehead.

It's gentle. Familiar.

But not what I want.

Disappointment curls her cold fingers around my chest.

"You haven't been back to Eden in a while." It comes out as an accusation, not a question, and I have no idea why I said it—my mouth's running ahead of my brain. I need a better filter.

"Have you been looking for me, Gigi?" His sly smile is wicked.

"Maybe." I shrug.

He runs a hand through his messy hair, shoulders sagging. "Work's been brutal. I haven't had a proper night off in weeks."

Now that he mentions it, the circles under his eyes seem darker.

"Thought we could do something different tonight," he suggests. "I've got admin to catch up on, and I haven't slept properly in days. Maybe you could help take the edge off."

"Of course. What do you have in mind?"

"Relax. Hang out. And... if you're up for it—cockwarming."

I blink. "Cockwarming? You're serious?"

"It's been on my mind. And... making you happy makes me..." He pauses, searching.

"Happy?" I take a guess for him, playful.

"I wouldn't go that far... more like content," he finishes with a small chuckle.

I grin. "How'd you convince Madame Anna to arrange a mid-week rendezvous?"

"A lot of cash," he deadpans.

I laugh. "Sounds about right." Madame Anna doesn't bend the rules for anyone, unless there's a very good reason.

I grab his hand, tug him over to the couch, and push him down until he's sprawled against the cushions. "Relax. Get comfy."

I kneel to untie his sneakers, slip them off one by one, then peel off his socks and prop his feet on the coffee table. I pour him a double of whiskey and hand it to him, loving the way he looks at me like I'm the best part of his day.

"Thank you." His voice is croaky.

I smile. "Lean back. Let me take care of you."

He tosses the drink back in one go and sets the glass on the table.

As he settles in, I circle behind the couch and place my hands on his shoulders. My fingers dig into the tight knots of muscle, drawing a low groan from deep in his chest.

"Fuuuck... that feels good."

A satisfied smile graces my lips.

"Your fingers are heaven."

"Shhh," I whisper. "No talking. Just let go."

I work his shoulders, thumbs pressing deep, gliding up the column of his neck to the base of his skull. Thirty minutes later, his head is slumped forward, eyes closed, mouth parted as his breathing slows. He's asleep, but hunched like that? It's not good for his back.

I kiss the nape of his neck. "Wakey wakey, Zaddy."

His hand shoots up, grabs my wrist, and hauls me over the back of the couch into his lap so fast I squeak.

Shit, I thought he was asleep.

"That was incredible," he rasps, the fine lines around his eyes crinkling. "Where'd you learn to do that?"

I shrug. "Just something I picked up." Muscle anatomy is one of the first things they teach in med school.

We're close enough to kiss, and I feel the pull in every fiber of my being, but he doesn't close the gap. I get it. Kissing's intimate in a way that Eden's rules don't always cover.

"You said you had admin to do?" I say to break the tension.

"Yeah." He pats my ass lightly. "Ten to twenty minutes. We'll see how you like it and how your jaw feels."

My pulse kicks up. "I'm in."

"On your knees."

I slide between his thighs as he pulls off his shirt and kicks off his sweats. I bite my lip. He's all hard lines and muscle, every inch of him cut and defined—and I'm definitely *not* disappointed that I'm seeing him naked for the first time. His cock—thick and angry—makes my lips part on instinct.

He reaches into his bag, pulls out his phone, and raises an eyebrow. "Ready?" I nod, already wet at the thought of being used like this. I wonder just how much extra he slipped Madame Anna to get electronics in here.

He feeds his shaft to me slowly, one hand on the base of his cock, the other tangled in my hair.

"Mouth so hot," he groans.

I can't help it. I start to suck, head bobbing instinctively.

"Ah ah," he warns, pulling back slightly. "No sucking. No moving."

I slip off his cock. "Shit, I forgot!" I huff a laugh. "Let's try again."

He guides me back onto his cock, and this time, I let him fill me, thick and heavy on my tongue. I shift into a more comfortable position, resting my head against his thigh, breathing him in. I want to be perfect for him, to show him I can be more than just another warm mouth—someone he can trust to relax around. The taste of him, the weight of him—I've been waiting for this since our first night together at Le Jardin. My knees adjust into a mermaid position, and I let the moment ground me.

"Comfy?"

I nod, not wanting to pull away. My jaw aches a little, but it's a sweet kind of pain.

"I'm going to catch up on emails. I'll check in at the twenty-minute mark." I just bob my head—what else can I do? "And you can stop anytime you need to."

I can't believe I'm living out one of my favorite kinks, and he's not just indulging me—he's *paying me* for it. We're supposed to be working through his fantasies, not mine.

He thumbs at his phone, typing while I try to stay still, his cock hot and velvety on my tongue. Saliva fills my mouth, and I swallow around him, fighting the instinct to suck. It's harder than I expected to hold him there and not take him deep. My job isn't to get him off—it's to keep him warm, to let him feel me wrapped around him.

My mind drifts. To tomorrow's to-do list. The medical journals on my reading list. Whether I need to overhaul my skincare routine.

"Fuck, Gigi," he groans. "No moving. I swear I'll come down that pretty little throat of yours if you don't behave."

Shit.

I stifle a laugh, remembering to keep still. I make a conscious effort to clear my mind and stay present. Steady breaths, slow and deliberate. I swallow again, running my tongue lightly along his length, savoring his taste. He's softened a bit, no longer a steel rod, but a gentle presence against my tongue. I love him like this—warm and heavy, but not completely hard.

I breathe in his scent, my mind blissfully blank. All I focus on is the sweet, simple pleasure of holding him in my mouth, of providing him with this quiet service. My body eases, one muscle at a time until I'm completely relaxed, eyes closed, and finally at peace.

Time slips away. Every now and then, he runs his fingers through my hair, stroking absently. It's almost tender. It's less like he's using me and more like he's letting me in—each absent-minded touch a silent promise that he sees me.

Eventually, he sets his phone down, leans back, and closes his eyes, his hand resting on my head. I'm floaty, my body soft and pliant. I could stay here forever, safe in the heat of him.

"You good?" he whispers.

The phone vibrates, jarring the stillness, and he picks it up. He types something out, puts it down again.

I hum a *yes* around his cock, and he smiles, lids heavy. "Attagirl."

A few moments later, he pulls me off him. I'm half-asleep, lips swollen and wet. I release his cock, slurping around it, swallowing the excess saliva.

"Did you like that, little one?"

I lick my lips, dazed. "I feel like I took a power nap. How long was that?"

His grin is indulgent. "Forty minutes. Didn't have the heart to bring you out of it."

"Could've been four hours or forty seconds," I sigh through a stretch, smiling.

A thumb grazes my bottom lip, lingering.

"Gigi," he says gently. "I wish I could stay, but I've been called in."

My smile fades. "Oh."

He frowns. "Next time, okay?"

"Let me make it up to you before you leave," I rush out. I don't wait for him to answer. Quickly, I take him back into my mouth, sucking him deep and fast, tongue working him over. I don't hold back.

"Fuck," he groans, hands fisting my hair. "You have no idea how much I wanted to bury myself in your throat. It was pure torture to keep still."

I smirk around him, determined to wring every last drop from his cock. I'm a woman on a mission—he might have somewhere to be, but I'm not letting up until I've tasted every bit of his release. Because when he looks at me like that—like I'm his escape—it's worth every ache in my jaw and every stolen breath. My tongue and lips work in perfect sync, fingers teasing his balls until they draw tight. With a long, low moan, he spills down my throat.

"Gigi..." he breathes, voice wrecked.

I swallow three times; there's so much of it. At last I pull away, licking my lips.

He's still catching his breath, eyes glazed, mouth open.

"Holy shit," he says, half-laughing.

I just smile, staying on my knees, waiting for him to collect himself.

He cups my cheek, stroking softly with his thumb. "I have to go."

"Will I see you again?" My damn motor mouth doesn't know when to shut it.

"Absolutely," he says, and... I believe him.

He gathers his things and slips out the door. I stay on my knees, my lips tingling and a smile curling at the corner of my mouth.

There will be a next time—and I'm already counting the seconds.

Chapter Seven

Chloe

Present, 10 a.m.

Swagger's not confidence—it's survival. And today, I'm faking it with everything I've got.

I'm bent over a chart at Central, chewing the end of my pen. Since I'm benched from seeing new patients, I'm pretending to be productive.

I'm finishing updating a chart when Olivia hooks a thumb toward bay nine.

"Got a woman in there with a three-year-old—Kayden. Kid's got a rash, might be viral. But the mom?" She tips her head meaningfully. "Red flags."

I follow her toward the curtain, but she stops me just outside. "I need five minutes with the mother alone. Can you keep Kayden company while I talk to her?"

I falter. "Uh… I'm not exactly great with toddlers."

"You don't need to be. Just distract him. Coloring books are on the nurses' station if you need. Apparently, he's obsessed with dinosaurs. Take a look at his rash too."

"Got it, you're the boss."

She chuckles. "Damn right I am."

Inside, the child is curled up against his mother's side, clinging to a battered blue stegosaurus plush toy. The mom's eyes are hollowed out, the skin beneath them purple and papery. Olivia steps in ahead of me, greets them both, and crouches to the kid's level.

"Hi, Kayden. I'm Olivia. This is Dr. Chloe. She's gonna hang out with you while your mom and I have a grown-up chat. That okay?"

He peers at us warily but gives a small nod.

"Kayden," the mom says gently, brushing his hair back, "you be good, okay?"

I smile and kneel beside him as Olivia leads her out of the bay. The kid's small, shorter and thinner than average, and covered in blotchy patches that spider across his arms. I grab the tiny plastic stool from the corner and sit on it.

"You like dinosaurs?" I ask.

He hugs the stegosaurus tighter, smiling.

"What's his name?"

"Spike," he whispers.

"Excellent choice. He looks tough. You think he'd win in a fight against a T-Rex?"

Kayden's eyes narrow as if I've said something deeply controversial. "Stegosauruses have tail spikes. They use them like swords."

"Ah. Of course. Spike would totally win, then."

A corner of his mouth quirks upward.

I pull out my phone and search Google for dinosaur pictures, sliding it toward him. He taps with eager fingers, naming each one under his breath.

"Hey Kayden," I say gently, "can I take a quick look at that rash on your arm?" He holds it out without glancing up from the screen. I palpate the skin—warm, but not hot. No swelling or tenderness. Olivia was right. Viral.

While he's distracted, I let myself glance toward Central. Olivia's sitting across from the mother, her body language low and open. She's talking gently, leaning forward with ease that comes from years of practice, not performance.

I can't hear what's being said, but I see the moment she breaks. The mother lifts her hands to her face. Olivia doesn't touch her; she allows her to cry. It's clinical, but warm.

Eventually, the mother dips her chin, wipes her cheeks, and they stand. I look away before they see me watching.

A few minutes later, Olivia rejoins us. The mother lingers at the entrance, lips pressed thin, but calmer than before.

"She's taking the social work referral. Hopefully they can secure her some financial aid," Olivia murmurs to me.

I nod, and Kayden hugs Spike to his chest.

"Bye, Kayden," I say. "Spike's a legend."

He gives me a small wave, then trails after his mom, still clutching the dinosaur.

Once they're gone, Olivia exhales and rubs the bridge of her nose.

"That was... intense," I reply, standing.

"She's not a bad mom. She's just drowning financially. And too ashamed to ask for help. Happens more often than you think."

"She said yes, though."

"Eventually. Most of them do. They just need someone to look them in the eye and tell them it's okay to not be okay."

We start walking back to Central.

"You're good at that," I comment. "The listening thing."

"You get better at it with time. I wasn't always like this." She lifts the water bottle strapped across her like a purse and takes a swig. "I used to get pulled up for being 'too direct.' One doctor said I was 'too cold to work in pediatrics.' I nearly smacked him."

I snort. I can totally picture that. Olivia swinging a clipboard at some smug doctor with too much ego and not enough sense.

"What changed?"

"Had my first kid."

I smile. "How many do you have?"

"Four." She grins. "All boys. Twelve, eight, six, and four."

"Wow. And you still have energy to run this place?"

"Energy? No. Caffeine and rage? Plenty."

I laugh. "Do your kids know you're basically a superhero?"

"They just think I'm 'Mom who yells a lot and forgets their footy socks.'" Her smile softens. "But when my youngest had appendicitis last year, I'd never seen three kids fight harder to get into the back of an ambulance with their brother. Suddenly, I was cool."

We reach Central, and she drops a note in the chart tray.

"Here's the thing, Monroe. You're sharp. Fast. You know your shit. But I can already tell that you take everything personally."

I bristle. "Is that a bad thing?"

"No. But it will be if you don't learn to manage it. You can't take every patient home with you."

I let the truth of her words sink in.

"Learn when to lean in," she continues, "and when to step back. Your job is to care. Not to combust."

"Did you combust?"

She quirks an eyebrow. "More than once. But the hospital's still standing."

I lift my chin slowly.

"And hey," she adds, tapping my chart. "Thanks for watching the kid. You were good with him."

"Didn't do anything. He did most of the talking."

"That's the trick. Listen hard enough, they'll show you what you need to know."

She turns to leave, then pauses. "And next time someone tells you you're too young, too soft, too emotional? Ignore them."

"Why?"

She glances over her shoulder, smirking.

"Because you remind me of me. And that means you'll be just fine."

Olivia disappears down the hall, and I exhale—shoulders a little looser, spine a little straighter. I don't know if she had planned to give me a pep talk, but it worked. I tuck it away, quiet and private, a secret weapon I can pull out when I need it.

I turn around and find Jax hunched over a chart, flipping through a file.

"What do you have?" I ask, planting myself beside him. I might be benched, but I'm not going to stand around doing nothing. I need to stay busy—plus, I'd rather help out Jax than Sienna. She's too perceptive; she'd sniff out that I'm not seeing new patients in a heartbeat. And once she gets a thread, she'll pull.

"Male, mid-thirties," Jax tells me, looking at the chart. "Knocked off his bike, skidded across the asphalt for a couple meters."

I let out a low whistle. "Ouch."

"You can say that again."

"Diagnosis?"

"Nothing broken, no tears—just road rash, a ton of gravel to remove, and monitor for concussion."

"That'll take an hour, at least."

Jax shrugs. "Yep."

"If you want, I can take him off your hands," I offer.

"Seriously?" he says, surprised.

"Yeah, I don't mind. You can jump in on the real action Sienna's getting and knock some names off that board."

He squints at me. "You know there's at least two hundred bits of gravel in this guy's leg, right?"

"I've got it," I confirm.

"Okay, bay eight. Liam Abbott."

"On it." I take the chart and head for the bay.

"Hey, Monroe."

I pause and glance back.

"Thanks," he says. "That's really cool of you."

I flash him a smile. "Anytime."

Making a friend while saving myself from looking bad—or from anyone catching on that I can't see new patients? Both wins in my book.

Road rash is easy-peasy lemon-squeezy. I weave through the madness of the department, and a few steps later, I'm at the curtain of bay eight.

Liam Abbott is sprawled in the bed, dark hair, dark eyes, muscle stacked upon muscle under skin-tight Lycra. He's a human anatomy chart come to life. My eyes flick down, traitorous, before I snap them back up, pretending I'm studying his file. His bits and pieces are all there, on full display.

"Well, hello, gorgeous," he drawls.

"I'm Dr. Monroe," I reply. "I'll be helping Dr. Wells by cleaning out the gravel from your leg."

"I approve of the upgrade." He gives me a slow once-over. "Much better package than that nerd."

Urgh. Here we go.

I keep my expression neutral. Some things only have power if you give them attention. "Your road rash looks pretty intense," I state instead. "Any pain?"

"Just in my groin." He waggles his brows.

I swallow a sigh and pull on gloves, determined to ignore him. I roll my stool closer. He's hard—straining against the Lycra, the head of his cock peeking out of the shorts.

Impressive, sure. But seriously? I roll my eyes and clamp my mouth shut.

"Can you feel this, Mr. Abbott?" I ask, picking up tweezers and pressing them into his thigh. Did I stab him harder than I should have? Maybe.

His grin stays fixed. "Nope. All numbed up."

Lucky him.

The rash stretches from his ankle to the bottom of his shorts. *Thank God it doesn't go further.* Asking him to remove his shorts would be a whole thing. I can tell.

I pull on the headlight, adjusting the strap until it's snug, and start plucking out pieces of gravel with tweezers—head down, mantra on repeat: *Confident. Capable. In control.*

Each tiny stone I pluck out hits the tray with a metallic clink, a rhythm that's oddly satisfying.

"What's your name?" he asks, trying to make small talk.

"Dr. Monroe."

"I mean your first name."

"First name's Doctor. Last name's Monroe."

"Aw, come on. Don't be like that. We're going to be stuck here for a while, with your face so close to my—"

"I'm concentrating, Mr. Abbott."

"Call me Liam."

I keep removing bits of gravel. If he'd shut up, this would actually be kind of... meditative. Like ASMR with tweezers.

Until he opens his mouth again.

"It's gotta be something sweet, like Cinnamon or Candy." His words are covered with an oily slickness. "I can see you on a pole, baby—tight ass, big tits, even under those scrubs. You know you'd make more money doing that, right?"

I already do, asshole. Minus the pole.

I pause, straightening up to look him dead in the eye. "Mr. Abbott, I'll only say this once. Stop being disrespectful. My appearance has nothing to do with the level of care I provide."

He laughs. "Come on, it's a compliment. No need to get your panties in a twist."

My jaw clenches. I force myself to look at his leg, holding my tongue that desperately wants to let loose. I know I shouldn't say anything. He's trying to get a rise out of me. But I've got at least an hour of this bullshit ahead.

"Why are all the hot ones so uptight?" he mutters, then louder: "I bet all you need is a good dicking to help you relax." He palms himself, cock still half-hard.

I drop the tweezers into the tray with a clatter. "Are you fucking kidding me?" My voice drops low. "If you don't knock it off, I'm calling security. What's it gonna be?" Maybe it's the day, or maybe it's that I'm already sick and wrung out, but my patience is on its last leg—and his words are scraping at me.

The smug smile slides off his face, replaced by the real him, cold and calculating.

"Do you know who I am?"

"Mr. Liam Abbott." I know that's not what he meant, but I'm not giving him the satisfaction.

"I own Accorder Finance, the biggest firm in the southern hemisphere. I could have a dozen bitches lined up to swallow me dry if I wanted."

A finance bro. How fitting.

"Good for you," I deadpan. "Your parents must be very proud."

His eyes go black, malicious. A shiver runs down my spine. Mocking him wasn't my intent, but I couldn't help myself. I've never seen eyes like that before; it's deeply unsettling. Alarm bells are ringing in my head, and red flags are waving everywhere. I look away first and focus on the tweezers. He stares holes into the top of my head while I work. My fingers start to shake—not because of him; because of the dehydration and the salt leeching out of my skin. But I refuse to show him any weakness. I refuse to give him that satisfaction. I try to block him out and concentrate on my work. What began as relaxing is now charged, and I can't wait to get the fuck away from him.

A scream slices through the air from Central.

"I need some help out here!" Olivia's voice, urgent.

I slide out of the bay and glance around to see who's available—no one else comes out of their bays.

Another scream: "Get it out! Get it out—I can feel it!"

Fuck it. I'm not supposed to be seeing patients; I gave Zac my word. But what choice do I have? The woman screams in agony again. No one is coming.

I snap off my gloves and headgear, stepping away. "I'll be back," I tell dickhead.

A hand clamps around my wrist, hard enough to make me flinch.

"You're not going anywhere," he snarls, fingers locking in.

"Let go of me," I grit out. His hold tightens, crushing the fine bones until my eyes sting with the threat of tears.

"This isn't over."

I twist free, leaving him behind as I jog toward Olivia.

The asshole's grip was brutal; my wrist throbs. But I don't have time to think about it now.

"What's going on?" I ask, arriving breathless.

"Everyone else is tied up and this patient's losing it," Olivia says.

The woman's clawing at her ear, shrieking.

"Please—make it stop! It's in my brain!"

I ease her into a chair in the hallway. "Ma'am, I need you to stop scratching, okay? Tell me what's going on."

I grab an otoscope and look. *Holy shit*—a huge black cockroach is lodged in her ear canal.

"Okay, deep breaths. I'm going to flush it out with saline."

Olivia nods and runs to get the syringe. I hold the woman's hands away from her head, murmuring calming nonsense. She's half-delirious, moaning in panic.

Olivia returns with saline and a kidney dish. I angle her head, carefully inject the saline, and watch in relief as the cockroach floats out.

"It's out. It's out." I tell her in a rush, relieved. "You're okay now."

That was kind of cool.

"I can still feel it!" she cries.

I stare at her. "No. It came out." I show her the kidney dish with the saline and the cockroach trying to crawl its way out of the puddle.

"The other ear!"

You've got to be kidding.

"Let me check," I say, shooting Olivia a look. She widens her eyes and subtly shakes her head as if to say, "fucked if I know."

I tilt her head the other way, peer inside. This time, her ear is blocked by something small and black, but it doesn't look like a roach. My blood runs cold.

"I can't take it anymore. Make it stop!" the woman yells.

"HELP ME!" A screech comes from another bay.

What the hell is going on?

Ignoring the other call for help, I say as calmly as I can, "Okay, let's flush it out."

I draw up another syringe of saline and flush her ear. This time, something with too many legs scuttles out. I drop the dish with a startled yelp, stumbling back.

I don't fucking do spiders.

The cockroach and spider take off in a slow crawl, and I'm too stunned into silence to move. Olivia is quick to react, crushes the spider with her boot, then stamps the roach for good measure. The last thing we need is for those things to be crawling around the ER.

"Holy shit," I breathe.

The woman sags, rubbing her temples. "Thank you. That's... so much better."

I nod, still shaking. "Ma'am, you had a cockroach *and* a spider in your ears." I don't know why I need to say it out loud, but some horrors need to be heard to be believed.

"Thank you," she repeats, half in shock.

"Dr. Monroe, can I see you for a moment?"

I turn to find Zac watching me, arms crossed over his chest—a stance I'm learning he defaults to in work mode.

Shit.

"Go," Olivia whispers. "I've got this."

We walk a few paces away, until everyone is out of earshot.

"What did I say about seeing patients?"

"I know, I'm sorry. But this woman was screaming, and no one else was around to help. It was just saline in the ears, nothing major. I swear."

A moment of silence passes between us.

"Fuck, okay." He drags a hand through his hair. "Your labs are back. Go to my office—I'll meet you there in ten minutes."

"All right," I say.

"Level five, suite 506."

Right.

I nod and turn to leave—then stop. Where the fuck are the elevators again?

I pivot back, and he calls out, low and dry, "Other way."

Trying not to laugh, I do an abrupt one-eighty. Passing him, I throw him a quick salute. "Got it, boss."

He just shakes his head, that wry half-smile softening his features. Then he schools his face back to neutral.

I head off in the right direction this time, the pulse in my neck thumping like a drum. My resolve is rock-solid. He could've sent me home—*should've*—but he didn't. No matter what happens behind that office door, I'm not backing down. I'm going to prove he didn't make a mistake in letting me stay.

Chapter Eight

Chloe

Past

Some nights, I'm a goddess, dripping in honey and gold. Other nights? I'm an extra in a zombie flick—dry chin, congested pores, one ill-timed sneeze away from my period, and bloated like a Macy's parade float.

"Guess who's here again?"

Madame Anna appears in the mirror behind me, her tone sly as she props herself against the vanity. I squeeze the tube of Paw Paw ointment onto my finger, dabbing it onto my chapped lips to make them extra soft.

"Who?" I play dumb, smacking them together.

I know who. Well, I *think* I do. But I refuse to say it aloud and be the clichéd sex worker who wets her panties over a client.

She lifts a brow, waiting.

I huff. "Fine. I know who." My grin is halfhearted, betraying the excitement bubbling under my skin.

She holds my gaze, unblinking.

"What?" I shrug, forcing nonchalance. "I like him. He's... easy to be around." I break eye contact, heat creeping up my neck. "It doesn't feel like work with him."

So much for keeping it all inside. It is easy and natural with Z—too easy. And that scares the shit out of me.

"So, you'd be happy to see him again for another private session instead of working the bar tonight?"

"If I must." I sigh dramatically. "Someone's got to take one for the team, right?"

"I can always ask another goddess to step in, if you'd prefer..."

"Fuck off," I shoot back, grinning.

She laughs, shaking her head. "That's what I thought." Pushing off the vanity, she walks behind me, her reflection in the mirror a calm motherly force. "Boundaries, Chloe. Strong, clear lines."

"I know, I know." I *do*. My heart just... doesn't want to listen this time.

She pauses, her expression hardening into something more clinical. "He's requested no condom. You okay with that?"

I nod, too quickly.

"You're on the shot, yes?"

"Yep, I'm covered."

I want everything between us to be real, no barriers. If living out his kink means giving him all of me, I'm not just willing—I need it too.

Madame Anna doesn't press further—she trusts me to know my own limits—but her gaze lingers. She's looking out for me. That's the thing about Eden. It's a job, but it's also like a family, protective.

"You remember what I said in our interview?"

I nod. "The moment you start blurring the lines between the job and real life is the moment you should quit. This job isn't sustainable long-term. Get in, make money, and get out intact."

She looks at me now the same way she did back then—like I'm nineteen and desperate to take back control. She saw through me in seconds.

I still remember the first time I walked through Eden's doors. My hands were sweating so badly that I had to wipe them on my jeans before I rang the bell.

Madame Anna opened it herself. She didn't look the way I'd expected—no severe dominatrix in heels, or sultry bombshell adorned with diamonds. She was elegance personified.

"You're younger than you sounded in your email," she'd said, eyeing me up and down.

"I'm nineteen," I had replied, lifting my chin. "Legal. Eager. And smarter than most of your girls."

She'd blinked once, unimpressed. "Virgin?" she asked. Her voice wasn't cruel. It was clinical.

I nodded.

"You have no idea what this job requires," she said, already turning to close the door.

But I caught it with my hand. "I'm not here because I'm stupid or reckless. I'm here because I want this. I've done the research. I've read every contract, every boundary clause, every screening protocol. I don't want flowers and a boyfriend and whatever bullshit romantic comedies shove down our throats. I want control over my body. Over my pleasure. This is my choice."

She'd stared at me that day. Long enough to make me squirm. Then, without a word, she let me inside.

"You were all nerve and theory," she recalls, pulling me back to the present. "But you sat across from me and told me exactly what you wanted. I respected that. I still do."

I smile faintly. "You didn't make it easy."

"Wouldn't have been worth it if I had," she replies. Then softer, "You were determined to choose your first."

"I wanted to choose it on my terms."

I remember the way she sat beside me that night, a guardian angel dressed in black silk, flipping through client profiles while I deliberated, using instincts I didn't know I could trust.

"Why this one?" she'd asked when I chose a silver fox with patient eyes and a teacher's smile.

"He looks like he'd ask permission."

She nodded once. "He will. He's gentle. Experienced. And respectful." Then she handed me a glass of water. "No alcohol tonight. You need to feel everything. Keep your head."

That first room smelled like lavender and leather. I remember how detached I felt—like I was observing myself from above. He touched my arm, just once, and asked if I wanted to stop. I shook my head. I was shaking all over. But I didn't stop. I breathed through it. I let it happen. I asked for what I wanted.

And when it was over, I let the tears fall. Because I had taken something back.

"I think about that night sometimes," I tell Anna now. "How weirdly empowering it was. To decide what was going to happen. To say yes."

She nods. "That's why I let you stay. Because you were ready and you knew why you wanted it."

"And now?" I whisper. "You think I'm forgetting that?"

She doesn't answer. She doesn't have to.

I look away. I can feel her watching me, trying to will me back into alignment with myself. It's a fantasy, that's what I need to remember. It's not real.

She squeezes my shoulder. "Room eight."

I blink. "Already?"

"Already," she repeats, gliding away to check on another goddess's costume.

Fuck.

My heart immediately launches into a sprint. He came back like he said he would. I try to tell myself it doesn't mean anything—that I'm just a familiar body in a luxury wrapper. But part of me secretly loves that he kept his word.

Of course he's here early. And I'm a hormonal bitch with a face to match. I hustle over to Edward, our resident stylist, because if I'm going to face Z looking like I crawled out of a crypt, I'm at least going to be wearing something that'll blow his mind. He's definitely a lingerie man—the kind who likes to take his time unwrapping his present. The way he looked at me the other night when he discovered I was wearing a thong? Yeah, I never got that back.

"Ed, I need something show-stopping."

He grins. "Got just the thing." He hands me a hot-pink lace set—bra, panties, suspender belt, and sheer stockings so fine they catch the light. "Honey Birdette's latest," he says. "A mind-melter on that body of yours."

"Perfect," I breathe.

He tosses in a pink silk robe and a pair of nude Louboutin pumps. "Knock him dead."

I grin. "You're a lifesaver." I've thought about "borrowing" Edward's Loubs before, but I'm not ready to die a violent death.

"You know it, baby." He flicks his non-existent hair over his shoulder and does a sassy pivot. Bald head shining, thick Tom Ford glasses perched on his nose—he should be dressing the Kardashians, not Eden's goddesses.

I slip into the lace, adjusting the stockings so the seams are arrow-straight, my reflection practically dripping seduction. *Much better.* I need this illusion to be airtight. He sees only Gigi—the fantasy, the confidence, not Chloe underneath.

Of course, the universe never lets me have anything too easy—my stomach cramps, hard. *Not now, dammit.* I chase two painkillers with water, muttering a silent prayer to Artemis, the menstruation goddess herself, to give me a few hours of mercy.

Standing outside room eight, my heart is doing its best impression of a trapped hummingbird. I take a breath, push the door open, and let the robe slide off my shoulders, striking a dramatic pose.

"You rang?" I purr, twirling with enough flair to make any Vegas showgirl proud.

Z bursts out laughing. "Holy shit. You look incredible."

I sashay over, hips swaying like I've just stepped off a catwalk. No idea if I'm pulling it off, but he doesn't need to know that.

His eyes drag over me in a slow caress, worshipful. That look alone has me wetter than any word ever could.

I settle on his lap, legs draped across him, cuddling into his chest and shoulder. He tips my chin up with his fingers, his touch gentle.

"Was this for me?"

I almost quip that it was for the last client, but I bite my tongue—no need to ruin the mood. "You bet your sexy ass it was."

"Stunning," he sighs, brushing his lips against mine. The kiss is soft, tender, and when I lean into it, I melt—our first *real* kiss, and it's everything I hoped it would be.

He pulls away, and his thumb slides across my bottom lip. I can't resist—I suck him in, my eyes fluttering shut.

"Fuck," he whispers.

When I reopen them, I grin, running my fingers through the gray at his temples. "You know what might be my favorite thing about you? Your hair. The soft grays coming in at the sides."

"Does it bother you?"

"Not even a little. It's sexy. Total silver-fox energy."

His dark eyes narrow playfully. "No, I mean the age difference."

I smirk, shifting my hips. "I wouldn't be here, half-naked in your lap, if I gave a shit about that. Does it bother *you*?"

His fingers skim the edge of my thong, his voice low. "Well, I wouldn't be here, hard as steel, with your sweet ass in my lap, if it did. The only things keeping me from being inside you right now is this flimsy lace and my jeans."

I rock against him, drawing out a low groan from his chest. I'm not pretending to be the seductress anymore. The lines between Gigi and Chloe have completely blurred.

"Fuck," he groans, "you gotta stop or I'm gonna blow before I get in your tight pussy."

"Then stop talking."

His hand tightens on my hip, steadying me. "Actually, I wanted to ask you something first."

"Oh?" I tilt my head, intrigued.

He leans back, mischief flickering in his eyes. "I'm heading out on a friend's yacht next weekend. I want you with me. No Eden. Just... you and me."

"Yes," I blurt. No hesitation. "I'd love that." My answer is too fast, too eager, but I don't care. The idea of being with him outside of Eden... it's dangerous in the best way.

His smile softens. "Good. Hey, I've got a gift for you."

"I love surprises!" I clap my hands and wiggle my hips in his lap, teasing on purpose.

He reaches into his jacket pocket, pulling out a handful of delicate clamps. "These are for you," he offers, tugging down one cup of my bra. "Your tits were made for these."

He flicks my nipple with his nail, and a tiny spark shoots heat straight to my core. I arch into him, desperate for more. He sucks the tip into his mouth, biting down gently before letting it go with a pop. Then he fastens the clamp, and I shudder. The pinch is pleasant. But I want more.

The second nipple gets the same attention, the diamonds on the clamp winking against my skin.

"They're beautiful," I gasp, breathless. "Thank you."

I'm dizzy with it—the way he looks at me like I'm precious. And I'm devouring it, craving more than I should.

"Your nipples were made to be pierced, made for jewelry." He pulls on them, and I suck in a ragged breath. Exquisite.

He chuckles, dark and deep. "You'd look perfect with them permanently pierced. Diamonds everywhere—your throat, your ears, your nipples, your clit."

Fuck.

I'm soaked, grinding against his thigh mindlessly. If he doesn't shut that dirty mouth of his, I'm going to grind myself to completion on his lap.

He lifts me, setting me on the couch. His knees hit the carpet, and he pushes the lace of my thong aside, his mouth finding me in one long, possessive swipe.

He's merciless on my bundle of nerves, and my hips buck in a reflexive protest before I force myself to go still, to give in and let him take me apart. My thighs quake, a gasp tears from my throat as he keeps going. He's relentless. Devouring me with a single-minded hunger that's almost too much. Sucking harder, over and over, until it's not only pleasure—it's a raw, searing ache, pushing me to the edge. My legs want to wrap around him, but I force them to stay open—offering everything.

Then he pulls back, breath hot against my skin, my clit swollen and straining for more. His fingers find the last clamp and snap it on. The bite is so sharp I gasp and see stars—white pinpricks that burst behind my eyes. Every nerve ending is alive, sparking for him.

He stands, tugging his jeans down to free that thick, glorious cock. His hand wraps around it, pumping once, twice. He shifts closer, bracing one hand on the back of the couch for balance.

As he leans over me, the heat of his skin and the faint trace of his cologne envelop me. I'm caged in, surrounded by him, exactly where I want to be.

His other hand fists his cock, guiding the head up and down my slick slit. My heart is in my throat—I've waited for this stretch, waited to feel his warmth—as he bends over me, pinning me down with that possessive look in his eyes.

Knock knock.

We both freeze, breath caught in our lungs. Our eyes meet, then dart to the door.

What the fuck?

He curses, head thrown back. "You've got to be fucking kidding."

In all my years working as a goddess at Eden, no one has ever knocked on the door.

He pulls the tip out, hissing, and tucks himself away. My legs are still spread, the air cool on my wet flesh as he walks to the door.

Madame Anna's voice drifts in, muffled but insistent. "Sorry to interrupt, sir. You have an urgent call."

"Fuck," he grits out. He closes the door and crosses back to me.

"Is everything okay?" I ask, sitting up and pulling my legs together.

"I have to go." Apology creases his face. "I'm really sorry to do this again." He reaches out and unclamps my nipples at the same time—pleasure blooms sharply; I gasp. Then he kneels between my legs, his fingers working the last clamp off my clit. The flood of sensation makes me shudder, a mini orgasm that leaves me breathless.

"Attagirl," he praises softly, lips quirking up.

He draws me into a kiss, deep and hungry, then he's gone. Out the door before I can even catch my breath.

I sit there, dazed. Aching for him. Almost feral with it.

I wanted to feel him inside me. To fill me so deep I'd leak when I moved.

But at least I got my kiss this time.

And there's still something to look forward to: next weekend, his friend's yacht.

Unless the universe cockblocks us again.

Which, let's be real... it probably will.

Chapter Nine

Chloe

I push open Zac's office door, scanning the darkness. My fingers find the light switch, and it's like any other office—plain wooden desk, minimalist décor, certificates lining the wall. But I know it's his. I can smell him. His scent lingers in the air, pressed into every corner of the room.

I close the door behind me, my eyes drinking in every detail, eager for a glimpse into who Zachery Bennett is. He's seen me in my comfort zone, but I've never seen him in his. And I'm like a kid on Christmas morning, I don't know where to look first.

I move to the wall of certificates, taking in each one. Pre-med at a top-tier U.S. university. Emergency Medicine. Cardiothoracic Surgery. Member of the Australian Surgical Board. He's not just good at what he does, he's exceptional. Not in that highbrow, academic way, either. He swears like a sailor and has the filthiest mouth I've ever heard. And don't they say the biggest swearers are usually the smartest? But it's his eyes that give him away—that sharp, perceptive gaze that says he's operating on another level. High IQ. Higher EQ.

I already had an inkling he was extraordinary, but seeing it laid out like this—a roadmap of his mind and success—ruins me. It's rare for anyone to swap fields or master more than one specialty, let alone as a surgeon. It's practically unheard of. My heart's already a casualty of this man, and this? Another blow.

I move to a tall free-standing cupboard, curiosity prickling. Two dry-cleaned suits. Crisp shirts. A stack of green scrubs. Socks and boxers folded with military precision. I pick up one of the shirts, lift it to my nose—hoping for a hit of him—but all I get is fresh detergent. Disappointed, I hang it back up and close the door.

I check the filing cabinet—only work files. No personal touches. The minibar's stocked with water, energy drinks, a fresh salad, and a sandwich. Everything neat, organized. The bookshelves are the same: medical texts, reference tomes, case studies. I flip through one, fingers lingering on the dog-eared page. A research paper published only a month ago. He doesn't just practice—he studies, he keeps up and earns the respect of his peers. And damn if that doesn't light me up. Heat coils low, my thighs pressing together, wet and wanting.

No personal books, though. I wonder what he reads for pleasure—if he even lets himself. Or if everything in his world exists to serve a purpose, even his downtime.

I find a door and peek inside—a bathroom, predictably immaculate. I open the vanity: cologne, mouthwash, deodorant. *Cologne.* I spray a bit into the air and close my eyes. It's *him*. Clean and masculine. My nipples harden, and I put it down before I get any dumb ideas. This shit is potent.

I unwrap a fresh toothbrush, brush my teeth, and rinse with mouthwash. My skin's clammy and pale in the mirror, so I splash it with freezing water, hoping it'll bring some color back to my cheeks. I take out my hair and retie it into a high ponytail, smoothing down the flyaways. My body's so dehydrated, I don't even need to pee.

Feeling like this is as good as it's going to get, I step out of the bathroom and drift over to his desk. The top is mostly clear, a neat stack of papers on one side. My fingers trace the polished wood, soaking in every detail.

Then I see a photo frame that stops me in my tracks.

Zac, head pressed against a stunning brunette's, both of them laughing. Eyes bright, cheeks pink. The kind of candid joy you can't fake.

The knot in my stomach pulls tight. My knees buckle, and I sink into his chair, the leather cold against my scrubs. They look close. And he looks happy. Doctors only ever have pictures of their families on their desks. Sister, maybe? But I already know that's not the case. They look too close, too intimate. I already know who this is.

I should've known. A man like him—early forties, smart, kind, and hot—of course he has someone. My fingers shake as I pick up the frame, turn it over, and take out the picture.

On the back, in delicate script:

To my one and only. Don't forget to celebrate the small moments. All my love, Casey xx

A bitter laugh slips out, half sob, half self-mockery.

Of course he has a wife.

Tears burn hot as they spill over, and I swipe them away with the back of my hand. I should be furious that he hasn't been honest. But I'm not angry.

I'm just... disappointed. Disappointed in myself for falling so hard, for letting my heart override what my head should have known all along. Disappointed that this revelation doesn't make me want him any less. I still care for him. I still ache for him, even though he doesn't belong to me. I wish I could hate him—cut out those feelings and be done with it. If only it were that easy.

Do I want to take him from her? I'm not that girl. I'm not here to destroy a home. But it doesn't stop my heart from wanting. I'm not a machine. It doesn't change anything.

He's a good man—I know it in my bones. Maybe they have an open relationship. Maybe she knows. Maybe she's okay with it. What do I know? All I have to go on is my gut, and my gut says Zac wouldn't cheat. He doesn't have it in him.

I put the photo frame back together and position it the way it was. My legs tremble as I move to the couch, curling up with a pillow that smells like him. I bet he's spent many nights on this couch. A deep ache throbs between my thighs, echoing the hollow ache of my heart. I close my eyes, mind spinning.

A few minutes later, the door clicks open. My heart jumps.

"Sorry, got caught up." His arms are full—supplies and an IV stand. He toes the door shut behind him, eyes scanning me. "How are you feeling?"

"Been better." That's the honest truth. Physically, I'm exhausted. And emotionally, I'm drained.

He drags the coffee table closer and sits on the edge. "You're low in magnesium and potassium, I'm gonna fix you up." He shakes the saline bag and flashes a reassuring smile.

"Thanks." My voice cracks, but I don't care.

He studies me for a moment. "What's wrong?"

"Nothing," I reply quickly, holding his gaze. He doesn't buy it, but he lets it go, jaw flexing.

That photo is burned into my mind. It's not my place to question him, is it? I bury the disappointment beneath the need to feel him again—just for a little while. I need him more than I need answers.

"I told Olivia you're on break. You've got half an hour to get this bag in and rest." He unwraps the bandage over my IV site and flushes it with saline. "I'm giving you 5 ml of Buscopan for the cramps and Maxolon for the nausea."

I nod, grateful for his help, though my stubborn streak makes it hard to accept. He works methodically, pushing the drugs one after the other. But when he adjusts the bandage over the cannula, his hand stills.

"What's this?" His voice drops an octave.

I follow his gaze to my wrist. The skin beneath the bandage is angry and red, already blooming in shades of purple.

"Chloe." His tone isn't soft now; it's steel. "What happened?"

I hesitate. "Nothing."

"That's twice you've lied to me." His eyes lock on mine. "I'm not going to tolerate it again."

I flick my gaze away. I don't owe him an explanation—not when he's still holding on to a bigger one.

There's a pause, long enough that the tension pulls taut between us.

He breaks first, exhaling through his nose. "Fine," he mutters, more to himself than me. A line drawn but not crossed.

He walks to the minibar and pulls out an apple juice, sets it in front of me on the coffee table. "Let me know if the drip burns and I'll reduce the speed." He doesn't look at me when he speaks next. "Start sipping this at the twenty-minute mark. The sugar will perk you up."

"I know, I'm a doctor, remember?" I quip, a small smile tugging at the corners of my lips. I know all of this because I've been dealing with this shit since I was a teenager. But hearing him say it, in that calm, commanding tone? I could listen to him order me around all day. My pussy clenches at his take-charge attitude. I know he cares for me and wants to take care of me. And I'm all too willing to say, "yes, Doctor."

"I'll be back in ten to check on you." He leans down and presses a kiss to my forehead, the tenderness in it gutting me. Then he's gone, the door shutting softly behind him.

Almost immediately, the pain ebbs, the nausea fading. My eyelids droop.

"How you feeling?"

I blink awake, disoriented.

Fuck, did I fall asleep?

My watch says fifteen minutes have passed, but it feels like I've been out for hours. My body weighs a ton, sinking into the couch. I obviously needed the nap.

"Surprisingly better," I admit, stretching my arms, careful of the drip.

"Good." He smiles, and it's like sunlight cutting through clouds. "I'm gonna have a quick lunch, do you mind if I eat in front of you?"

"Go ahead."

He grabs his salad and sandwich, settling into the armchair across from me. He props his feet on the coffee table, biting into his sandwich like a starving animal.

I finally manage to move my muscles, swinging my legs to the floor and sitting upright on the couch.

I sip my organic cold-pressed apple juice, the sweetness a shot of energy. "Damn, that tastes amazing," I mumble, savoring every swallow. I can almost feel the glucose working its way through my veins.

He chuckles low.

"What?"

"You have the same look of relief when I come inside you."

"I do not." A laugh bursts from my chest, my cheeks flush hot.

His deep laugh is like molasses on my skin, sticky, warm, and wet, and I feel it in places I crave for him to be.

"You can't say shit like that. We're at work," I hiss, but I can't help the grin tugging at my lips.

He shrugs, finishing his sandwich in two bites. "We're in my office. Who's going to know." He opens his salad, shovels a big bite into his mouth. His mouth works—chewing, licking his lips—and my mind wanders.

"Watching you eat might be my new favorite hobby," I murmur, mesmerized.

He arches a brow. "That's because you know what I can do with my tongue and lips."

Oof. My nipples pebble, and I shift in my seat.

My brain conveniently conjures up the image of him and that woman—*Casey*—but my body doesn't care. Not right now. I just want his hands on me.

"You gotta stop turning me on," I mutter. "My nipples are already sensitive. They're a constant distraction when you're around."

He sets his food down, wiping his mouth with a napkin. "Show me."

I stare. "What, now?"

He beams. "Yeah. I want to see my handiwork."

This man.

For a moment, it's easy to forget the photo, the note. But it's there, a tiny blade of grief under all this tension.

Slowly, I shimmy my scrub top up and unclip my bra, letting it fall open. My breasts spill free, and the relief is instant—no more chafing, no more pinching. The cool air hits my sensitive nipples, and they tighten harder. I moan softly, running my fingers over the aching buds and the jewelry that always keeps them a little too alive.

"Oh God," I whine, lightly pinching them. "They ache so bad."

"Want me to make it better?" His voice drops, dark and hot.

"Yes, please," I breathe.

"So polite. How can I resist?"

He circles the table, dropping to his knees and gently nudging my thighs open. "So fucking gorgeous," he whispers. His palms cradle my breasts, thumbs sweeping over the sensitive piercings—his handiwork—sending sharp, delicious jolts straight to my core.

He leans in, kissing one nipple, then the other. His mouth is hot, the stubble on his jaw scraping deliciously against my skin. I arch into him, my fingers tangling in his hair.

"Whenever I see these, they take my fucking breath away," he says, reverent. Since he pierced them they've been ultra-sensitive. He trails his mouth across both breasts, licking and softly biting, leaving me gasping.

My hips rock, desperate for more, needing pressure, needing release. He pauses to grab his water bottle, takes a swig, then latches onto one nipple. The shock of cold water in his mouth makes me cry out, my body jerking in response. He does the same to the other, and I buck helplessly, seeking that final push.

"Can't wait to pierce your clit next."

God, I want that too, more than anything. The thought of my clit pulsing all the time, of it throbbing and needing constant friction, has me breathless.

I lift my hips and he yanks off my scrub bottoms and panties in one go, sneakers and all, then drags my hips to the edge of the couch. Two fingers drive into me, curling and pounding as his thumb grinds against my clit. His mouth latches onto one nipple while his free hand tugs at the piercing in the other.

Instantly, my orgasm rips through me. My back arches, head thrown back, eyes squeezed shut as I try to keep the scream from bursting out.

I shudder through the aftershocks and open my eyes to find his dark ones fixed on me.

He brushes a knuckle down my thigh. "Better now?"

I manage a nod.

"Good. Playtime's over. Let's go." He slaps my thigh and heads for the bathroom.

I move quickly, unhooking the IV and putting myself back together. I'm still lacing up my sneakers when he steps out of the bathroom, face relaxed—but the hard bulge in his pants says otherwise.

"You've got your color back."

"An epic orgasm will do that," I shoot back, unable to hide my grin.

He chuckles and reaches for my arm. "Let me take out your cannula." His hands move efficiently, stripping the tape and sliding the needle out, pressing down to stem the blood. As he works, he shifts slightly, adjusting his scrubs. My eyes flick down, catching the thick swell straining against the fabric, hard as steel.

"You can't go out there like that," I tease.

He shakes his head, a low groan in his throat. "We don't have time."

"Let me take care of it," I coax, my tone jovial. He checks my arm, the small bandage neat and tidy. "I'll be quick," I promise, giving my voice the sweet lilt that I know he can't resist.

"I've already been gone for too long."

"You'll be distracted, come on."

His lips twitch in a grin. "Okay. Drop your scrubs and pull open your panties."

I quickly unlace the drawstring of my scrubs, tug them over my ass, and peel the front of my panties down while he frees his cock. God, it's beautiful—thick, hard, veins standing out, the head flushed and slick. My mouth waters at the sight, but I know he won't let me have it there. Not now.

He rubs the tip along my clit, slow and deliberate, each stroke making me whimper. Then he drags it through my folds, back and forth, gathering my wetness until he's glistening with it. My hands hold my panties, and I'm trembling, biting my lip to keep from begging for more.

It only takes a minute, maybe less, before he positions the head at the edge of my panties and comes. Hot and thick, it spurts across my slit and pools into the gusset, soaking me with him. His jaw slackens, eyes locked on the mess he's made.

"Fuck," he groans.

I don't wait for him to tell me. I pull my panties into place, the wet, sticky heat of him snug against my folds. It's filthy, and it's perfect. I love it—the weight of it, the way it claims me. I know he wants me to feel it for the rest of the shift. To be owned by him, to carry him with me.

"That's my girl." He sighs, tucking himself into his pants.

He kisses me, slow and sweet, like we've done this a hundred times... and maybe we have. My chest tightens at the tenderness in it.

"Let's go save some lives, Gigi," he says, lines at his eyes and mouth eased.

And just like that, we're back in the real world—seamlessly, as if I'm not walking out of his office with a literal load in my panties and a heavier load on my heart.

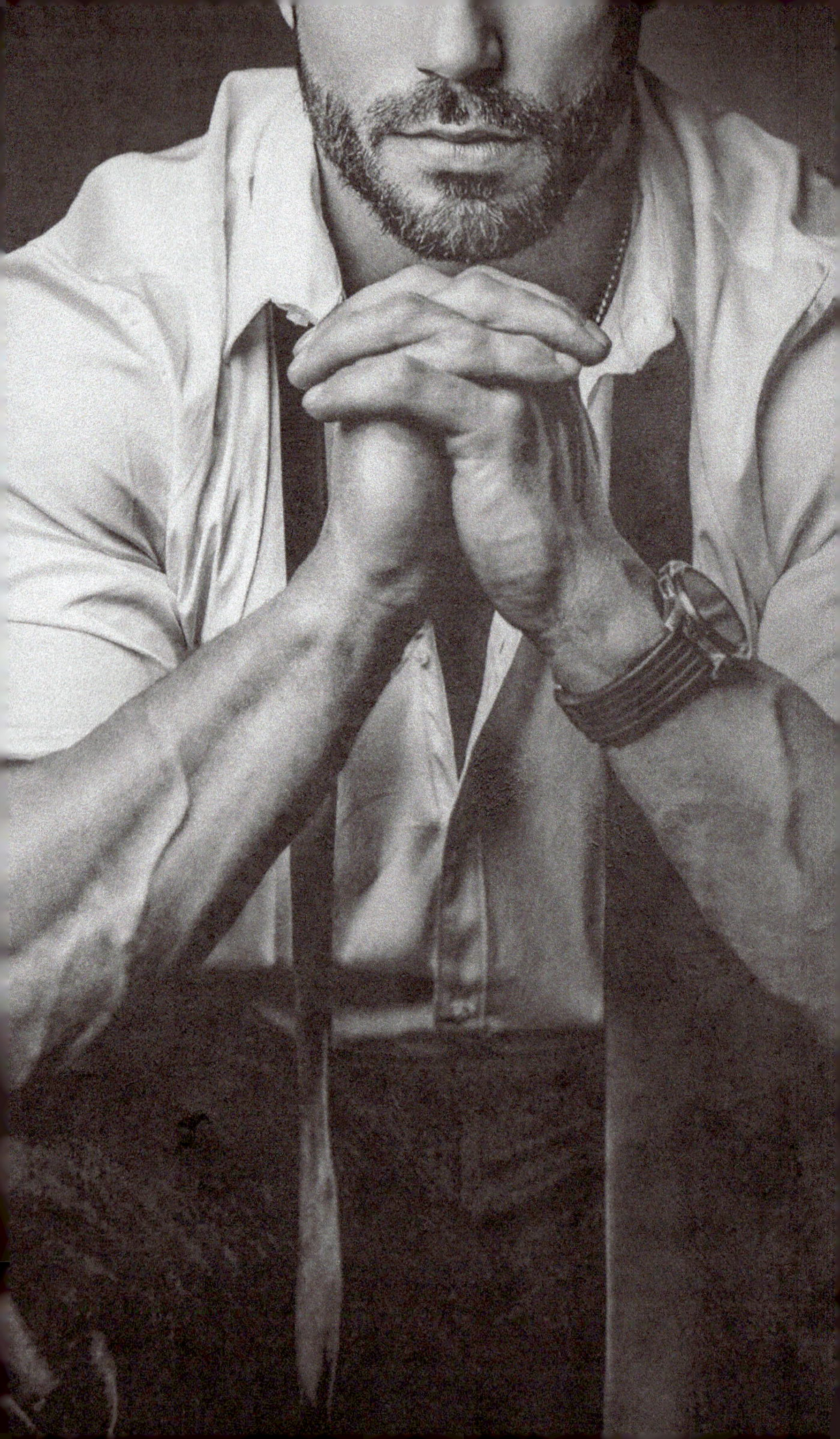

Chapter Ten

Zac

Gigi's body is a work of art—lean, sculpted by countless reps at the gym, yet still soft in all the right places. She's the perfect mix of strength and curve, and, fuck, if it doesn't make me hard every time I look at her.

We should work out together sometime. Take her to my gym. I can see it already—tight leggings hugging her curves, sweat glistening on her skin as I bend her over the barbell bench and fuck her from behind. Get her sweaty for a whole other reason.

Fuck me, another kink unlocked.

It's not entirely her body though; it's how she is. Magnetic without effort. She pulls me in without even noticing.

She's mid-laugh, head tipped back, hair damp from the ocean. Hailee clinks a glass against hers while Cora and Blaire lounge nearby, all of them naked and glowing.

Sunlight bounces off the water and catches on the sheen of sunscreen and sweat coating their skin. Gigi keeps stealing glances at me—hot, hungry looks that go straight to my cock, even though she sucked me off not twenty minutes ago.

It was the perfect start to this weekend on James and Dameon's yacht. Dameon's idea to have Hailee naked set the tone perfectly. The rest of the girls had to join in—no one wanted to be the odd one out. The only downside is that it's distracting as hell. My focus should be on the poker game, not the way Gigi's thighs glisten in the sun.

"I'm out," James says, tossing his cards down.

"Same," Carter echoes, throwing his cards onto the pile.

I've got two aces. I toss in a couple of chips. "Raise."

"You guys coming to the show next week?" Carter asks.

"Wouldn't miss it," I reply. Everyone else nods. Carter's world tour kicks off in Sydney next week—it's rare to catch him in our own city, and none of us would dream of skipping it.

My eyes drift back to the women. Gigi's sprawled on one of the loungers, her pale skin shimmering like diamonds. I'm painfully hard in my board shorts, my mind nowhere near the game. It's on her—on those thighs, and how I want to spread them wide.

"You win," Dameon says, snapping me out of it. His pair of eights lies face up.

I toss my cards down.

"You know, I haven't seen you look at anyone like that since you met Casey," Dameon notes, watching me over the rim of his glass.

I still.

My stomach clenches. The sun suddenly feels too hot.

"We're not doing this," I mutter, gathering the deck and shuffling.

Of course he brings her up. She's always hovering, waiting for any excuse to be remembered. Her laugh, light and dry, always cracked when she was tired. The way she'd roll her eyes when I left my scrubs on the floor, but would throw them in the wash anyway. How she never asked for anything... and then the one time she did.

Come away with me, Zac.

If I had just listened.

She believed in me when I didn't deserve it, and I let her drown in the emotional debris of who I became.

"She would approve, you know. If you asked."

I shake my head, firm. "Drop it, Dae. We're not talking about this." A lump lodges in my throat.

He doesn't push it. None of them do. They know better than to poke at old wounds. Especially the one named Casey.

I drain my glass—Dameon's top-shelf whiskey, smooth and warm—and slap the cards down hard.

"I'm out." I push back from the table.

Dameon nods. "Look, I'm just saying—the whole Daddy Dom thing you've got going on with her? It's working."

I grunt in reply, but don't deny it. He's not wrong.

It still catches me off guard—this pull toward someone younger. But it's not surface-level. It's rooted deep in that part of me that needs to take care, to protect. And somehow, she makes me feel more awake than I've felt in years.

Which is its own kind of fucked up.

I shouldn't feel this alive because of someone who isn't my wife.

I love Casey more than anything. But she can't give me what I need. The guilt is there, low and constant. But not strong enough to stop me.

I cross the deck, eyes locked on Gigi. She's already watching me, head propped on one hand, lips parted—and when I strip off my shirt, her gaze drops to my chest. Her tongue darts out, wetting her lips, and she doesn't even realize she's done it.

"Come here," I command, softly—because sometimes softness is more potent than a barked order.

Her breath catches. She moves with slow grace, every muscle strung tight like a bow.

"Over my knee, little one."

I take her spot, dragging her face-down across my thighs. Her legs kick a little, but I pin her down with one of mine. She's soft, pliant, already trembling with need.

I start warming her up with gentle swats. Then I let go—my palm cracking against her ass, sharp and stinging. Her skin flushes pink, heat radiating from her. She gasps—part shock, part pleasure—then exhales on a moan that goes straight down my spine. My balls draw up tight, my cock throbbing at the sight.

She doesn't just take it—she welcomes it. Presses back into my hand, needing it more than her next breath. And I give it too eagerly. With too much force behind it, because it's not only lust fueling me. It's the guilt of everything I haven't said to Casey. Everything I still want. I was too numb to feel anything until Gigi crawled between my thighs and cracked me open.

When I'm satisfied with the color of her ass, I pause. "On the lounger, Gigi, hands and knees," I order. "Face the water. Knees wide. Ass up." I tap her gently to get her moving.

She crawls into position, arching her back beautifully. I kneel behind her on the sun lounger, my hands gripping her hips. "You're soaked, little one." My dick springs free from my shorts and I slide the head along her folds. I groan low in my throat. "You should see how you glisten."

She's too gorgeous for words. Around us, the other women shift into similar poses—naked and open, ready for their men. The poker game is long forgotten.

I push into her slowly, savoring every inch of her tight heat. She's on fire. Her cunt grips me like it doesn't want to let me go.

"Ah, fuck—yes," she moans.

"Is this what you needed, baby? My cock stretching you?"

She whimpers in answer, and I don't hold back. I thrust into her, hard and fast, my fingers holding her hips steady, so I don't fuck her clean off the lounger. Her moans mix with the slap of skin on skin, the sun hot on our backs. I glance over and see the guys are fucking their women just as hard, the air thick with sweat and sex.

"I need to come," she gasps.

"Not yet," I growl, pulling out. She whines at the loss, but I'm already looking at Carter.

"Swap with me," I say. He grunts, pulling out of Blaire, and we trade places. He sinks into Gigi, her mouth dropping open in a silent moan.

"Oh my God," she breathes, eyes wide as she glances over her shoulder at him, then back to me. I've seen the way she looks at Carter—no surprise there. Women get starstruck around him all the time, and if I were a betting man, I'd wager she's a Pulse fan, too. Giving her this fantasy is what I'm here for.

But still, I watch her closely—focusing on her face, the micro-expressions, the way her body responds. She's not playing, she's right here with me, trusting me. *Mine.*

I slide into Blaire, her pussy warm and welcoming. It's good—hell, it's great—but it's not Gigi. A few minutes later, I'm itching to be back where I belong. Carter and I swap again, wordless understanding passing between us. I sink into her, and it's like coming home. Her breath catches, her body recognizes me before her mind does.

My hand slides from her shoulder to her spine, feeling the tremor in her muscles. I reach under, fingers finding her clit, pinching gently. She shudders, her cunt gripping me tighter. She starts to break apart, her orgasm building in shivering pulses. She keeps on coming and coming, her body shaking, soaking my cock in the process, and I can't hold it back any longer.

Electricity zaps down my spine. My balls draw up. I explode inside her with a groan, jaw tight and eyes squeezed shut. My cock jerks with every spurt until there's nothing left. My head tilts back, the sun blinding me even through closed lids. For a moment, there's no one else—just Gigi and me, everything else forgotten.

CHAPTER ELEVEN

Chloe

I'm floating somewhere between sleep and sun-drenched bliss, everything soft and hazy, like clouds slipping through fingers. The yacht rolls gently beneath me, each splash of water against the hull syncing with the steady thump of the heart beating inside the bare chest I'm curled up on. Z's chest. Solid. Warm. Rhythmic.

The heat from the sun cloaks me in silk, slow-baking me in SPF and sweat. My Audrey Hepburn hat shields half my face, oversized sunglasses covering the rest. It must be mid-morning, judging by the sting of the sun. Hard to tell through the haze of last night—cosmos, skinny-dipping, sex. A highlight reel of hedonism. Worth every headache this hangover's gifting me.

After two Bloody Marys and a breakfast fit for royalty, we scattered across the deck like lazy cats. Z and I staked out a patch of sun and haven't moved since. Just dozing and touching.

I lift my head from his chest, stretching with a quiet yawn. No need to wake him. He's still asleep—arms tucked behind his head, chest rising and falling in slow, steady waves.

I trail a fingertip across one nipple, watching it tighten under my touch. He doesn't stir. Just a flicker of his lashes, then stillness again.

I smile.

Watching him, relaxed and unaware, does things to my heart.

"Mmm, where you goin'?" His voice is deep, scratchy, and scares the absolute shit out of me.

"Jesus Christ," I gasp, hand flying to my chest. "Every time I think you're asleep, you open your mouth and try to kill me."

He chuckles and pulls me into him, arms and legs wrapping around me like a human octopus.

"How do you stay so still when you're awake? It's creepy."

He grins against my ear. "Meditation. Slows the brain. Sometimes better than sleep." He nuzzles my neck. "You should try it."

"I can *guarantee* my scattered ass can't sit still for that long."

He laughs lazily. Silence drapes over us again, easy and unforced.

Lying here with Z, tangled up in warmth and skin, doesn't feel like a role I'm playing. Doesn't feel like a performance. It feels... like me.

My thoughts drift back to last night: the laughter, the drinks, the nudity, the insanity. Carter. I still can't believe *Carter fucking Ashford* had his dick inside me. My teenage self would faint.

I loved listening to the guys swapping stories and teasing each other like brothers. Carter's virginity story? Comedy gold.

"You're smirking," Z notices.

"Huh?"

"That look. What's going on in that gorgeous brain?"

I laugh. "Just remembered how Carter lost his virginity."

He snorts. "Yeah... poor bastard. That can't have been a good experience."

"Speaking of... how did you lose yours?"

He pauses. "High school girlfriend. First love, I guess." His tone shifts, stiffens.

"You don't want to talk about it?" I ask gently.

"Nope."

Got it.

But now I'm curious as hell.

"What about you?" he asks, redirecting.

I shrug. "Eden."

He turns toward me and blinks. "Seriously? How old were you?"

"Nineteen." I laugh. "Relax."

His eyebrows go north.

"I missed all the teen milestones. No dates, no awkward dances or first kisses. My priorities were... different."

"You weren't in a cult, were you?"

I snort. "Why the hell is that your first thought?"

"In my line of work, I've seen it all."

Now I really want to know what his line of work is.

"By the time I hit nineteen, romance wasn't on the radar. I just wanted to be fucked. Get it over with. No flowers, no candlelight, just dick."

He huffs a quiet chuckle, but stays silent, giving me the space to share.

"I basically blackmailed Madame Anna. She said I was too young and inexperienced. I told her I'd find someone off the street, get it over with, and come back." I grin. "She caved. Offered a safer option—with a client."

There's a moment of silence.

"Do you regret it?" he asks softly.

"Hell no." I shake my head. "I wasn't really going to fuck someone off the street, I'm not stupid. I wanted to work there, and it ended up being on my terms. I had a list of kinks I wanted to try. Eden was safer than one-night stands. Plus, I had no time for dating or hookups, not with my studies and everything else going on in my life."

He's quiet for a moment.

"Have you ever had sex without being paid for it? A real relationship?"

It's a simple question. But loaded.

I blink. I'm paid for sex for so many reasons: power, control, curiosity, and pleasure. But never for love.

In my rush to chase pleasure, have I screwed myself emotionally? What if I've trained my brain to perform, not connect? With clients, I always find something: a trait I can admire, something in their personality I can anchor to. I look for a feature I can latch on to, a sliver of humanity to make it feel real. But that's not a true emotional connection. That's strategy.

And yet... with Z, I don't have to search. I don't have to pretend. It's just *there*. Natural. Unfiltered. All-consuming. I feel it everywhere—in my body, mind, and chest.

"No," I whisper.

He nods slowly. "Fucking someone you love... it's different. Like breathing underwater. Everything changes."

His voice is low. Not bitter. But... knowing. The way someone sounds when they've been wrecked and rebuilt by life. Someone who's been burned and is still carrying the scars.

I don't answer.

I have nothing to compare it to.

But I wonder—who did he love? And is he still in love with her?

It stings.

Swallowing the pain, I offer a smile instead. "I'll take your word for it."

He shifts beside me, the moment folding into something lighter. "I've got a surprise for you."

"Oh?" I arch a brow, grateful for the change in current. "You know I love surprises."

His thumb drags across my nipple, and it tightens instantly. "I brought my kit."

"Your *kit*?"

"These gorgeous nipples are begging to be pierced."

Oh, fuck.

My body lights up. I've always wanted this—for me. But for him, too. The way he looks at me, like I'm his canvas.

His to mark. His to claim.

I'm already dripping.

"Do you want to?" His thumb circles again, winding me tighter with every pass.

"I do. But... is it safe?"

I mean, I'm going to be a doctor. I know what could go wrong. Infection. Rejection. I know how to care for them, too. But still...

"I'm trained. Everything's sterile. I'd never risk your health, Gigi. Not for anything."

I believe him. I trust him with my life. "Let's do it."

He kisses me—deep, slow, and intense. Then pulls away. "Stay here. I'll get the kit." He pecks my lips, untangles himself, and disappears below deck.

Excitement buzzes through me, making the fine hairs on my arms stand up. By the time he returns with the black case and settles beside me, I'm practically vibrating.

"Kneel," he instructs, jutting his chin to the space between his thighs.

I drop down without hesitation, settling between his legs. He opens the case and snaps on a pair of gloves. The sound alone sends a jolt straight to my clit.

Oh fuck. Medical kink? No. No, no—too close to home.

But the look in his eyes—focused and in control—I'm melting.

"I'm going to rub your needy little clit and get you nice and ready." His gloved fingers slide between my folds, gathering slick and circling my clit. It's clinical, but holy fuck, it's hot.

When I'm trembling on the edge, he pulls away. "Ready," he says simply.

I bite my lip, aching for more.

He changes gloves, then disinfects my nipple with an alcohol swab.

"Hold still." He pulls out a surgical marker and dots the entry and exit points. "I want it to be perfect."

I peek down to inspect his work.

Not bad, Z.

He clamps my nipple gently with forceps, then coats the needle in sterile lube. I don't need to touch it to know it's cold as ice. Then, he pushes the 14-gauge needle through.

White-hot pain.

I gasp—sharp, shocked—but it passes quickly. He replaces the needle with a bar, and screws on the ball, securing it in place.

I knew it would hurt. My nipples are overly sensitive on a good day—but goddamn, this is next level.

I look down.

It's beautiful.

Two tiny silver spheres gleam against the tender skin. The sting lingers, softened by the heat still thrumming through my veins.

"You okay, little one?" he asks, stripping off his gloves, fingers drifting over my clit once more.

A moan slips past my lips. The pain fuses with pleasure, twisting hot together, turning it molten.

"Yeah... good." I breathe, my lids fluttering as my body bows into his touch.

"Can you come for me?"

I nod, but it's shaky. The ache is still there, pulsing behind the pleasure, and I'm close, but not quite there.

"I need more," I whisper.

"I've got you."

He presses deeper, fingers curling where I need them most. His other hand slides up to my chest, palm flat over my heart.

"Come for me, baby. Let go."

The pain dulls, the pressure snaps, and I splinter—shaking and panting.

"That's it."

My nipple throbs in time with my clit, and I ride it out, trembling, soaked and completely under his control.

"Good girl, Gigi." He cradles my face with both hands and presses a kiss to my forehead. "Let's take a break before we do the other one."

He strips off his shorts, kicks them aside, and guides my head to his lap. I don't need to say a word. He knows I need comfort.

I take him in my mouth and suckle gently, eyes burning, chest full. I don't know why I'm overwhelmed—but he does. Z gets me on a level I didn't think was possible with anyone. No judgment, completely in tune with me and my needs. He gives me space without asking.

I stay there, wrapped around him, breathing through it. Letting the pressure ease. Letting him hold me, without actually holding me.

His cock stirs, slowly thickening against my tongue. I keep going, easing into the motion until he pulses, his release warm and thick. I make sure to lick him clean, pouring every ounce of gratitude into the act.

"Stunning," he exhales, eyes locked on mine. "Absolutely fucking stunning." He reaches out and brushes his thumb carefully over the new piercing. "Just imagine all the fun we'll have with these."

A shiver races down my spine.

He snaps on a fresh pair of gloves.

I draw in a breath and brace myself for the next one.

I'm ready.

Chapter Twelve

Chloe

Physically, I'm fine.

Emotionally? I'm one breath away from eating ice cream in the supply closet and calling a therapist.

The nausea's gone, the headache's fading, and thanks to saline, pain relief, and an apple juice, I'm practically human again—like Popeye after a hit of IV spinach.

But the real ache? That started the second I saw that photo on Zac's desk.

One image. One tiny frame. And my stomach dropped. Not cute little butterflies fluttering around, more like bowling balls bouncing.

Did I seriously let a married man come in my underwear? Am I casually walking around with his cum soaking into my panties like some deranged souvenir?

My gut says he's not married. But if I'm wrong? Then I've fucked up.

I press a hand to my forehead and groan quietly.

Nope. Not going there right now.

I shake off the thought, trying to recalibrate as I round the corner—and catch sight of trouble.

Bay eight. Mr. Abbott. The human embodiment of a hemorrhoid.

He spots me and glares, eyes like heat-seeking missiles.

Damn it. No escape.

I grab a fresh set of gloves and push the curtain aside, stepping into his bay.

"Where the *fuck* have you been?"

"Sorry, Mr. Abbott. I had a medical emergency to attend to."

"This is an ER! Everyone here has a fucking emergency!"

God, if eye rolls could kill, this man would be a chalk outline.

"I understand, but some patients need urgent intervention."

"You said you'd be gone a minute. That was over an hour ago!" he shouts.

"HELP ME!" someone screams nearby.

"And who the fuck is screeching like that?" He grips his hair like he's about to tear it out. "I'm losing my goddamn mind."

"Calm down, Mr. Abbott. I'm here now. You'll be done in twenty minutes."

"Don't tell me to calm down! I'm leaving this place the worst fucking review."

Like the ER's on Tripadvisor. "You do that," I say, the sarcasm in my voice so baked in, it startles even me.

I suit up and get back to work on his leg. At least he's quiet now—silent fuming is a massive upgrade. I know waiting in the ER sucks. I've done my time in here on the other side, clocking hours on hard plastic chairs while staff dashed past, juggling meds, charts, and whatever fire needed putting out. Once, I waited nine hours for a set of bloods. The staff were slammed, one urgent case after another. It wasn't their fault—they were doing their best under the circumstances. That's why I'm making it my mission to see every patient as quickly as I can.

But this dude? Zero sympathy.

He probably yells at baristas and writes Yelp reviews like it's his civic duty.

And the fact that I'm sitting with Zac's cum between my legs while I dig gravel out of this asshole's shin? Poetic justice.

He hisses as I pull out a particularly deep piece. The anesthetic's wearing off, but I'm not going to wait another twenty minutes for numbing cream to finish the last stretch of his leg. Not for the last fifteen minutes. He can suck it up.

My hands keep working, but my mind drifts—of course, straight to Zac.

The way his hand cradled the back of my neck. The way he took care of me in his office.

Have I misread deverything? Were there signs—subtle cues—that he had a partner, and I refused to see them?

But then I think about the way he looked after me at my place a few months ago when I was sick. Sat with me when I couldn't even move. That doesn't scream married man sneaking around. That's someone who cares. Isn't it?

Unless he's just really good at compartmentalizing. Some men are experts in double lives. I see it all the time at Eden.

Maybe I've deluded myself into thinking he could be mine. I should've just asked—*Is there someone waiting for you at home?* I had the perfect chance today, alone with him in his office, his attention solely on me. I got too wrapped up in how good it felt to be wanted, to be looked after. Instead of talking, I caved to his touch.

I want to know the truth. My feelings toward him haven't changed. But I need to know. Or I'm just going to keep driving myself in circles, obsessing, spiraling. I don't think I can wait until the shift is over.

I adjust in my seat, aware of the wetness between my thighs—his and mine mixed together. My pussy clenches around nothing at the memory.

Get it together, Chloe.

"Hey, I'm talking to you."

I snap out of it. "Sorry, what was that?"

"How much longer is this going to take?"

"Almost done. A nurse will flush the wound, clean it, and bandage it. She'll also go over care instructions. I'll prescribe antibiotics to prevent infection."

I pull out the last two fragments.

"All done."

"About fucking time."

This fucking guy.

"Alrighty then. Take care, Mr. Abbott." I snap off my gloves, strip off my gown, and ditch the headlamp. "The nurse will be in shortly."

I don't wait for a response, just hightail it out of there. Out of the bay. Out of that energy. Out of the mess inside my own damn head.

Back at Central, I drop off Mr. Abbott's chart, but I can't help my thoughts looping back to that photo. What it means.

I need to know.

"Hey, Olivia, can I ask you something?"

"Shoot. What do you need?" She looks up from behind her computer screen, grabbing a protein bar and tearing it open.

I hesitate, scanning the triage board for cover. There are more patients than when I started. It's a Hydra—cut one head off, and three more take its place. Healthcare edition.

Before I can ask, Sienna and Hannah stroll over.

I grab the next file: abdominal pain.

"Ugh, abdominal pain? Boring," Sienna groans, peeking at the file in my hand.

"Better hope Dr. Zac doesn't catch you cherry-picking," Olivia chastises around a mouthful of protein bar.

"Ooohh, I'm taking nosebleed guy!" Sienna lights up, snatching the chart and strutting away.

Hannah shakes her head. "She's going to learn the hard way." She grabs the next file and trails after her.

"Seriously, though," I continue, quieter now. "Can I ask you something? How long have you known Za—Dr. Zac?"

"A long time now, over ten years, I think. Why?"

I hesitate again. My fingers toy with the edge of my sleeve, twisting the fabric tight.

She gives me her full attention, taking another bite of her bar. "If you want to ask something, just ask it. If I can't answer, I'll say so."

Right.

I take a couple of seconds to contemplate how to ask what I want to know, while she takes a sip of her water and waits.

"Do you know why he left cardiothoracic surgery for emergency medicine? I mean, ER's cool and all, but if I had the kind of talent he clearly does, I wouldn't be down here in the trenches."

She smiles gently. "He was one of the best—top cardiothoracic surgeon in the country, maybe even the world. Chief of Surgery. Then, a few years back, he walked away. Switched to Emergency when the position opened."

"Why?"

"People burn out. Lose the spark. Or they run from something."

Before I can reply, her phone buzzes. She picks up.

"Trauma. Two minutes out. Crushed foot, cement truck," she yells out.

Zac emerges from a bay. "I'm on it. Dr. Monroe, you're up."

Crap. No time to think about framed photos or ex-surgeons. It's showtime.

"You too, Dr. Wells," Zac calls as Jaxon passes us, pushing a patient in a wheelchair.

"Right behind you," he says.

On cue, the medics barrel in through the double doors, rolling in our patient.

"Male, mid-thirties, construction worker, cement truck rolled over his left leg." They call out vitals as we wheel him into a trauma room.

My stomach gurgles at the sight of his leg—or what used to be one. From the knee down, it's a pulp of flesh, muscle, and blood at an awkward angle. Unrecognizable. I gag, bile rising, but swallow it down. It's one thing to study this in textbooks; it's another to see it up close.

"O2 dropping. Heart rate falling," a nurse warns.

"Monroe. You're up. Intubate," Zac orders.

I nod, throat tight but hands steady. *Confident. Capable. In control.*

I move to the head of the bed. The equipment's ready and the nurse has already administered the sedative.

Scope in. Cords in sight. Tube threaded in under twenty seconds.

"I'm in." I attach the bag and start oxygen.

"O2 stabilizing," someone confirms.

My hand twitches with the urge to fist pump the air, but I rein it in—professionalism barely winning out.

"Nice work, Gigi."

Oh.

Fuck.

Me.

The name hangs in the air like a dropped grenade. My eyes flick around the room in a quiet panic. Two nurses trade loaded glances. Another coughs quietly. Jax frowns, confused. And I freeze, my heart tripping over itself. I don't dare look at Zac; I'm not ready to see whatever's written on his face.

"Heart rate still dropping," a nurse calls.

Thank God for distractions.

"Let's save this man's leg." Zac climbs onto the table, grips the crushed limb, and realigns the knee with a sickening crunch. I wince, but I'm wholeheartedly impressed. The strength, the precision... the sheer command of saving the patient's limb.

Then, a thud.

I glance down. Jaxon. Out cold on the floor.

My instinct is to call out, but I stop myself. This is a trauma room, and we're trying to save a life. A fainting doctor isn't the emergency here.

"Check his head," Zac instructs one of the nurses, barely missing a beat.

No one else pauses. No fuss. Triage instinct kicks in. I'm glad I kept my mouth shut.

"Diagnosis, Monroe?"

"Surgical repair, definitely. But why was he run over?"

"Exactly. Did he faint? Trip? Context is critical, let's find out."

"I'm on it." One of the nurses leaves, no doubt to talk to his buddy who came in with him.

"You want me to take over?" asks the nurse who just checked on Jax.

"Please." I hand off the bag, the transition seamless.

"We'll call if anything changes," she says.

"Thanks." I smile and squat next to Jax to check his pulse. Strong and steady. I give him a sternum rub, and he comes to with a groan.

"What happened?"

"You fainted."

"Oh no..."

"Come on, I got you." I help him up.

"Take a fifteen-minute break, get something to drink, and stabilize your sugar levels. It happens to the best of us." Zac squeezes his shoulder.

"Sorry, Dr. Zac."

"It's fine." Zac waves him off.

I still can't bring myself to look at him. I can't believe he let that slip—in the middle of a trauma, no less.

Heat climbs my neck as I steer Jax toward the staff lounge.

"You okay?" I ask him.

"Yeah. Except for my bruised ego," he mutters, flopping onto the couch, knees splayed, head hanging low.

"It *was* pretty gross," I admit. "I nearly puked."

"At least you didn't face-plant in front of everyone," he groans, pressing his thumbs into his eye sockets.

I twist my lips to hold in the snigger.

Poor guy.

Humble pie always tastes worse with an audience.

"Whatever you do, don't say anything to Sienna. She'll never let me live it down."

"Your secret's safe with me. But... four other people saw."

"Ugh, don't remind me." He drags his hands down his face, pulling at his cheeks in defeat.

"Hey," he says suddenly, "why did Dr. Zac call you Gigi? That's not your name, is it?"

My stomach drops. I keep my face neutral, but it's like someone yanked the curtain back on my double life.

"Nope. It's Chloe."

"Thought I was losing it."

"You weren't," I assure him.

"Still... weird."

"Totally." I bite my lip.

The door bursts open. Sienna storms in, grinning.

"Napoleon, I heard you stacked it. That's priceless." Her eyes are bright. She's ready to eat him alive.

"I'm fine, thanks for asking," he replies dryly.

"I should start calling you Stacks."

"It's Jax. Like I've told you before."

"Come on, we're friends! That's what friends do." She winks at him. "Sounded like a wicked case, shame I missed it." She sighs dramatically. "Anyway, I'm off. You snooze, you lose." She leaves the staff lounge room the same way she entered it, in a whirlwind.

"She's a psycho, right? It's not just me?" Jax groans.

"She's definitely... something." I grin. "See you out there in ten?"

"Yep," he exhales, sinking into the couch, eyes on the ceiling like he's questioning every life choice that led him to med school.

Chapter Thirteen

Chloe

The crowd's gone feral—seventy-thousand bodies jumping in sync, one heartbeat, one beast. Fans are losing their collective minds, and I'm right here, soaking it in. From our air-conditioned VIP suite, the vibe couldn't be more different—wild energy out there, chilled champagne in here. I've never been in a suite before, but God help me, I may never go back.

Carter commands the stage below, black tee plastered to his chest, sweat-slick hair flinging back as he belts out one of Pulse's hits. That voice—gritty, raw, soaked in sex—rips right through me.

I can't believe I've had that voice inside me.

Literally.

Last weekend on the yacht? One for the books. Not just because of Carter's rockstar anatomy, but because of Z. Sleeping wrapped in his arms, warm and wanted, I got a glimpse of what *real* could feel like. I've always known, theoretically, what having a boyfriend means. But experiencing it—even just a sliver? Yeah. I liked it. A lot.

I sway to the beat, hips loose, the music rolling through me.

A strong arm snakes across my chest from behind. I drop my chin to his forearm to hide the smile stretching across my face. We move together, perfectly in sync.

His lips brush my ear. "You know, I've never been jealous of Carter."

That gets my attention.

"Oh?"

"The fame, the fans, the no-privacy: I wouldn't wish it on my worst enemy. Poor bastard can't even take a piss without a security detail. Not for me."

On the stage, Carter cradles the mic like a lover's face, sweat glinting under the lights as women scream their hearts out.

"Until last weekend. For a few minutes."

My ribs lock around my heart.

Damn, this man.

He doesn't elaborate, so I lean down and kiss his forearm. A silent thank you.

I was starstruck at seeing Carter. And instead of being possessive, Zac gifted me the fantasy. He offered me to him. *Because of me.* Just like when I keep him warm in my mouth. That's my kink, not his. He's generous in the most twisted, thoughtful ways. He gave me exactly what I didn't know I needed.

And then, before I can overthink it, his voice is low in my ear.

"I want to talk to you," he says, "properly. Not just at Eden."

I glance up at him over my shoulder, brows drawing together. "Okay..." The word comes out slower than I mean it to. I'm not exactly sure where this is going or what he means.

He pulls something from his pocket—a small, sleek flip phone. A burner, brand new.

"This is just for us. You can use it or not. I won't push. But if you want to talk... I want to hear from you. I'll pay for your time."

I take the phone, fingers brushing his, and slip it into my purse.

"Thank you," I reply quietly. "You don't have to pay me. I want to talk to you, too."

He nods slowly.

I don't know what to call this thing between us, but it's no longer transactional. We're breaking the rules, pushing all the boundaries. I know it's real. And real is rare. So I give him the one thing I know he needs.

"I'm not going anywhere, Z. Until you say so."

In front of us, the crowd roars and the song crashes to a close. The girls behind us let out a whoop. We turn to find Hailee and Cora twirling with their drinks, cheeks flushed and eyes shining.

God, I adore them. If I had time—if I had the luxury of health—I'd pour myself into friendships like that. But studying medicine is brutal. Add a chronic illness and my Eden shifts on top of it? I'm barely surviving. Any scraps of free time I get, I spend at the gym, trying to keep my body strong enough to carry me.

I know Hailee better than Cora as she's Madame Anna's right-hand woman. Cora only worked at Eden briefly, so we never really had a chance to connect. Still, if I ever had the bandwidth, I'd claim Hailee and Cora as my ride-or-dies in a heartbeat. Low-maintenance, real, down-to-earth. Unlike Blaire... she's different. I never get good vibes from her. That smug, mean-girl energy? Yeah, I steer clear. Feels like high school all over again, and I graduated from that drama years ago.

Actually... where *is* Blaire tonight?

The next song's a slow one. The girls pounce, yanking James and Dameon away from their work talk and onto the makeshift dance floor before either can protest.

I turn in Z's arms, letting him draw me into a slow, easy sway. My hands slide behind his neck, our eyes locked. The music fades, the crowd disappears. It's just us.

Everything about this feels right. Right place. Right man. Right time.

The glint in his eyes says he's about to drop something downright dirty and delicious, and I already know I'm going to love whatever comes next.

"I've got an idea. If you're game."

I smirk. "I'm always game."

"Come with me."

He grabs my hand and leads me to the couch tucked away at the back of the suite, still with a clear view of the stage, but semi-private. He takes a seat and draws me into his lap so I'm facing away from him, my back nestled against his chest.

"I'm going to open my zipper. You're going to lift your skirt and sit on my cock. Got it?" he whispers, his mouth brushing the back of my neck.

My heart skips. "Here? Now?"

The waitstaff are still bustling around, clearing glasses and refilling platters. I've got no problem getting fucked in front of his friends and the girls. We spent the whole weekend naked on a yacht—this isn't exactly new territory for me. But that was private property. Trusted staff. This? This is a civilian zone.

Z told me to wear a long skirt and skip the panties for tonight. He clearly had a plan. I can already feel the thick press of him beneath me, rock-hard inside his jeans. He's ready. Honestly, I've been wet since I walked in and saw him looking like sin in that T-shirt-and-jeans combo.

Still, if we're doing this, we've got to be quick. And clever.

"Move forward a little," he instructs, helping me shift.

I twist to look over my shoulder, as he undoes his zipper and pulls his cock free. My body shields him from view, so no one sees when he wraps his fist around his shaft—stroking from base to tip, collecting the bead of pre-cum with his thumb and offering it to me.

I latch onto his thumb like a hungry lioness, tongue swirling, sucking hard. His eyes drop to half-mast.

One hand gathers my skirt. The other braces the base of his cock. He casts a casual glance around the suite, cool and composed. "Okay. Now."

I raise slightly while he guides his thick head to my entrance. I sink down—slow, smooth, until I'm fully seated, completely filled. He drapes my skirt over us like a curtain, and I face forward, melting back into his chest.

We both sigh.

From the outside? Just a couple cuddling on the couch during a concert.

Inside? Filthy, beautiful, perfect.

For a split second, I was worried I wouldn't be wet enough—that I'd get stuck halfway down, awkward and exposed.

I move a little. We both groan.

He feels too good. Too thick. I want to roll my hips, ride him hard, chase the high already curling in my belly.

"Don't move," he growls into my ear, gripping my hips.

"Why not?"

"Clench."

"What?"

"Your muscles. Clench for me."

I do as I'm told.

"Oh, fuck. Make me come like this."

I don't bounce or grind on him. Instead, I hold him deep and tight, coaxing him with nothing but the way I clench.

Challenge accepted.

I tighten. Release. Tighten again. Slow and steady. Good thing I've got Kegels of steel.

He pants against my neck, barely holding on.

A waiter approaches. "Another drink, miss?"

He's young and kind of cute, blissfully unaware of the filthy scene unfolding under my skirt. And if he does suspect anything, he's got a poker face worthy of Vegas.

I don't miss a beat. "Long Island iced tea, please."

And for you, sir?"

Z's voice is tight, after a particularly hard clench. "Whiskey. Neat."

The waiter nods and walks off, apparently none the wiser.

"Jesus, baby. Your cunt's heaven. I could live inside you forever."

Fine by me.

I crane my neck and twist, lifting my face to his, and nip at his bottom lip. "Give it to me. I've been a good girl. I want your cum, Zaddy."

He makes a pained sound in between a moan and a groan. His eyes flutter, and his breathing picks up until he's panting into my lips.

Three sharp jerks. His cock pulses inside me, coating my insides and filling me up. His orgasm sets off mine, my body automatically taking over the clenching, and I milk him through his aftershocks as my own orgasm overtakes.

"Fuck," he whispers.

"Mm-hmm."

I fuse my lips to his, bringing one hand up behind me to bury in his hair as I claim his mouth.

But the music swells again, thumping louder into the suite—reality edging in, pressing at the seams of our cocoon.

Z breaks the kiss, his lips drifting to the side of my head, where they linger.

"You okay to walk?" he murmurs.

My pussy aches in the best way, but I push up anyway, smoothing my skirt. Z slides free, his cum leaking down my thighs.

"Yeah, but if I limp, we're blaming the heels. Not your... enthusiasm."

He chuckles, tucking himself back into his jeans with all the stealth of a marching band in a church.

I bite my lip, fighting a grin.

Just a clench and a well-placed "Zaddy."

God, I'm a menace.

"No cleaning up," he reminds me.

I blow him a kiss.

"Please, I'm always wearing you. At this point, I'm basically marinating."

We rejoin the group as the next track crashes through the speakers and the crowd outside erupts again. Inside the suite, it's just us and our circle—warm, fizzy energy and champagne sweat. Hailee's ditched her heels and is dancing barefoot with Cora, both spinning like tipsy fairies. James and Dameon are still locked in a work debate.

Z glances over at Dameon. "Backstage?"

Dameon lifts his drink in a lazy salute. "Already arranged."

"Afterparty?" James asks, leaning in. "Where?"

"Dressing room," Dameon mutters, tapping his phone. "Apparently we've been summoned."

"I'm in," Hailee sing-songs, arms still mid-spin.

Cora laughs. "We talking open bar? Because my liver's only half-dead."

"Come on." Z catches my hand. "It's not a real Pulse concert until someone licks tequila off a groupie."

I arch a brow. "How many groupies have you defiled, exactly?"

He grins. "Not enough to compare to what I've done to you."

Hailee shrieks, "Too much information!" but she's grinning, flushed and giddy.

And just like that, the night shifts.

We make our way downstairs, the thump of bass growing louder with each floor. The elevator dings open, and boom—straight into backstage bedlam. Sweaty bodies, spilled booze, and at least one half-naked groupie.

Crew members weave through the crowd with headsets and clipboards, already packing up, ready to ship out for the world tour.

The backstage lounge has a bar built from battered amp cases with neon lighting casting everything in a haze. The walls vibrate with basslines. To our right, someone's yelling about a missing drum key.

I stick close to Z. This world isn't mine—not like Eden. Eden is ordered and controlled; this world is untamed.

He drapes an arm around my waist in a casual claim, fingers resting above my hip bone. I lean into him without thinking.

Carter finds us within minutes—shirt off, dog tags swinging, slick with sweat and charisma. He's sex and trouble, the human personification of a rock ballad. The two women hanging off him look reluctant to let go when he approaches us.

"How was the suite?" Carter asks, smirking. "Bet it smells like sin in there now."

Z shoots him a look. "What, you want a sniff test?"

Carter grins. "Depends—are you charging by the finger?"

Dameon sighs. "Jesus. Can you two not flirt like deranged frat boys for five minutes?"

"Honestly, this *is* their version of foreplay." James lifts his glass.

I flash a saccharine smile. "With Z? Foreplay's just a formality. He can slide in anytime."

Z's eyes lock on mine. "Don't tempt me, little one. You're already walking proof."

Carter groans, clutching his chest like he's been shot. "Aww, you two."

James mutters, "Get a room."

Dameon adds, "Preferably one that's soundproofed."

Z flashes them a smug smile. "Already had one."

We claim a sunken leather couch in the corner—one that's probably seen more naked bodies than a strip club booth on amateur night.

It's been hours. We've drunk enough to kill a lesser liver, and played voyeur to so much casual cock-sucking I stopped noticing it after round three.

But now, the debauchery is simmering down. The music's quiet, the crowd's thinned, and half the band has wandered off—each with one, two, or more groupies in tow. Finally, the night's coming to an end.

Hailee's perched on the armrest, feeding Dameon chocolate from her purse. Why she has chocolate in her purse, I have no idea. Cora's half-asleep in James's lap. Carter's splayed across a beanbag with a bottle of scotch and two naked girls tracing the tattoos on his chest. I sip my drink and lean into Z's side. His hand drifts lazily up and down my thigh. He's always touching me, like he needs constant contact.

"This feels... nice," I say quietly.

Z's mouth brushes the edge of my jaw. "It is. I haven't had this much fun in a long time."

I hesitate, then glance up at him. "Think anyone knew what we were up to?"

He smirks. "Only anyone who saw your 'I just came' face."

I huff a laugh.

We don't leave with the others. We linger, letting the moment stretch between us, neither of us quite ready to say goodnight. To let go.

Z helps me into my jacket, his hands warm on my shoulders.

"You sure you're okay heading back alone?" he mutters. "I can take you home."

"I'll be fine," I reply. "Besides... I've got a burner phone now, remember?"

He gives a devastating smile, one that reaches all the way to his eyes. "Use it."

I rise onto my toes, brushing a kiss to his cheek. "Count on it."

As I turn to leave, his voice follows me.

"Goodnight, Gigi."

"Goodnight, Z."

I press my lips together, trying—and failing—not to smile as I walk away.

Chapter Fourteen

Chloe

Present, 1 p.m.

Abdominal pain guy is a total sweetheart. He reminds me of my grandfather—same thinning white hair, sun-spotted skin, and motor mouth. If he didn't have a Russian accent, they could be twins.

He's managed to outline his entire family tree and half his life story in the span of walking from Triage to his bay. But I don't mind. I'm used to having my ear chewed off; it comes with having a grandfather who thinks storytelling is a competitive sport.

"...Olga used to say my food would be the death of me," he chuckles, wincing slightly. "Turns out, she was right."

Olga is his late wife. She died five years ago, collapsed in her GP's waiting room while Borris was parking the car. Gone before he made it inside.

"Let's not jump to conclusions, Borris," I reassure him, wrapping a blood pressure cuff around his arm. "Could be a dozen things causing your stomach pain."

"If I can't eat borscht anymore, you may as well kill me now." He winks. "Food's all I've got left." He pats his belly with theatrical flair. "You know, Olga and I opened the first Russian restaurant in Sydney? Ran it together for thirty years—until she passed."

I grin. "Let's run some tests before we ban beets. Your bloods should be back soon. We'll start with an ultrasound; if that doesn't give us answers, we'll move on to CT or MRI. In the meantime, the nurse is going to give you something for the pain."

"The good stuff?"

"The very best." I wink back.

I leave the nurse with him and head off to hunt down the scan machine.

"Hey, Olivia, where's the ultrasound?" I call out.

"Bay thirteen!" she replies over her shoulder.

I glance at the board and cringe. I should be moving faster, clearing more patients. I pull back the curtain at bay thirteen—and immediately wish I hadn't.

"Oh shit. I'm so sorry!" I whip the curtain shut again. "Do you, um, need assistance in there, sir?"

Please say no. Please say no.

The image is seared into my brain: a squat gone wrong, shit everywhere—bed, gown, legs, the pan. That was some explosion.

The *smell* alone nearly knocks me flat. I bury my face in my elbow.

Sweet mother of mercy.

"Can't a man get any fucking privacy?" the patient snaps.

"Apologies, sir."

"Don't mind him," a nurse says, already gloving up. "He's all bark, no bite. What do you need?"

"Ultrasound."

She nods, hauls it out, and wheels it over to me. I pointedly keep my eyes *anywhere* but on the war zone behind her. Once was enough.

"What crawled up his ass and died?" I whisper, removing my nose from my elbow.

"Two weeks of crap," she replies flatly.

"Seriously?"

"Fourth enema."

"Holy shit." My brows lift.

"Exactly. Not so holy—just shit. And buckets of it."

"Good luck. And thanks." I grip the machine and flee back to Borris, thanking every cosmic force that I didn't pull that chart. We're not supposed to pick patients, but that was more fecal trauma than I can handle in my state on day one.

Back in Borris's bay, I squirt some gel onto his belly and get to work.

"Monroe?" he asks, reading my badge. "Like Marilyn?"

"The very one. My parents are huge fans. They joke they almost named me Marilyn, but I like to believe they wouldn't be that cruel."

"Well, you're just as lovely—if not lovelier—than your namesake."

"Borris, you silver-tongued devil."

He laughs, his gaze warm as I move the wand across his abdomen.

"You're a young thing, aren't you? Your parents must be very proud."

"They are. Ridiculously so. I lucked out—best support system I could've asked for. I might be young, but you're in safe hands, I promise."

"I believe it. You've got that spark in your eyes, you're one bright kid. Are your folks in medicine too?"

"God, no." I laugh. "Mom faints at the sight of blood, and Dad wouldn't step foot in a hospital unless something was falling off. She's a kindergarten teacher with the patience of a saint. Dad's a retired builder, totally gruff on the outside but mush on the inside. I'm an only child, so yeah... I had a monopoly on their attention."

"And what made you want to be a doctor? Or is that too personal?"

I glance up, amused. "Borris, you told me your wife 'had a great rack', and your daughter once choked out your son over pirozhki. I think we passed 'personal' five minutes ago."

He chuckles. "Fair enough."

"I was diagnosed with Crohn's disease as a kid. Spent a lot of time in hospitals. Met some amazing nurses and doctors who made it bearable. I just... wanted to do that for someone else, you know?"

"You already are," he states gently.

My throat tightens. I blink fast and smile, shifting my attention to the monitor. I've worked and studied while sick more times than I can count. Nausea, joint pain, fatigue—I push through because I've always had to. That's the thing about growing up with a chronic illness: discomfort becomes your baseline. You learn to function through the fog. So I keep my body strong. I lift, train, move—whenever I can—because I need muscle to carry me when nothing else can. Because when my body crashes, I need it to know how to fight. And it does. Because I'm strong. And stubborn. And I've got shit to prove.

I pause, wand hovering mid-sweep.

"There was this one doctor," I explain. "Back when I was thirteen. No one could figure out what was wrong with me. I'd lost weight, was running fevers, and was always exhausted. Most of them thought I was being dramatic. That it was anxiety. Or hormones. You know—*girl stuff.*"

Borris watches me closely, expression sobered.

"But this one female doctor didn't. She was working a shift here—in this exact ER." My voice thins a little at the edges. "Took one look at me and said, 'I don't like how this feels.' Ordered a bunch of tests when she could've just sent me home, like every other doctor had."

He lets out a low sound, almost a hum.

"If she hadn't caught it when she did…" I trail off, letting the reality sit between us. "I might have ended up in emergency surgery. Or worse."

His gaze softens. "That's quite the guardian angel."

"She was," I whisper. "Didn't treat me like a kid. She saw *me*. And she put me on this… path. Showed me how powerful medicine can be, when it's done right."

I glance at the wand in my hand, the cold gel sliding across his abdomen. "So, yeah. That's why I'm here. I don't want to be another set of scrubs. I want to be someone who cares. Who listens."

Borris reaches for my free hand and gives it a firm squeeze. "Well, I hope the next kid who walks through those doors gets someone just like you."

"Thank you," I reply softly. "You know, you remind me of my grandfather. He calls me his little firecracker." I smile. "He's stubborn, opinionated, and swears too much—basically, your spiritual twin."

"Sounds like a stand up guy." He winks. "Though I'd upgrade you to flamethrower."

I laugh, the tension breaking. My eyes flick back to the monitor, and I finish scanning his abdomen. Four stones—nasty ones.

"Well, looks like we found your culprit—gallstones."

He groans. "Does this mean no more borscht?"

"You might have to make a few diet changes. Sorry."

"Ah, *blyat.*" He sighs.

"The good news is, none of them are blocking the duct and you don't have a fever, so no emergency surgery. But you'll need to follow up with your GP to figure out a long-term plan."

I squeeze the back of his hand in sympathy.

"Do you have any chest or back pain?"

"Actually, yeah—right here." He taps his sternum.

"Gallstones can mimic heartburn or chest pain. But I'll order an ECG to be safe."

"So... what now?"

"We keep you on fluids, continue the pain meds, no eating or drinking to give your gallbladder a break. We'll also give you anti-nausea meds if you need them. But once the pain settles, you can go home with a plan to follow up with your GP."

The sound of the curtain being pulled back makes me glance up. Hannah pokes her head in. "Hey, you free?"

"Give me two minutes."

I turn to Borris. "A nurse will come by soon for the ECG. I'll be back to go over the results."

He pouts dramatically. "Who will I talk to while you're gone?"

"You'll survive." I grin. "I won't be long."

I step out and lean against the wall. It's uncanny how much Borris reminds me of my grandfather. They have the same gift for making a stranger feel like family in under five minutes. One moment, I'm charting his vitals; the next, he's made his way into my chest.

I take a breath and shake it off.

Hannah's waiting with Sienna and Jax, so I head over to join them.

"Dr. Zac asked me to show you the morgue, the hospital's private tunnels, and how we handle helipad pickups. We've got an organ delivery arriving in ten," she explains.

Sienna gestures ahead. "Let's go."

We follow Hannah down the corridor toward the elevators. She points out the double fire doors. "Private tunnels. Swipe your pass to get in. We use them mainly for patient transfers." She keeps moving, and we trail behind here.

"So," I say, "where did you all study?"

We've only just met, but working side-by-side in the ER makes it feel like we've known each other longer. There's a connection, even if I barely know anything about them.

"Melbourne Uni," Sienna says.

"UNSW," Jaxon adds. "You?"

"Sydney Uni."

"You from Melbourne originally?" I ask Sienna while we wait for the elevator. She's not my favorite person, but I'll give her this—she's a solid doctor. Shame her personality doesn't come with the same credentials.

"Yep. Born and bred. Wanted a change, so I moved north for my internship."

"What about you, Hannah?" I ask as the elevator doors open.

"Sydney Uni, too. I'm in my third year," she replies, indicating the basement level on the panel. "That's where the morgue is."

I nod. "How's the ER treating you so far? Think you'll stick with it?"

She shrugs. "Fast-paced, chaotic, borderline traumatic... But I love it. Good for my ADHD brain."

Sienna gives a sharp snort and nods.

"What about you, how are you finding it?" Hannah asks.

"As far as first days go? No complaints," I reply.

Would be better if I weren't exhausted and in the middle of a Crohn's flare.

"I thought we'd be doing cooler shit," Sienna mutters.

"It's *literally* your first day," Hannah points out.

Sienna rolls her eyes. "Well, at least my day is going better than Stacks here, hitting the deck mid-trauma."

Jaxon drags both hands over his face, then tips his head back like he's praying for divine patience. "Seriously? Again with this?" he grumbles. "Put a sock in it, Sienna. And stop spreading gossip."

She smirks. "Call it gossip if you want—I call it live reporting."

"And I call it unprofessional," Hannah mutters, arching a brow.

The elevator dings open, and we step into a blast of sun. My first breath of fresh air since starting the shift. I tilt my face to the sky and close my eyes for a moment.

Hannah's giving the rundown, and I'm half listening, half taking stock of my body while basking in a rare moment of calm.

Overall? Not too bad. Exhausted, a little achy, but holding steady. I'd kill for a sandwich, though. A crusty, carby, melt-in-your-mouth kind of sandwich. But I can't risk it. Not until I'm off shift.

The whoop-whoop of the chopper blades builds as the helicopter descends onto the pad. A crew member hops out with a cooler and hands it to Hannah. Smooth. Efficient. Over in sixty seconds.

"Well, *that* was a waste of time," Sienna mumbles.

"You needed to know not to cross the red line. Now you do," Hannah replies evenly.

Sienna rolls her eyes again.

Sure, that trip to the helipad was a total waste of time, but I got a few precious seconds of sunshine. I'll take it.

"Later, losers," Sienna calls, as we step out of the elevator, already in search of her next patient. I do the same—heading in to treat a horrible burn on a woman's forearm.

I'm elbow-deep in a burn dressing when I catch Jax hovering outside the curtain, fiddling with his stethoscope.

"Spit it out," I say, peeling off my gloves.

He hesitates, then jerks his head toward the next bay. "Can you give me a second set of eyes?"

I follow him, curiosity already piquing. "What's the case?"

"Ten-year-old boy, vague abdominal pain. No fever, no vomiting. He says it's a six out of ten, but he's barely wincing. No rebound, no guarding. Bloods are fine. Urine is clean. No infection. Normal ultrasound."

"And?"

He blows out a breath. "Nothing's lining up. Kensington has already walked by once. And I don't want to call Zac in and sound like I've got no clue."

Ah. There it is. I glance sideways. "You're worried he's going to think you're not cut out for the ER after the fainting incident?"

He flinches.

"I'm not trying to throw shade," I add quickly. "We're in this together."

"I know." His voice is tight. "And yeah. I'm trying to stay ahead of it. I don't want that one moment to be what people remember… especially if Sienna keeps giving them something to talk about."

He exhales hard. "Honestly? I think he's playing it up. Trying to stay overnight. Mom says he's been different since the dad moved out—extra reserved."

He pulls back the curtain, and I step inside. A slim boy is lying on the bed, curled slightly, one arm across his stomach. His mother sits at his side, concern etched deep into her face.

"This is Chloe, one of our doctors." Jax steps aside so I can introduce myself.

"Hi," I say gently. "Mind if I ask a few questions?"

The boy nods. His name's Ethan. His pain has been there since last night. No recent falls or injuries. No family history of abdominal issues. But he's tired. Didn't want breakfast. Skipped soccer practice.

I press carefully around his abdomen. No specific tenderness, but he does flinch a little near the right lower quadrant.

"How's your appetite, Ethan?"

He shrugs. "I'm not hungry."

"Any issues with the toilet? Pooping? Peeing?"

"No."

"Does your tummy feel worse after eating certain things?"

He shrugs again. "I guess."

"Gluten?" I ask. "Like bread or pasta?"

His mom perks up. "Actually, he has complained before about a sore tummy after pasta. But the GP already ruled out a gluten intolerance."

I nod, thinking. Catching Jax's eye, I tip my head toward the curtain. He gets the message.

We step outside of the bay, and Jax crosses his arms. "We've ruled out appendicitis, renal, and even constipation. Everything's come back fine."

"He's not fine," I say. "It's just not obvious."

Jax frowns. "You don't think he's attention-seeking?"

"No," I affirm. "I think you're missing the quiet diagnoses. Could be mesenteric adenitis. Or atypical celiac."

He looks at me. "Really?"

"I've seen it before. The TTG antibodies and ESR might tell us more."

"We already did a CBC and CRP."

"Then add a celiac screen, ESR, and a repeat ultrasound—focused on the lymph nodes."

He hesitates.

"If you're wrong, it's still non-invasive," I point out. "If I'm right, you're not sending a boy home in pain."

Before he can respond, Dr. Kensington comes up behind him.

"Dr. Wells," he says smoothly. "Update on bay seven?"

Jax straightens. "Vitals stable. No acute distress. Labs and imaging pending. We're screening for less-obvious GI pathology."

Kensington's eyes flick to me. "And you're consulting a fellow intern for that?"

"I've come across something similar before," I jump in. "The symptoms didn't align at first, but it turned out we just needed a better look. Jax is on the right track."

Kensington stares at us for a moment. Then gives a clipped nod. "Let me know what comes back."

He walks off. Jax exhales so hard it's almost a groan.

"You didn't have to cover for me," he says.

"I didn't. You had it—you just needed some backup," I reply.

We walk toward Central. He drops into a chair and scrubs his face.

"I hate this," he mutters. "The whole... not knowing thing."

"You mean, being a doctor and a human?"

"No." He stares at the wall. "I mean, being the guy who's supposed to know it all."

I sit next to him, our knees brushing.

"You ever feel like everyone's waiting for you to screw up?" he asks.

I lift my chin. "Constantly."

He sighs. "Back at uni, I was top of every class. My parents act like I've cured cancer. But now, I'm scared to sneeze wrong in front of Kensington. Or Zac. Or you."

"Me?" I snort.

"You're super smart. Don't think no one's noticed."

I shift in my seat. "Want the truth?"

"Always."

"I've got Crohn's. Diagnosed as a kid. I'm working through a flare right now, actually."

"Shit." His eyebrows hit his hairline.

"I've learned how to function through the pain. You'd be amazed what adrenaline and caffeine can cover up."

He tilts his head. "Why are you telling me this?"

"Because I know what it's like to feel like you're not allowed to falter. That if you don't show up perfect, you'll lose everything. But that's bullshit."

Jax's jaw works, then he lets out a breath.

"Yeah," he says quietly. "It is bullshit. But it's hard to unlearn."

I playfully slap his arm. "Good thing you've got me."

He snorts. "God help me."

I gesture toward the curtain. "Come on. Let's ultrasound again. I've got a hunch."

Fifteen minutes later, we're huddled around the screen as it loads.

"Well, damn," Jax mutters. "You were right. Mesenteric lymphadenopathy."

"Some cases play hard to get." I try not to boast, but I'm grinning.

He explains it to the mom while I chart. She's grateful, emotional. Ethan looks relieved that someone finally gets what he's feeling.

As we walk out, Jax nudges me.

"Dr. House in a ponytail," he says.

I laugh. "You saying I'm brilliant and insufferable?"

"Weird and useful. But yeah, that too. I owe you one."

I snort. Napoleon calling me weird is a whole new level of irony.

"Thanks, Monroe."

"Anytime, Wells."

Chapter Fifteen

Chloe

Past

It always starts the same. A cramp, sharp and sudden, like barbed wire twisting under my skin. Then the nausea, creeping up slowly, sour and metallic. My whole system coils tight, my body folding in on itself. But I breathe through it. In. Out. Pain isn't new—it's practically a roommate at this point. Still, every flare brings a new flavor of betrayal.

It doesn't matter what day it is or how carefully I've scheduled my life—when my stomach decides to play up, everything stops. Uni, Eden, gym, family plans... all gone.

I'm curled up on the couch in the fetal position, cold sweat damp against my skin, with an almost-empty IV bag sagging from the coat rack I jerry-rigged into a drip stand.

Usually these episodes land me in the hospital for five to seven days. But since starting med school, I've learned how to manage at home when I can—my GI specialist prescribes the saline bags, and I keep a few on hand for bad days. I've built this little war-bunker setup. Pain meds, sick bags, a makeshift IV setup. A thermometer I trust more than most people. Everything within arm's reach. Control, or the illusion of it, is the only thing that makes this bearable. Plus, home has my bed, my own bathroom, and none of the constant cacophony of a hospital ward. There are only so many times you can handle a night nurse shining a light in your face, taking obs.

Don't get me wrong, I don't cut corners. I hydrate, monitor my vitals, push fluids and anti-nausea meds intravenously, and I always go into hospital when I *have* to. I'm no martyr. I'm just... practiced. This is my version of control.

I scroll endlessly through streaming services, eyes half-lidded, trying to land on something mindless. I settle on a rewatch. Familiar noise that's comforting.

Then my *other* phone pings. The one Z gave me.

Z

> Sorry for the late reply.

I messaged him hours ago to cancel our plans at Eden tonight. No details. Just: *Can't make it. Sorry.* He left me on read. And now... this.

I hesitate, thumb hovering over the keyboard.

I'm sick, but I don't want to tell him. It's too personal. But if I say nothing, he'll think I'm brushing him off.

Was it something I said? Or did? Or didn't do? Help me out here, little one.

Despite myself, I let out a dry laugh. Then grimace. Pain slices under my ribs like a rusted knife.

I'm sick. That's all. No need to panic.

I opt for the partial truth, even though it's vague.

Keep your fluids up. Can I send you soup?

Not that kind of sick.

What are your symptoms?

Oh my God. Seriously? What's he going to do—Google it and diagnose me over text?

I'm fine. Could use a distraction though…

Want company?

Me

> Not unless you can bring morphine.

Z

> And if I could?

I frown. What does that mean? That wasn't flirting. It felt... serious. He doesn't seem like the type to use recreational opioids. His eyes have always been clear, grounded. But damn, am I tempted. Not for the morphine—for *him*.

Do I really want him here?

My place—this version of me—isn't the one I show people. I'm not Gigi, the goddess at Eden, not Chloe the med student. Here, I'm stripped down. Sick and spent.

The thought of curling up with him on the couch—breathing him in, letting him wrap around me—wins out.

Me

> I'm not exactly sparkling company tonight.

Z

> I get it. But looking after people is my thing. I just got off work, and I can't go home knowing you're sick. Let me take care of you. Let me be there. Please.

That word—*please*—hooks me.

I know that feeling. The ache to *do something*, to take back power when everything is out of your hands.

I send him my address and the door code, then slowly peel myself off the couch. The IV bag's done, so I disconnect and clean up the supplies. After stripping out of my rumpled clothes, I rinse my face and put on fresh PJs. It's the best I can manage. I take out the cannula. He said I don't have to tell him what's wrong, but I don't want to *show* him either. I don't want him seeing the tubes, the syringes, the reality.

Twenty minutes later, there's a soft knock on the door.

"Gigi, it's me."

He steps inside, bringing with him a gust of clean air and his signature scent. Rolled-up shirt sleeves, tailored black pants, that calming presence I've come to crave—it's all so *him*.

His gaze lands on me and softens.

"Hey," he starts. "How are you feeling?"

"Better now," I lie with a weak smile.

He doesn't buy it. His eyes scan me, arms crossed over his chest. I've never seen him this serious before.

"What can I get you?" he asks, the crease between his eyes deepens.

"Nothing. Come join me?" I lift the blanket in invitation.

He settles in beside me, gently lifting my legs and laying them across his lap, tucking the blanket around us. Warmth spreads across my body from the contact. His hand finds my knee and stays there.

"I need to know what's wrong," he pleads after a long moment studying me. "I know it crosses the line—boundaries and all that—but I *can't* not know."

His voice is rough. His hand trembles slightly as he rubs his scruff.

Why does he need to know?

He doesn't look worried—he looks haunted. Like whatever he's seeing is pulling him somewhere else entirely. There's sadness in his eyes, and I want to ask. I really do. But now's not the right time.

"Hey..." I sit up, wincing, and take his hand in both of mine, lifting it to my lips. I kiss each knuckle. Slowly. "I'm okay, I promise. I've done this before. A lot, actually."

I search his face. He's still not convinced. So I give him more.

"I was diagnosed with Crohn's when I was thirteen. This is a partial bowel obstruction. It sucks, but it's not new. I know the signs. I know when to worry."

"You need to go to the hospital." Panic flickers behind his eyes.

"I *will*—if I get worse. But right now, I've got it under control with pain relief and anti-nausea meds."

He narrows his eyes. "Promise me that you'll go if you're still like this in twenty-four hours?"

"Promise." I squeeze his hand. He closes his eyes and exhales.

His reaction is sweet. But you don't freak out like this over a partial bowel obstruction. Something else is going on with him.

"You just got off work, right?"

He nods.

"Go take a shower, order something to eat. I don't have whiskey, but there's wine in the kitchen. Take a breather and come back to me. Keep me company."

I lift my feet so he can get out.

"All right, I'll be back." He hesitates. "Where am I going?"

"Down the hall. Bedroom's on the left—you can use the ensuite."

He gets up, still distracted, eyes flicking around. "Nice place."

"Thanks."

He says it like he means it, eyes lingering on the details. I love this apartment. Exposed brick, steel accents—an old warehouse turned loft. I saved every cent of my first few Eden paychecks to afford the deposit to purchase the place and furnish from scratch. Decorating it became my obsession. For once, I let myself splurge—not on clothes or nights out, but on something that actually mattered. My space. My sanctuary.

The first thing I renovated was the bathroom. It's the one room I knew I'd spend the most time in when I'm flaring. I went all out—double rain shower, deep spa bath, twin sinks, and yes, even a bidet (basically unheard of around here). I also had heated towel racks and heated floors installed. It's a goddamn oasis. If I'm going to be folded over in pain, I might as well do it in paradise.

He disappears down the hallway, and I slink back against the cushions. The second he's out of sight, another cramp rips through me. My whole body locks. I double over. Grab the sick bag. Dry retch. There's nothing left in my system, only bile and pain.

Cool fingers press my forehead. Strong arms scoop me up, settling me on his lap. One hand holds my head, the other sweeps my hair away.

"I've got you, baby. I've got you."

I collapse against him, limp with exhaustion.

"I bet this wasn't what you pictured when you paid for the full goddess experience," I croak.

He grins. "I don't know... you kind of make this look sexy."

I groan. "Ugh. I'm disgusting."

"Still hot. Just... slightly more bile."

I laugh—weak and hoarse, but real. It hurts. But in a contented way.

He ties off the bag, sets it on the floor, and gently runs his fingers through my hair. It's hypnotic, each stroke calming the storm still rumbling beneath my skin.

"Talk to me," I whisper.

"About what?"

"Anything."

"Okay… When I was six," he starts, "my dad took me to a planetarium. I threw up in the theater. Best night of my life."

His voice is low rumble. I don't register the story so much as the rhythm of it—the anchor it becomes. And just like that, I drift off.

I don't know how long I've been asleep. But when I wake, the apartment is quiet. Dark. Except for the light in the kitchen.

Z is in there, washing my glass at the sink. His shirt is damp, hair still wet from the shower. He moves through my space like he's always belonged here.

"You stayed," I murmur.

He turns, startled, his mouth lifting. "Where else would I be?"

There's a fresh glass of water on the coffee table. My blanket is folded neatly at the foot of the couch. The sick bag has gone.

I wonder what it would feel like to let someone take care of me more than once. This isn't how I pictured his first time in my apartment—me curled up, pale and puking. But here we are. And he's not here out of pity or obligation. He's here because he wants to be.

I've spent years learning how to hold it all together, how to carry myself through the worst of it without leaning on anyone. Strength has become my default. But tonight, there's comfort in being held. In not having to be the one doing the holding.

Z needs control. I see it in the way he watches me—the set of his shoulders, the flicker of panic in his eyes. But his control isn't about power. It's about purpose. He needs to help, to do something, to take care of someone. And for once, I let myself be the one who needs it.

We're different kinds of strong—his is action, mine is endurance. And somehow, in this moment, we fit. We balance each other.

It's not weakness, letting someone peek behind the curtain. I don't have to carry it all alone. And he doesn't have to hold the world up by himself.

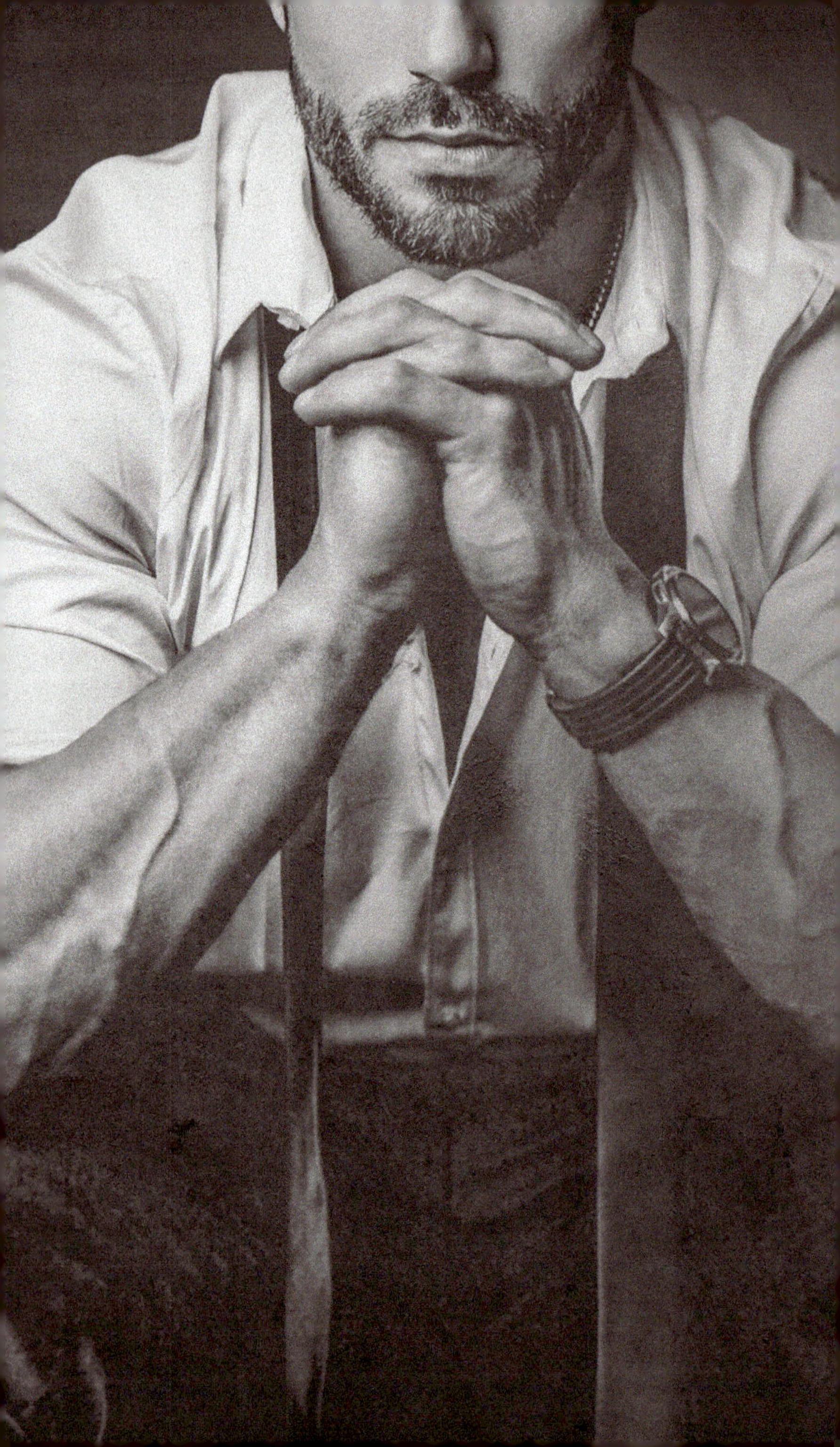

CHAPTER SIXTEEN

Zac

Present, 2 p.m.

For fuck's sake.

First, the kid faints in my trauma room, and now Ellis goes and drops an oxygen tank on her foot. My team is dropping like flies.

I rip off my gloves, dump them in the bio bin, and push open the staff lounge door with my shoulder.

"Ellis," I call out.

She's on the couch, a bare foot propped up on a rolled-up towel, a half-melted ice pack clenched in both hands. Her ponytail's lopsided, cheeks flushed.

"It's my toe," she groans before I can ask. "Throbbing like a bitch."

I crouch beside her and pull on a new pair of gloves.

"Let me take a look."

Under the nail, her toe's black, but there's no swelling. I guide her through a few movement checks, watching her face for pain.

"The good news is there's no break. The bad news is that we'll need to drain the pressure under the nail to ease the throbbing."

She winces. "Great. I'm such a dumbass. I'm so sorry."

"Accidents happen. Don't beat yourself up. Try not to pick fights with oxygen tanks next time."

Her mouth twitches.

"And how do I relieve the pressure? Scalpel?"

I raise a brow. "That'd be overkill. Something a lot simpler, but you're still not going to like it."

"That's comforting."

"Stay put."

I head out toward the supply cabinet, weaving through the usual ER madness. Crouching next to the cabinet, I rummage through drawers until I locate a paperclip and a small butane torch.

WHUP-WHUP.

Something flaps. Hard.

I freeze.

"Oh, fuck no."

Perched on the curtain rail of bay two is a judgmental feathered gargoyle, glaring down at me. Sonny is back.

We lock eyes.

I don't move. Neither does he.

He fluffs his wings slowly. Menacingly. Like he's winding up for a second round.

"Don't you fucking dare," I mutter.

He tilts his head.

I grab what I need in one hand and slowly back away, maintaining eye contact like I'm dealing with a velociraptor.

He doesn't follow. Just watches me retreat. He's probably disappointed I didn't offer a proper challenge.

Back in the staff room, I hold up the paperclip and torch.

Ellis stares. "Seriously?"

"Dead serious."

I straighten the clip and spark the torch until the end glows orange. The hiss of heat hits my ears. That acrid scent of burning metal curls into the air, biting at the back of my throat.

"On three," I say, voice firm. She flinches back slightly from the glow, eyes wide. I don't wait. "One, two—"

She yelps as I quickly push the tip through her nail. Blood spills out, bright and thick.

"Ow, Jesus—" Then she exhales. "Actually... that's starting to feel better."

I hand her a dressing pack. "Wrap it up and get back out there. You good?"

She nods, already reaching for the gauze. "I'm good."

"Excellent. Thank you, Dr. Ellis."

I step into the corridor and finally head toward the one thing I've needed since noon: a goddamn piss.

Should've gone when I was in my office with Chloe, but things escalated and... I got distracted.

I'm halfway to the staff bathroom when I spot Jaxon—head down, pacing nervously near the curtain of bay twelve, a chart clutched in his hand. His eyes flick toward me, then away.

He's about to do something stupid.

I sigh and reroute. My bladder can wait. Again.

"Everything okay, Dr. Wells?"

He startles, eyes wide.

Definitely about to do something dumb.

"Oh. Uh. Yes. I mean—sort of? I've got a patient with chest tightness and dizziness. No cardiac history, stable vitals, but she's convinced she's having a heart attack."

"Age?"

"Twenty-one. No significant history. No risk factors."

"ECG?"

"Clean. Troponins ordered. Just came back—negative."

I nod. "Anxious presentation?"

He exhales. "Says she's been having palpitations for weeks. Thinks she has some rare heart condition TikTok convinced her of."

Ah, the new age of medicine.

"Let's take a look."

We pull back the curtain. A young woman sits upright in bed, clutching her chest. Eyes wide. Breathing shallow.

"Hi, I'm Dr. Zac. Mind if I ask you a couple more questions?"

She seems nervous, bobbing her head. "Is it my heart? I googled it, and everything matches."

"I hear you," I offer calmly. "But your ECG is clear, and your bloodwork looks good. No signs of a heart attack."

"But it still feels tight."

"Anxiety can do that," I suggest. "Have you had any major stressors lately? Lack of sleep? Caffeine?"

She hesitates. "Finals. And my boyfriend broke up with me last week. I haven't eaten much in a couple days."

I nod slowly. "This is your body's reaction to the pressure. It's normal, even if it doesn't feel that way."

"So I'm not dying?"

"Not today. But let's make a deal: water, food, and at least six hours of sleep. Come back if things get worse."

She relaxes slightly. Jaxon watches, taking it all in.

Outside the curtain, I clap him on the shoulder. "Your instincts weren't wrong. You did everything right. Now, add context to the data. Not all chest pain is cardiac."

He nods, visibly relieved.

Then he blurts, "Hey, uh... can I ask something weird?"

Here we go.

"Shoot."

"Is Dr. Monroe your ex or something?"

I blink. Hard.

"What makes you ask that?"

He flushes immediately. "I mean—sorry, that's none of my business. I just—when she walked in this morning, you both looked like someone had dropped a defibrillator in a bathtub. I've never seen two people avoid each other's eyes that hard."

I bark a laugh despite myself. "Good diagnosis."

He grins, sheepish. "So?"

I consider it. The kid's green, but not stupid. And this ER has ears.

"We've... crossed paths."

He nods, clearly dying for more but smart enough not to press.

"Back to work, Dr. Wells."

"Yes, sir."

He scurries off, and I finally—*finally*—make it to the staff bathroom. And it's damn near spiritual. I brace one hand on the wall, groan under my breath, and let the tension drain out of my shoulders. Ten seconds of silence and relief. Best part of my shift.

Well. Not quite.

Coming in Chloe's panties wins. She better still be wearing me—my mess—under those scrubs.

I zip up, rinse off, and step into the corridor again, refocused, only to be stopped cold.

Sienna.

She's elbow-deep in a central line insertion. Solo.

Fucking hell.

Every instinct goes on high alert. This isn't just cocky; it's reckless. I've seen what happens when confidence trumps caution. I've held the hands of grieving families while we tell them their loved one didn't make it, knowing full well it was because an intern thought they knew better. Not on my shift.

I stride over. "Dr. Rhodes—update me."

She doesn't flinch, simply rattles it off. "Septic shock. BP tanked, heart rate spiked, skin mottled. Administering norepinephrine."

She pushes the meds through the IV while a nurse calls out, "BP's coming up. Stabilizing."

I clock the tremor in her left hand as she tapes the line. Her brow's damp, a fine sheen collecting at her hairline. The tension in the bay coils tight—like the moment before a code blue.

"Good save. Chase the blood cultures—we need to ID the bacteria. Start broad-spectrum antibiotics."

She nods. But she knows she crossed a line.

From across the ER comes that same screech that's haunted me all day. "HELP ME!"

My jaw locks. "Why is that fucking bird still here?" I mutter under my breath, already heading to Central.

"Olivia, get all junior doctors into the staff lounge. Now."

"Got it, boss." She salutes.

By the time I hit the staff room, the juniors are assembled.

They straighten when I step in.

"Okay, everyone, quick huddle," I announce. "Listen up."

I look at them—bright-eyed, green as hell, buzzing from adrenaline. They don't know how fast things can go sideways. *Yet*. I want to shake them and protect them in the same breath. God help me, I think I actually care about this lot.

"This is a teaching hospital, and you're here to learn. You are *not* here to show off or pretend you know more than you do. Because you don't. None of us does. I've been doing this for years, and I'm still learning every day."

I sweep my gaze across them. Chloe. Jaxon. Sienna. Hannah.

"The moment you stop learning is the moment you should quit. You're going to make mistakes. Try not to make them fatal. But if you do, own it, learn from it, and move forward. That's how we do it. But if I catch *anyone* ignoring protocols—performing procedures unsupervised—you're out. Am I clear?"

Their heads all bob in understanding.

"You're dismissed. Doctors Ellis and Rhodes, stay back."

Jaxon files out with his head low. Chloe meets my eyes—for a second—then quickly looks away, following him without a word. Not angry or cold. But... distant. I know what avoidance looks like.

What the hell did I miss?

I turn to Hannah. "Status on the parrot patient? I honestly can't take that damn bird screeching for help again."

"Ready to go. I was on my way to discharge her."

Thank fuck for small mercies. "Thank you, Dr. Ellis."

As soon as she leaves, Sienna doesn't wait for an invitation.

"I knew what I was doing," she fires off, arms crossed like a shield. "I've seen it done a dozen times."

I raise an eyebrow. "And *that* qualifies you to do it alone?"

"I reacted," she snaps. "The patient was crashing—what was I supposed to do, wait for backup while he died?"

"There's a difference between reacting and playing cowboy," I growl. "You wouldn't be the first intern to panic under pressure. You could've hit the lung. Missed the vein. Caused an embolism. Do you know how many ways that could've gone wrong?"

She opens her mouth to argue—then clamps it shut.

Her eyes flick away. And I see it land. The weight of what could have happened. The trace of shame beneath the bravado.

I drop my tone, but not my intensity.

"You do *not* touch a central line again unless you're supervised. Understood?"

She nods stiffly, swallowing hard. "Yes, Doctor."

"Good." She still looks stunned, but I let her sit with it. Better to feel it now than freeze in the next code. Rules exist for a reason. And I'm not here to coddle anyone, I'm here to teach. This is how people die—when someone thinks the rules don't apply to them.

I scrub a hand over my jaw, exhaling hard. That's my job—holding the line, even when it makes me the asshole in the room.

When I step back into the department, my focus shifts the second I catch sight of Chloe. She's at Central, already walking toward a bay, head down.

Not yet.

I jog to catch her.

"Hey," I call. "Can we talk?"

She stops but doesn't turn. Just stands there a moment before slowly facing me. "Sure. What's up?"

"In private." I scan for an open trauma room and gesture toward one. "In here."

We duck inside, and the air constricts.

I step closer. "Are you okay?"

She crosses her arms. "Yep."

"You sure?"

A shrug. "Yeah. Why?"

I search her face, trying to read past the mask. "No reason. It... doesn't hurt to check in. It's part of my job."

She flashes a smile, all teeth and tension. "Then you've done your due diligence, Doctor. I'm fine."

Doctor? What the fuck?

That smile's too polite. I've seen her real one, the one that lights up her eyes.

This isn't that. She's slipping behind glass, shutting the door from the inside. I can't lose her, too. Not when I've only just started figuring out what the hell this even is.

She turns to leave, and instinct takes over. My hand lands on her forearm—warm, soft, a little clammy. Her skin jolts beneath my touch like she wasn't expecting it. Neither was I.

I smell the faintest trace of her shampoo, a clean citrusy scent that's familiar. Impossible to ignore.

"Are you pissed that I accidentally called you Gigi?"

She stops and exhales deeply through her nose before turning around. "No. No one knows what it means. They probably think you forgot my name." She tries to smile, but it doesn't quite land.

I don't care what anyone else thinks. What matters is *her*. Why she's closing herself off from me.

"Then what is it? And don't lie to me again."

She looks up at me, and there it is. The wall. The flicker of sadness behind her eyes. Hurt.

"Now's not the time, Zac."

She says my name softly, and it slides under my ribs and lodges there.

"Later, then?"

She hesitates long enough for it to sting.

"Later, I promise."

She walks out, closing the curtain behind her. I don't follow. Don't move. I stand there, stuck in place.

That wasn't a brush-off. That was a retreat. And I felt it in my bones.

What the fuck has happened?

I know how to stop a heart. Restart a lung. Clamp an artery with seconds to spare. But I don't know how to stop this. Whatever just slipped between us?

It felt a lot like the beginning of goodbye.

Chapter Seventeen

Chloe

Past

I could watch this man all day.

Z stands at the barbell, shoulders stacked, muscles flexing with every clean rep. Not gym-bro inflated—he's functional strength, clinical efficiency, sharp angles and sweat-slicked skin. Every time his abs contract, I picture them pressed against mine. I wouldn't mind him pushing me to the floor right here. Right now. Pinning me down... hard.

"You're drooling, Gigi."

"Can't help it. Your body's ridiculous."

"Your turn." He starts loading the bar, guessing my weight range.

"Add two more."

He lifts a brow. "You sure?"

"Heavier."

He loads up the bar without another word. I step up, plant my feet, and lift clean to the hips. Twelve reps—smooth. No puffing. No struggle.

I drop the bar, hands brushing the back of my leggings. When I glance up, he's watching me like he wants to bend me over and prove gravity has nothing on what he can do to me. His expression mirrors what I imagine mine looked like when it was him exercising: molten. Focused. Ready to devour.

Game on.

"Chin-ups. Let's go." He smacks my ass as he walks past. "Be right back."

I watch him walk away, toward reception, and bite my lip. Watching him move is a study in temptation.

We're at his gym—all polished chrome and glowing LED panels. Mine's basically a glorified storage closet in my building: one treadmill, some dusty free weights, and a decrepit fan that rattles as it works.

I never bothered with a real gym membership. No point paying for something I can't always use. With an autoimmune disease, your body's a roulette wheel—could be fine today, but floored tomorrow with a random infection, virus, or flare. This place, though? I'd happily fork out a chunk of my salary. It's a temple. Polished floors, state-of-the-art machines, everything gleaming. Even the air smells clean. There's no sweat, chemical bleach or stale locker-room funk. I breathe in cool, crisp, expensive air instead.

"You ready?" He jogs back, grinning.

"You first. I want a show."

He pulls off his shirt, and I whistle, unashamed. That body. Every ripple of muscle, the sheen of sweat—he moves like sex.

He grabs the bar and pulls up, slow and deliberate. His lats fan out like wings, abs flexing as he controls every inch of the movement. Each pull-up is poetry. Dirty, filthy poetry that I could recite by heart.

Getting sweaty is now officially my second-favorite thing to do with him.

He drops down. "Your turn."

His hands grip my hips as I jump and catch the bar. Our eyes lock. Fingers linger, brushing from my waist to my ribs, then—

"Z—"

His thumbs find my piercings, and even through the padding of my sports bra, I shudder.

The gym is empty. Somehow, somewhere, everyone disappeared.

"Pull it down," I whisper.

The last hour has been a cock tease for him as much as it's been a clit tease for me.

He wrestles the bra down, baring my breasts. They spill out, high and tight from the compression, nipples pebbled and waiting.

"Fucking gorgeous," he mutters, brushing his thumbs across them again. This time, I feel it all the way to my core.

"Start the set."

I grip the bar tighter and begin.

One. Two.

Pull-ups while turned on? Torture.

By the third, I'm gasping. Z's hands steady my hips, guiding my rhythm. As I lower myself, he leans in to suck a nipple between his lips—hot, wet, and greedy.

"Keep going. You stop, I stop," he warns.

I whimper, the burn of the workout eclipsed by the burn beneath my skin. I'm shaking, and not from the exertion.

He switches sides—tongue circling, teeth grazing. His mouth is all heat and hunger, leaving my chest wet and tingling.

The music pumping through the gym is bass-heavy and low. I glance around again. Still alone.

My arms burn as I pull my chin to the bar, then lower with slow, controlled focus. His breath scorches across my stomach as I lift again, muscles straining. The heat of his body presses into mine, making every nerve hum. I drop down once more—he meets me there, mouth locking around the left piercing, pulling a moan straight from my throat.

I'm barely holding it together by the time I finish my set. Slick and throbbing.

"Fuck me already," I heave, still holding on to the bar.

He slips off my sneakers and socks, then peels my leggings and panties down—both soaked through.

"Wrap your legs around me." He's already freed himself—thick and flushed. I slide onto him in one deliberate, stretching thrust.

My head falls back. "Z—"

"Fuck—so hot," he growls.

I cry out, clinging to him with my legs. It's frantic, urgent, and feral. He fucks me hard, his hands gripping my ass, my arms holding the bar above us to balance as I ride him.

My shoulders burn from the pull-ups, and my thighs are already trembling.

"I can't," I pant. "My arms—"

He's got most of my weight, but I'm spent. My grip falters. My muscles burn. I'm seconds from giving out.

"Let go."

My hands finally peel away, my biceps grateful for the relief, and I wrap my forearms around his neck. Z's still inside me as he carries me across the gym, past the rows of machines, to the yoga section in front of the floor-to-ceiling mirror.

"You know what I fantasize about every time I train here? You. In this mirror. Writhing. Taking every inch while I watch you fall apart for me."

I strip my bra off, baring everything. He lays me across the yoga ball, pulling out, making me whimper.

"Zaddy's got you, little one."

The nickname slides under my skin like a wire pulled tight. I clench around nothing.

He drops to his knees and drapes my legs over his shoulders, rolling me back until my head tips upside down and my arms dangle, boneless, to the floor. The world tilts. I'm completely weightless and under his control as he keeps me steady on the ball.

Z dives in like a man starved, tongue hot and hungry, licking me open. Moaning like I'm the feast he's waited for. It's filthy, obscene, and beautiful.

My palms press flat to the mat. They're the only thing grounding me. I watch upside down in the mirror—his face buried between my legs.

"I couldn't wait any longer to taste this pussy."

There's something insanely hot about a guy who stops mid-fuck just to eat you out—who couldn't wait any longer to taste you.

He's in his element—devouring me on instinct—and I'm not about to drag him out of it. So I let go. Close my eyes. Let the weightlessness take over as his tongue glides through my folds, cleaning me up just to make a mess of me again.

Then his mouth seals around my clit and sucks—hard—stealing the breath from my lungs. A beat later, his teeth scrape over it, just enough to spark. The third time he does it, my whole body clenches. Muscles coil tight. White-hot stars explode behind my eyelids.

He rolls the ball forward, wiping his mouth, lowering my legs from his shoulders.

"Turn over."

His cock is red and angry, jutting from his shorts. He quickly rips them off, so he's completely naked.

I lie on my stomach over the exercise ball and place my hands on the ground. He's taller, so he lifts my legs wheelbarrow-style to line us up. He enters me from behind in one thrust.

"Z—"

"Fuuuck, Gigi."

The ball rocks beneath us as he moves. I raise my head, meeting his eyes in the mirror. He's locked on me—burning bright and setting me on fire.

"You wreck me," he growls hoarsely.

"Right back at you."

Looking into his eyes, I know this man is going to destroy me when it ends. And maybe I'll let him. A part of me is already hoping he breaks me—so I don't have to keep pretending this is casual. We're past any line. Boundaries have not only been blurred, they've been fully erased. We're so far past *that* point now, it's laughable to think there was even a line to begin with. I'm completely myself when I'm with him; it's no act. Every time I think sex with him can't get any better, Z takes it to the next level and blows my mind.

He fucks me until my muscles give out. The ball rolls, the world clouds, and I forget everything but him. He spills inside me with a strangled grunt, then keeps thrusting, dragging it out, working it in. The way he comes is phenomenal, I could watch it on replay over and over again.

He hits a spot deep inside of me, and I fall apart again. The orgasm ambushes me—violent, blinding, and so good it's almost cruel.

He pulls out slowly, his cum spilling down my thighs, hot and thick.

Everything burns. My muscles spasm, shot to hell from the workout, from him. My arms give up. I drop, hard, onto my knees, my forehead resting against the ball. I cling to it, panting, dizzy, and drenched in sweat, every nerve still vibrating.

I can't breathe. Can't think.

All I feel is *him*.

Then, he drops to his knees behind me.

"What are you—"

The words barely form before he slides his head between my thighs and pulls me down, seating me on his face as if it's a throne.

His tongue drags through the mess, groaning.

I jerk from the overstimulation, thighs twitching. "Z—fuck—"

He *moans*, mouth sealed around my pussy, tongue pressing deep. He moves out from under me and grabs my jaw. "Open," he rasps.

My lips part without hesitation.

He leans in and spits it onto my tongue.

I swallow.

My whole body convulses with something I can't name. It's obscene. Tender. Raw.

Mine.

He pulls me onto his lap on the mat and wraps his arms around me. I melt into him—nothing but a pool of sweat, soreness, and satisfaction.

"Look at you... ruined and radiant," he praises, brushing sweaty strands of hair from my face.

I hum, too boneless to speak.

I'm sure my face is red and flushed, and I'm sweating like a pig. But I appreciate the compliment. I would tell him that if I could open my mouth to form the words.

"I'm not done with you yet. One more set." His chuckle is almost evil, which makes a laugh burst from my chest.

"How do you still have stamina, old man? I'm almost half your age and I'm ready to collapse."

He scoops me into his arms, bridal style. "Old man? Watch your mouth."

After everything, his strength still amazes me. I press my lips to his throat.

He lifts me onto the treadmill, hooking my legs over the handrails so I'm suspended and wide open for him.

My thighs are already trembling. My eyes go wide.

I won't be walking tomorrow. And honestly? I don't care.

I'd crawl home with his name on my lips if it meant just one more minute in his arms, pretending this is something we never have to give up.

Chapter Eighteen

Chloe

Present, 3 p.m.

Four hours to go.

I've almost made it through my first shift.

If this is what I can handle running on no sleep and a flare, imagine what I'll be able to do at full capacity.

I helped patients today. And that's what matters. It's rewarding and satisfying on a soul-deep level.

Don't get me wrong, I could sleep for a week. My muscles hate me. My feet might stage a rebellion. All I want is a scalding bath with Epsom salts, something warm and pureed to eat, and to sleep like the dead.

I'm back in at seven tomorrow morning. But I did it. And I'm proud of myself. So proud I could cry.

I know I told Zac we'd talk later, but I can't face him right now. I'm drained—physically, mentally, emotionally. I don't have the strength to hear the word *married* and protect my heart from fracturing.

I'll text him instead. Ask if we can talk tomorrow before the next shift. I know I'm avoiding the inevitable. Postponing it. But tomorrow is a new day. With food and hopefully sleep, I'll be better able to face the fallout.

The staff lounge smells like microwaved tuna, and I resist the urge to gag. We're crowded around the small table, elbow-to-elbow, everyone half-slouched.

Jax is shoveling down a suspiciously beige pasta. Hannah's nursing a sad-looking salad. Sienna, of course, has perfectly sliced avocado on sourdough toast. And me? I'm sipping electrolytes and pretending it's a choice.

"That all you're having?" Sienna asks, eyebrows raised as she clocks my bottle of water and nothing else.

I cap it slowly. "Not very hungry."

"How can you not be hungry?" she observes, too close for comfort. "You've only been sipping water all day."

"Had a dodgy slice of pizza last night." I shrug. It's only half a lie. "Still not feeling quite right."

Jax looks up from his pasta. Our eyes meet for half a second. He's the only one who knows about my Crohn's. He doesn't say anything—just quirks a brow and goes back to his meal.

"Well, sucks for you," Sienna comments, licking some avocado off her thumb. "The vending machine is down, and all they've got left in the café is egg sandwiches."

"So, business as usual," Hannah mutters.

We sit in silence for a few moments. Then, as if on cue, the postmortem begins.

"All right," Jax begins, his mouth half full. "Craziest case so far?"

Sienna grins. "The woman with the parrot. It bit the nurse trying to triage her. Still cackling about that."

"She was my patient!" Hannah exclaims. "And her blood pressure was sky-high because of that damn bird screaming 'HELP ME' on repeat."

"Okay, fair." Jax nods. "But Chloe wins. No contest."

"Me?"

"I heard you pulled a Bluetooth speaker out of some dude's ass."

God, that feels like forever ago.

I blink innocently. "Technically, I extracted a foreign object from the lower gastrointestinal tract."

"I heard it was playing Pitbull when you pulled it out." Sienna laughs.

"That wasn't even the worst part of today," I moan. "Cockroach Spider Lady takes the crown."

"Oh my God," Hannah whispers. "Was that real?"

"Very." A shiver runs down my spine. "They were nesting in her ear."

Jax pushes his pasta away. "Thanks. Now I'm done."

"You're welcome."

There's a lull in conversation until Hannah glances over at Sienna. "So... what did Zac say to you?"

Sienna groans, dropping her fork. "He *eviscerated* me."

"You performed a central line, unsupervised, on a crashing patient. What did you expect, a gold star?" Hannah deadpans.

"I saved his life."

"You got lucky," I add quietly. "And Zac's not wrong—we're still learning. That line could've gone south. Fast."

"I had it under control," Sienna insists. "It was fine."

"This time," I say.

She goes quiet, tapping her nails against the side of her plate.

I take another long sip from my bottle, buying myself a moment. I know Jax is watching me. He waits until the others are distracted, then leans in, voice low. "You okay?"

I nod.

"You sure? Because... I know. About you and Zac."

My head snaps toward him.

"Relax," he rushes out. "I'm not going to tell anyone. But... maybe keep the hallway eye-fucking to a minimum."

I open my mouth, equal parts horrified and defensive, but the door swings open before I can speak.

"Dr. Monroe—Mr. Andreev's ECG came back all clear," a nurse announces, stepping into the lounge with a folder.

Grateful for the interruption, I rise. "Thanks, Kara."

I don't look back as I leave.

There wasn't any eye-fucking going on, was there? I thought we were showing restraint.

Clearly, I was wrong. Who else saw?

I force my thoughts aside and tug back the curtain, pasting on a smile.

"Borris. Good news, you're all clear. You can go home."

He's slumped in the bed. Eyes closed, skin pale.

"Hey, Borris. Wakey wakey."

No movement.

I step closer and shake his shoulder. Still nothing.

"Hey, Borris, wake up for me," I call out louder this time. I press my knuckles hard into his sternum. He doesn't flinch,

Panic slices clean through me. I press two fingers to his neck.

No pulse.

"Shit. Shit. SHIT."

I slam my fist on the emergency button and lower the head of the bed, flattening him out. "I need help in here!" I shout, launching into compressions.

Dr. Kensington bursts in, gloving up. "When did you last check on him?"

"I don't—I don't know. Maybe an hour ago?" My voice is too high. Too fast. I can't think. My hands are moving at lightning speed, and my mind is working double that pace.

Zac rushes in. "What happened?"

"Gallstones. His ECG was clear. I don't know how long he's been down," I stammer.

"Crash cart!" Zac yells.

I keep pumping. "Come on, Borris. Stay with me."

The cart arrives. A nurse fits the mask over his mouth while Zac preps the paddles and hands them to Kensington.

"Hold compressions," Zac orders.

I yank down Borris's gown and step back. Kensington applies the paddles.

A long, steady beep.

Kensington frowns. "Asystole. Resume compressions."

I get back on his chest. Arms burning. Forehead slick with sweat.

Don't fucking do this, Borris. Your family needs you.

"Amp of epi," Zac instructs, passing the syringe to Kensington.

"Pupils fixed and dilated," calls the nurse on the oxygen bag.

Zac lowers his voice. "He's been down a while."

No. I keep going. Harder. Faster.

Another nurse connects the heart monitor. Still flat.

"Switch out," Kensington offers, stepping closer, ready to take over.

"I've got it." My arms shake.

"Hold compressions."

I freeze.

The long, droning beep swallows the bay. Flatline.

"Still in asystole," Zac states.

I dive back in. "Come on. Please. Come on."

Kensington looks at Zac. "Time to call it?"

"No, wait—" My voice cracks. "Please. Let's try another amp. Just one more." I glance up at Zac, *begging*.

He stands at the foot of the bed, arms crossed tight. His eyes meet mine for a few seconds before he nods.

"One more. Then we call it."

Kensington gives the second dose. I keep compressing. My arms are lead, and I'm drenched in cold sweat.

"Hold compressions," Zac says softly.

I step back.

The flatline tone drones out again.

Zac looks at me, gentler than I can handle. "You ready to call it?"

His expression is full of compassion, and I hate it. I hate how soft his voice is. I hate that he's treating me like I'm fragile. I want to scream at him.

I drop my gaze.

No, I'm not ready.

But I nod.

"Time of death, 3.26 p.m.," I call out, voice hollow.

I shake my head. Swallow the sob crawling up my throat. This can't be real. I turn and walk out without sparing a glance at poor Borris, Zac, or anyone else in the room. Kensington squeezes my shoulder as I pass, but I can't feel anything except the weight of failure.

I can't fucking do this.

I walk fast, nearly breaking into a run, and lock myself in the women's staff bathroom. I sit on the closed toilet lid and fold myself in half as the sobs come crashing out. They're loud. Ugly. Painful.

I cleared him.

I told him he could go home.

And now he's gone.

Because of me.

I'm so sorry, Borris. I'm so fucking sorry.

This is all my fault. I don't know what I missed, but I fucking missed something.

The bathroom door creaks open.

"Chloe?" Zac says gently. "Let me in."

I cover my mouth to smother the sound and shake my head, even though he can't see me. I don't want him to hear me or, worse, see me like this. Weak.

"I'm not leaving until you open the door."

A shudder rips through me, but I unlock the stall.

He steps in. And the second I see his face—those warm brown eyes, heavy with sympathy—I fall apart all over again.

He pulls me into his chest. Holds me like he means it. One hand on the back of my head, the other across my spine. I cry into him. Ugly, ragged sobs that shake my whole body. Silently, he rocks me.

Eventually, the storm inside me begins to quiet. Each breath comes a little easier. My sobs soften into hiccups, my body no longer trembling. I stay wrapped in him for a moment longer, letting the safety of his arms anchor me.

Then, slowly, I lean back. He tips my chin up.

"How are you feeling?"

I shake my head. "I was just talking to him. He told me about his family. His wife. His kids…" My voice breaks. "And now he's gone."

"It's the hardest kind of loss," he assures me quietly. "When it's personal."

"Especially when it's your fault."

"It wasn't."

"I missed something. I must have."

"You didn't. I spoke to Kensington—you followed every protocol. Nothing in his chart or test results indicated this. He must've had a silent condition, something nobody caught. You did everything right. I know it hurts. But today was his time. Sometimes, no matter what we do, we can't change the outcome. Every day, around a hundred and fifty thousand people leave this world—and today, he was one of them. It's unfair, and it feels personal. But you'll learn to live with it, and you'll eventually learn to accept it."

"I'm not cut out for this," I whisper. "I thought I was. I really did. But I'm not." Angry tears sting my eyes again. This time they're not grief-fueled, they're full of shame.

"You're doing better than you think," Zac tells me. "Emergency medicine's not for everyone. But choosing another field doesn't stop you having to deal with death. Patients will die on your watch, and you must accept that. Trust me, I'm speaking from experience."

I swallow hard.

"How do you deal with it?" I ask. "How do you live with it?"

His smile is rueful. "I'm the worst person to answer that."

"Why?"

"I'll tell you another time." He glances around. "Preferably not in the women's bathroom."

I snort.

"Last place I want to be caught with an intern." He lifts his eyebrows.

Fair point.

"You okay?" he asks. "Want to go home?"

"No. I need to finish the shift." It's the right thing to do, the only thing that makes sense.

He nods. "I'll see you out there. Come find me when you're ready—we'll finish this conversation."

He wipes the tears from my cheeks with his thumbs. Kisses my forehead. And slips out.

I take a deep breath and exit the stall, washing my tear-streaked face. My reflection is a disaster. Splotchy, red, and haunted.

Somewhere out there, they're clearing Borris's bed. Making space for the next patient.

One moment you're promising someone they're okay.

The next, you're signing off on their death.

And I have to walk back out there like none of this ever happened.

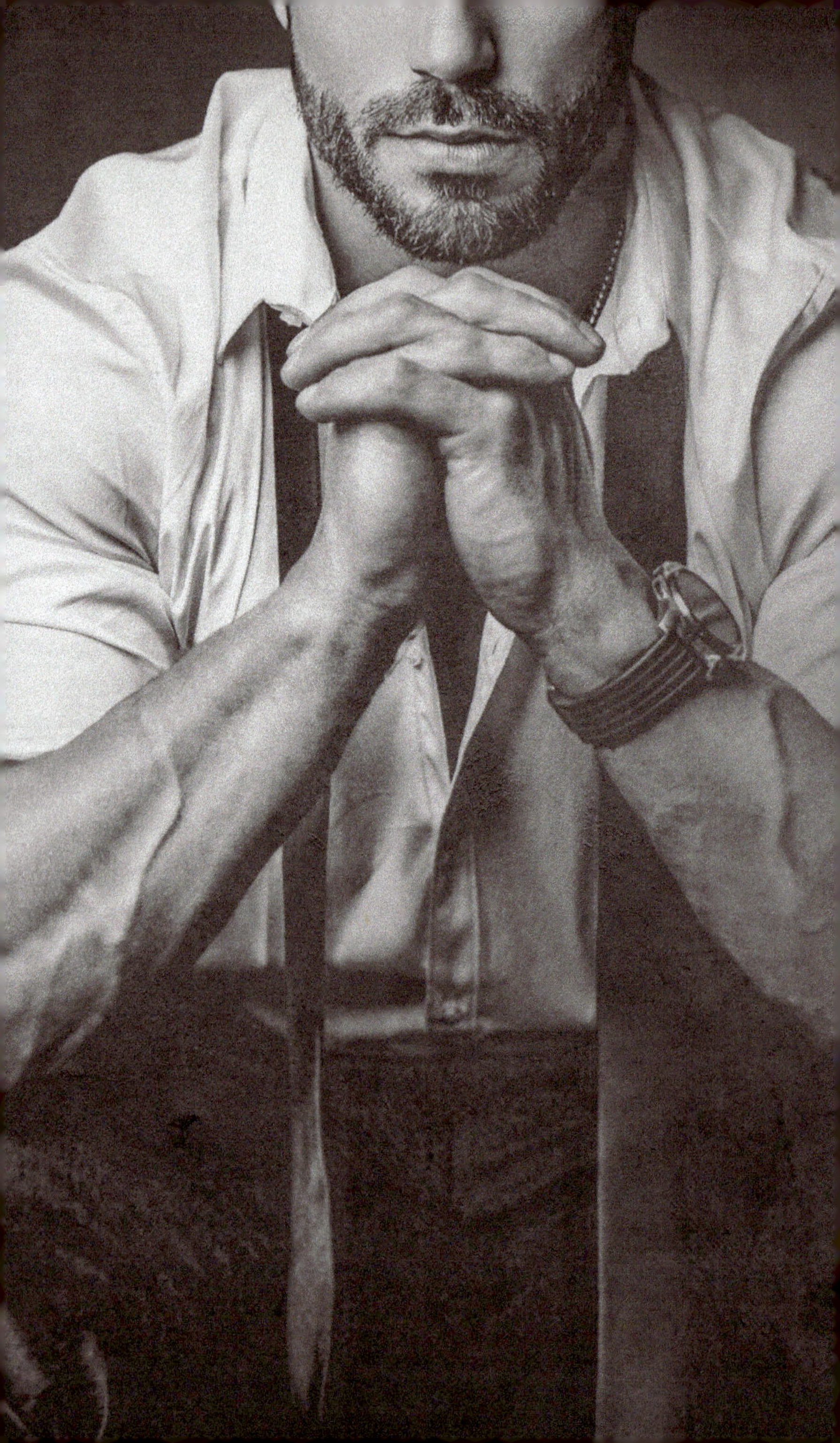

Chapter Nineteen

Zac

Past

I don't come here often.

Not because I don't want to—but because when I do, it destroys me.

Tonight, the air is crisp, laced with the damp bite of turned soil and eucalyptus from nearby gum trees. Wet leaves stick to my boots, and my breath fogs out in puffs.

Sydney's winters rarely demand much. No snow, no black ice, only the illusion of cold. But now, the polar blast cuts through my coat and bites at my skin. I blow into my hands, rub them together, anything to feel warmth. Anything but this.

"Hey," I say softly. "It's late. I know. Couldn't sleep."

The words fall flat against the silence.

Somewhere in the distance, a bat chirps. Something rustles in the grass. But all I can focus on is the way the cold settles deep in my bones. This place doesn't just hurt—it hollows me out. From the moment I turned the car onto the gravel drive, I felt it in my chest. A phantom pressure. My body knows what's coming before my mind lets it in. The ache isn't metaphorical. It's cellular. My chest constricts. My throat burns. My legs get heavy, dragging me down before I even reach where I'm going.

Every step toward her feels like I'm walking barefoot on broken glass. And yet, I come back. I always do. Even when I swear I can't anymore. Even when the guilt claws at my insides, whispering that I don't deserve to speak her name.

I've been dreading this visit for months. Dreading what I'd have to say and what I might feel. Dreading the fact that I don't even know if I'll feel anything at all—and how that scares me more than the pain ever could.

Because this isn't just a conversation. This is a confession. A reckoning. And deep down, I know that once I start—once I say the thing I've buried inside me—I can't take it back. I can't un-feel it. I can't un-know what it means.

"I'm sorry," I apologize softly, shaking my head. "I've got no one to blame but myself. I put us here. No one else."

Casey doesn't answer.

I've been picking up double shifts just to think straight. Twenty-four-hour madness in the ER is easier to manage than twenty-four minutes alone in my own damn head. At least at the hospital, I know what needs fixing. At least in a trauma room, there's no risk of calling a patient the wrong name.

Because that's the fear now.

That I'll slip. That I'll call Gigi *Casey*, or worse—call Casey *Gigi*. They look nothing alike—different hair, different laugh—but somehow, my mind blurs the lines anyway. One day I'll forget which set of eyes I'm drowning in, whose voice is echoing in my ears, whose hair I'm threading between my fingers in the dark.

And God help me... I don't want to forget either.

They deserve better.

I drop my gaze, the wind whistling through bare branches overhead. "I've been trying to keep it together—for you. For me. For the idea of *us*. But I can't keep splitting myself in half like this, pretending."

Eden was never supposed to be anything but a pressure release. The guys have been members for years, always trying to drag me along. I resisted—until two years ago, when I finally gave in. Because I had nothing left in the tank.

It wasn't only about sex. It was a place where I didn't have to feel for a while. To not carry every loss like a second spine. Rules, control, and the illusion of calm.

Eden gave me that. And it worked—for a while.

I could have my needs met quickly and quietly with no fuss. Without putting in the effort to get to know someone. As fucked up as it sounds now, I didn't care who they were. Not their names, their stories, or their lives. They were background noise.

There was no risk of connection, the kind I had with Casey. She was my heart, my home. Until I picked the wrong goddess.

And suddenly, everything that had been clean got messy. Everything that was numb came roaring back.

Because she wasn't background noise.

She was color. Loud, blinding color in a world I'd let fade to grayscale.

And after that night, nothing—not even Eden—felt the same again.

"I didn't mean for it to happen," I add quietly. "With her."

The wind picks up around us, and I squint against the cold air burning my eyes, making them water.

"I can't lie to you anymore. I tried to keep it surface-level. I did. But there's something about her, Case. She's..."

My hands push into my coat pockets as I angle my body away from her, my eyes fixed on nothing.

No matter how hard I try to trace it back—what made Gigi different, what made her stick—I come up blank. She's kind and beautiful. Funny in a dry, sarcastic way that always makes me laugh. But a lot of people are those things. It's not just that.

Maybe it was fate. Or my soul catching the echo of its missing piece.

I press the heel of my hands into my eyes and try to make sense of the confusion swirling around my brain.

I don't even know her real name. Where she grew up, what she wanted to be as a kid, who broke her heart first. But none of that stops me from falling.

Those details don't even matter. Strip away the labels, the past, the formalities—what's left is the core. And her core... it's good. Soft but fierce. I feel it in my gut every time I look at her.

And I want to know her. Not just touch her. I want to be near her, protect her, make her laugh when the world is shit. I want to give her everything.

Even our kink—this whole Zaddy thing—is new to me. Casey and I tried it once. It felt staged. Like we were both playing roles we didn't audition for. But with Gigi, it's like something I forgot I already knew how to do. It was always there, waiting. For her.

It's not only about dominance, but about care and instinct too. I want to guide her and watch her thrive. I want her safe. Held. Unshakable.

It's fucked up how little I know about her. And how sure I am that she's already part of me.

"I feel like I'm betraying you."

Pausing, the shame creeps up my spine. Because saying it aloud makes it real.

"I'm scared," I admit. "Of letting go. Of forgetting the sound of your voice. Of loving someone else. Of not loving you enough if I do."

Silence answers me again.

"I miss you," I tell her. "Every fucking day."

The earth is soft here, sunken slightly from time and weight. Moss growing into the lettering etched into stone.

"I still hear your voice, you know," I whisper. "When I'm tired. When I'm alone at night."

My head shakes in disbelief.

Come away with me, she'd asked the night before she died. That's what I hear, day after day. For so long I wished that I had. Until Gigi.

"I haven't stopped loving you. That hasn't changed. And it never will."

I exhale slowly.

"But you don't own my whole heart anymore."

The words are a betrayal, even as I whisper them. I shake my head again, ashamed—not of the truth, but of how it happened. I let my guard down and Gigi broke through. Just a sliver. Enough to slip through the crack. And now that she's in, she's not leaving.

"I didn't plan this."

I wasn't looking. Wasn't ready. But the universe shoved her into my life anyway, and I've been spiraling ever since.

"But it's happened. And I can't undo it."

Kneeling down, the cold seeps through the knees of my pants. I adjust the bouquet—pink gardenias, her favorite—until they sit just right in the vase. Casey hated anything crooked.

The wind bites at my skin and I pull my coat tighter around me. "I hope... someday, you'll understand. And forgive me."

I used to think you could only love one person at a time. That for someone new to take root, the old love had to wither, or at least make space. But I know now that's bullshit. There's room for both.

What I feel for Gigi doesn't diminish what I have with Casey. It's different, but it's just as real. Just as powerful. Just as consuming.

Time doesn't matter much when it comes to the heart.

"I love you, Casey."

I brush away the wet leaves clinging to the granite.

The headstone is simple. Her name. Her short years. And one final line we stole from our vows.

LOVE FIERCELY. LOVE WELL.

I kiss two fingers and press them to her photo—smiling, radiant, forever thirty-nine.

Until we see each other again.

"Always will," I murmur.

And for a moment, I swear the wind stills around me.

CHAPTER TWENTY

Chloe

Present, 4 p.m.

I wish I could say I'm numb.

That would be easier than this. That would mean I could coast through the last three hours of my shift on autopilot—present, but not *really* here. But no. I feel everything—too much.

Guilt and sadness are in a tug-of-war, each trying to pull me under. One moment I'm on the verge of tears, the next, I'm furious with myself for not doing more. My fingers tremble as I try to finish my notes, the adrenaline finally bleeding from my system.

I glance up at the board. The backlog stretches on like a to-do list from hell. We've barely made a dent.

"You doing okay, hon?" Olivia asks gently, appearing beside me.

"I'm fine," I lie, offering a half-smile.

She doesn't push. Just rests a warm hand on my back. "We take a moment of silence when we lose a patient. Not just to show respect, but to remember that they mattered. Once you're done with your notes, head to the staff on-call room down the hall. Ten minutes, that's all. Clear your head. Don't take this home with you. Trust me."

"Thanks. I will." Her hand rubs a slow circle on my back, and it's the most maternal gesture; it nearly breaks me again.

Olivia had asked if I wanted to be the one to call Borris's kids. I said no.

Am I a coward? Probably.

But I couldn't do it. Not with their names in my head, their stories in my heart, and the crushing belief that I'm the reason they didn't get to say, "I love you" one last time. The reason they'll never see him again.

I finish my notes. I consider moving onto the next patient to distract myself, but Olivia's right. I can't help anyone until I get my head back in the game.

The on-call room sits behind an unassuming door in a quiet corridor off the ER; it's easy to miss if you don't know it's there. I open the door slowly and peek inside—two sets of bunk beds, neatly made with hospital linen. No one's inside, but I don't turn on the light. I need the dark.

The door clicks shut, swallowing the room in complete darkness. I toe off my sneakers and sink onto one of the lower bunks. My feet and back practically sigh with relief. This—lying flat—is what I've craved since seven this morning. But my body's wired, even as my limbs beg for stillness.

I close my eyes anyway.

I don't sleep. I can't.

Olivia's right. I need to leave Borris here. I can't carry it home and let it unravel me all night. My body needs rest. My mind needs peace.

I've never dealt with death, not up close. Even my grandparents are still alive—one of them out of pure spite, I think.

That doesn't mean I got to this point in my life untouched—being sick has messed with my head in ways I still don't fully understand. I've spent most of my life in denial about my own mortality. I knew death was always a possibility with my illness, but knowing and accepting are two very different things.

Maybe that's why losing Borris has hit me so hard.

I let myself think of him for a moment. His strong Russian accent. His stories about the restaurant. His love for food and his pride when he talked about his kids. He promised to bring me pelmeni one day, said it would change my life.

I swallow around the lump in my throat.

I hope he found his wife. I hope he's talking her ear off, just like he said he used to. He didn't deserve to die alone in a hospital bed while I was sitting in the staff lounge, congratulating myself for helping him.

The door creaks open. I don't move.

Zac steps inside, immediately spotting me in the dark. He shuts the door and climbs onto the bunk. I shift to make room, curling into his side, resting my head on his chest. His heartbeat beats a steady rhythm beneath my ear.

"I can't stay long," he murmurs, rubbing circles into my back. "But I wanted to check on you. See how you're holding up. If there's anything I can do."

In here, in the dark, he's not Dr. Zac. He's not the Director of Emergency Medicine. He's Z. Or Zaddy, when we're playing. And right now, I don't need medical advice or logic. I need comfort.

I shake my head.

"You sure?" he asks, voice low, coaxing. He loosens the tie on the waistband of his scrubs. "I'm here if you need it."

His meaning is obvious. It spreads between us with heat. Do I need *it*? It never crossed my mind, but now that he's here and offering.

The truth is... I *do* need it. I need to float. To forget how it felt when Borris flatlined under my hands. I want the sadness to cease consuming my mind. I want the comfort he's offering.

I slide down his body, then help him shove the scrubs over his hips. I take him into my mouth gently, to be close. To be quiet. His taste, his scent—they're strangely calming.

His fingers slide through my hair, loosening my ponytail and massaging my scalp until the tension bleeds out. I sigh into him.

Then his voice breaks the dark.

"I want to tell you something."

I freeze. Panic rising.

I know what's coming... He's married.

Shit.

I start to pull away, but he gently presses a hand to the back of my head.

"Please. Stay. I need to get this out."

I let my head settle against his thigh. He wouldn't dare tell me he's happily married while I have his dick in my mouth. Right?

"There's a reason I left cardiothoracic surgery and moved to emergency."

He exhales slowly.

"I used to pride myself on connecting with every patient. I made the effort to get to know them as a person, rather than by their illness. I thought it made me a better surgeon. And maybe it did. But every time I lost one, it gutted me. I didn't have boundaries. I brought my grief home. I stopped sleeping. Started resenting the job."

His voice wavers.

"And I took it out on my wife, Casey."

My stomach drops. I move to sit up.

"Wait—please."

He'd better start talking. Fast. Because I'm not about to be the other woman in someone else's love story.

"She was everything to me. We met in high school. Stayed stupidly in love through uni. We didn't get into kink until after we were married and had moved to Australia. But once we did—nothing was off-limits. She was an attorney. Brilliant and intense. She scared judges and turned grown men into stammering messes. But at home, she just wanted to let go. I gave her that. And I needed it, too. To be the one she could let go with. We grew into it together. Explored everything together. And I thought I had forever with her."

He pauses.

"The day she was brought into the ER after a car crash... everything changed. Catastrophic chest trauma. No other cardiothoracic surgeons were available. Hospital policy states you can't operate on your own family. But if I'd waited, she wouldn't have made it."

He trails off.

"Didn't matter. She died on my table anyway."

My heart cracks. I scrunch my eyes shut, but otherwise don't move a muscle. He needs to get through this; this is therapeutic for him in a way, too, without me jumping up to comfort him and shoving my sorrow for him in his face.

"After that, I couldn't go back into the OR. Couldn't risk connecting again. So I moved to the ER. Here, patients come and go. Most of them, I don't even learn their names. It's fast and detached."

His words drift into the dark like a confession.

"That's why I'm telling you this now: protect yourself. Set boundaries. You can't grieve every loss like this and survive. It'll eat you alive."

His cock slips from my mouth, and I crawl up his body, curling against him, hand on his chest.

"I will," I whisper. "And thank you for trusting me."

There are so many questions I want to ask. *How long ago did Casey die? What was your relationship like?* I want to know the woman who first held his heart. I want to make space for her, too. But now's not the time.

I can't see his face in the dark. Maybe that's why he told me all this in here, because the dark is softer. Safer. Less exposing.

And even without the light, I feel everything in the way his chest rises beneath my palm.

The hospital PA system suddenly crackles overhead, shattering our stillness.

Attention all staff: Code Black. Code Purple. Emergency Department.

Zac bolts upright, scrambling to tuck himself back into his scrubs. "Shit!" His face is white.

Attention all staff: Code Black. Code Purple. Emergency Department.

"What's a Code Black? A Code Purple?" I ask, flicking on the light and scrambling for my shoes.

I should know what that means. I *did* know. But the hospital induction video feels like a lifetime ago.

"Chloe, get out of the hospital. Now. And take as many people as you can."

"What? No, I'm not leaving!"

"Now, Chloe, I'm serious."

There's panic in his eyes. He opens his mouth like he's about to say something else—then clamps it shut. He bolts through the door without looking back.

I tie my sneakers with shaking hands, twist my hair into a bun, and chase after him.

Straight into chaos.

Chapter Twenty-One

Chloe

My phone pings on the nightstand, and I practically leap for it. Anything to save me from the dry, soul-sucking article I've been pretending to read. I toss the medical journal aside and swipe open the message.

Hailee

> Hey, wanna go out tonight? Cora and I are thinking Club Ivy.

It's sweet that they keep including me. They've been making a real effort, and I love them for it. We even started a group chat, which—*just quietly*—made my inner teenager squeal.

I've always struggled to make friends. Years in and out of hospitals meant I missed out on slumber parties, friendship groups, and pretty much all the social milestones that glue girls together. I turned inward. Introversion became my way of survival. If I hadn't been sick, maybe I wouldn't be this way. Or maybe I'd still be the kind of girl who finds peace in solitude. Who knows? Letting people in isn't easy. But these two? They haven't given up on me yet.

Perfect. A hangover isn't on my bingo card for tomorrow—I need to be on my A game. I do a quick check of the apartment.

Not that it needs much to be ready for visitors; I don't exactly throw wild parties. I take out some plates and wine glasses and set them on the coffee table.

Forty minutes later, I buzz them up.

"Fuck me, this place is *nice*," Cora says as she steps in, loaded up with brown paper bags.

"Thanks." I try to play it cool, but I'm glowing. I'm stupidly proud of my place.

"The comforts of Eden, hey?" Hailee snorts, slipping off her heels and passing me a stack of steaming pizza boxes.

"I know, right?"

Cora holds up a bottle of red and a stacked cheese board. "Where should I put these?"

"Table's fine."

They wander around, cooing over the furniture and décor as though it's an article in *Architectural Digest.* I don't entertain much—okay, ever—so it's nice to have someone appreciate it.

We settle into the couch, pass around plates, and pour glasses of wine. I stick to water—no way I'm starting my internship with wine breath and a migraine. I take a bite of supreme pizza and groan as the sweetness of pineapple hits my tongue.

"You excited for tomorrow?" Hailee asks, adding more wine to her glass.

"I am," I reply around a bite. "It's surreal. After all the studying and theory and clinical hours, I finally get to *do* the thing. Help real people. Be a real doctor."

I pause, chewing slower now.

"But?" Cora prompts.

"But I'm also shitting myself," I admit. "My first rotation in the ER. It's intense. What if I freeze? What if I fuck something up and someone dies?"

"They're not gonna throw you in solo," Cora reasons. "There'll be other interns, right? And senior doctors, too?"

"Yeah, I know. But still. It's terrifying."

"Which hospital?"

"St. Vincent's."

Hailee freezes mid-bite and gives Cora a sideways glance.

"What?" I narrow my eyes. "What was that look?"

"Nothing," Hailee says, way too fast. "Just... I got stitched up there once by a ridiculously hot doctor."

"What happened?" The question slips out before I can stop it.

She shrugs, too casually. "I was attacked by an acquaintance of Dameon's. He tried to rape me."

I drop my plate on the coffee table, cheese stretching off the crust in gooey strings.

What the actual fuck?

Cora doesn't even blink, still chewing. She's clearly heard this story before.

"Are you... okay?"

"I'm fine." Hailee waves off my concern. "Long story short, I got glassed in the thigh. Dameon took me to St. Vincent's, and a Doctor McHottie patched me up."

I blink. "That's... so messed up."

"Right?" Hailee spits, throwing her hands up.

"Jesus." I shake my head, trying to process it.

We fall quiet for a moment.

Cora clears her throat gently. "What are your hours like?" she asks, shifting the mood.

"Usually twelve-hour shifts, but I've heard they can stretch to fifteen or sixteen if things go sideways."

"Yikes. What are you gonna do about Eden?"

"I don't know yet," I say. "I don't want to give it up. Actually, I *can't*. I need the money. Intern pay is literal trash."

I glance around my apartment. I'm not losing this place. Period.

"If I can squeeze in one bar shift a week, maybe it'll work. But Le Jardin's out. No way I can pull an overnighter after a full hospital week."

The thought alone drains me. Holding an intelligent conversation and being emotionally dumped on by a client after back-to-back shifts in the ER? Hard pass. Even a healthy person would burn out on that schedule. Add a chronic illness to the mix? It's a suicide mission.

But my one day off won't be rest. It'll be laundry, groceries, and life admin. Am I really going to have the energy to stand for six hours slinging drinks?

"You'll figure it out." Hailee pouts theatrically. "I don't want to lose you."

"Same." I sigh.

Madame Anna and Eden have been my safety net since I was nineteen; stepping away would be a huge adjustment. And if I'm really honest about it, I'm not ready to lose Z. He's more than a client. He's my calm. My addiction. My heart. But reality's a bitch. I won't have the time—or capacity—for our dates anymore.

As if reading my mind, Cora eyes me. "What are you going to do about *him*?"

I shake my head, suddenly quiet. "I don't know."

The tears sting before I can blink them away. The pain of not seeing him again is too raw and real to process. I refuse to acknowledge it. There must be a way. We're not going to end like this.

"You love him," she suggests softly.

I don't answer. I can't.

"Hey, trust me. Everything has a way of working out," Hailee offers gently. "Even when it doesn't feel like it at first."

I appreciate the comfort in her words—the way she's trying to make me feel better. I *want* to believe her. But I'm a doctor.

I don't run on hope. I run on logic. Proof. A plan. And right now? I've got none.

I wipe my eyes on the back of my hand. "Ugh. I hate getting weepy."

"It's kind of nice," Cora says, bumping her knee against mine. "Means he matters."

"All right, enough sap," Hailee adds, grabbing the remote. "Let's watch something before this one starts bawling, too."

"Hey! I can't help it. My hormones are all over the place," Cora protests.

"Wait... are you pregnant again?" I ask, half-joking.

"Maybe. I don't know. I'm late, and honestly, I'm too scared to check. But my boobs? Hurting something *vicious*."

"You're totally knocked up," Hailee declares, rolling her eyes.

"James will kill me if I take a test without him."

"What are you waiting for then? Just do one with him."

"I don't want to be wrong and disappoint him."

"Babe, you could literally shit on his head and he'd still worship the ground you walk on."

"Thanks for the visual, bitch."

We dissolve into laughter, tears leaking from my eyes for a very different reason this time.

We put on a thriller and spend the next two hours curled up on the couch, yelling at the screen and stress-eating pizza. It's exactly what I needed.

They leave and I start cleaning up, putting dishes in the sink, tossing empty boxes in the bin. Then a sharp pain slices through my stomach.

I freeze.

Did I chew properly?

Shit. Pineapple. That stuff's a nightmare to digest.

Another agonizing wave hits.

No. Not now. Please not now.

Chapter Twenty-Two

Chloe

Present, 5 p.m.

Alarms shriek around me—deep and pulsing, not the usual hospital beeps. People are shouting over each other, rapid footsteps pounding past me, and all I can think is: *this is not a drill.*

I barely make it three steps out of the on-call room before a nurse barrels past me, eyes wide, pushing a patient on a bed. I call out, "What's happening?" but she's gone before the words leave my mouth, swallowed up by the storm of people racing in every direction.

Zac's nowhere in sight. He's disappeared into the swarm. Just gone.

What the hell is happening?

I stumble forward, trying to get my bearings, trying to *think*, but every corridor is the same, a blur of motion and noise. My sneakers slap against the floor, and I'm swimming against a current of bodies and rolling beds and clipped commands being barked into the air.

Then I catch sight of Hannah. *Thank God.* She's halfway down the corridor with a clipboard clenched between her teeth, pushing a bed with one hand, adjusting the IV pole with the other. Calm and efficient, like she's done this a hundred times.

"Hannah!" I sprint toward her, heart jackhammering in my chest. "What the hell is going on?"

She doesn't stop. She whips the chart out of her mouth just long enough to say, "There's an active threat in the department. The hospital is evacuating."

"What?!"

She shoves the clipboard between her teeth again, leans into the bed like a linebacker, and pushes it toward another nurse, who seamlessly takes over.

"Tunnels," she calls over her shoulder, already turning away. "Take them to the private hospital. There are nurses waiting."

Tunnels. Right. The underground hallway that connects our hospital with the private one across the block. Five-minute walk on a good day. Less if you're sprinting.

"Where's Clarke?" I ask. "And Kensington?"

"No idea." She shrugs. "Get as many patients as you can—we need to clear the department now."

"On it." I pivot, scanning for the nearest bed.

My hands are shaking. I don't notice until I reach for a woman's IV line and knock it sideways. The saline bag wobbles as I fumble to unclip it from its hook and transfer it to the bed pole. The heart-rate monitor gives a protesting *beep-beep* as I tangle the cords.

My first day. My first goddamn day.

When I bend too fast, a sharp pain flares in my lower abdomen. It blooms like fire, nausea bubbling at the back of my throat. A dizzy edge creeps into my vision.

I don't have time for this.

I don't have time to be sick.

My body, clearly, disagrees. I briefly press a hand to my stomach, clenching my teeth. I still move, still work as fast as I can. But I can feel the pressure ratcheting up with every second. It's like my intestines are folding themselves into origami.

The adrenaline buys me a little time—fight or flight overrides pain. It always does. But I can't outrun my body forever.

I grit my teeth and keep moving.

The patient's name—Mrs. Parker—is written neatly on the whiteboard above her bed. She's in a deep sleep, blissfully unaware of the panic exploding around her. *Lucky her.* I finally get the drip secured, tug the monitor's plug free, and wheel it with the bed as best I can. My arms are too short, the angle awkward.

Another bed zooms past me, nearly clipping the end of my bed.

"Shit." I dig my feet in, halting the momentum, my stomach protesting the sudden move. I shove forward again and take off down the corridor.

The red emergency lights have been activated. My feet slide on a wet patch. I don't look down, I don't want to know what it is. There are too many voices yelling at once—some calm, most not.

Overhead, the PA system comes to life again: *Repeat: Code Black. Code Purple. Emergency Department.*

Even though everything feels like a disaster movie, there's a rhythm within the chaos. The nurses and senior staff are a well-oiled machine—fast with no time to waste. They must have done drills for this. I remember a slide from induction, a passing mention of lockdown procedures, but I'd quickly flicked through it.

I should have paid attention.

But I'm not the only one. Jax runs past me, white-knuckled, pushing a bed with one hand and supporting a panicking family member with the other, his brows drawn in full-blown panic. Sienna's wrestling a gurney, two IV poles wobbling violently. She swears under her breath as one of the wheels catches on a stray power cord, jerking the entire rig sideways.

"Fuck," she mutters, eyes wild. "Fucking—" She cuts off when she sees me watching. Her mask slips. And underneath all that steel and smugness is a scared woman barely holding it together.

I rush toward her. "Here," I offer, grabbing one of the poles and stabilizing the IV lines. "You've got the gurney—I'll handle the meds."

Her lips part like she might argue, but she doesn't. She exhales sharply, relief flickering across her face.

"Thanks," she mutters.

"No problem," I say. "Let's get them to evac."

Moving in sync, we guide her patient, the mess of equipment, and Mrs. Parker through the corridor.

We push through two sets of double doors to the tunnel. A nurse I don't recognize is already there, clipboard in hand. She grabs the side of Mrs. Parker's bed as I roll it toward her.

"Got it," she says briskly.

"Thanks." I turn and run.

I need to find Zac.

Where is he?

I scan every corridor as I rush through the ER. The adrenaline makes everything sharp and hyperreal—every beep, every shout, every face. But not *his* face. Not anywhere.

I swing back to Central. It's a mess of scattered equipment, unplugged monitors, and empty supply carts. The ER is starting to empty out, but the panic? Still thick in the air.

I make eye contact with Olivia. She's shouting orders, voice clear and sharp.

I jog over. "Have you seen Zac?"

"Yes," she says, barely sparing me a glance. "He's in Triage, finding out what's going on."

The phone rings, and she snatches it up.

"Zac? What's happening?"

I resist the urge to grab the phone from her hand. Instead, I listen to her side of the conversation, my heart lodged in my throat.

"Jesus." Her face tightens as she listens. "You sure you want him in here?"

What does that mean?

"Okay," she tells him. "We're almost clear. Chloe and I are taking the last two through now."

She hangs up and finally meets my eyes, her expression grim.

"There's a guy with a knife and a homemade vest—Zac thinks it could be a bomb."

My jaw drops open.

"He's bringing him back here to talk until police arrive."

He's out there? Alone? With a bomb?

"Why would he do that?!"

She shrugs, grim. "Because he's either brave or insane."

A chill threads down my spine.

"Miller! Final sweep—get everyone out, now!" she barks at a nurse, pointing toward the tunnels. Miller snaps into motion, moving to usher the last of the ER staff through the exit.

She turns to me. "Let's go." We run toward the trauma rooms. There are two patients left—one thrashing, awake and panicking. The other unconscious, monitors bleeping softly.

"You take the left bed," Olivia instructs, "I'll take the right."

I nod, hands already gripping the rails. I start to move, steering the bed to the tunnel exit.

"Come on," Olivia urges, already pushing her bed ahead.

And then—

The double doors to Triage swing open behind me.

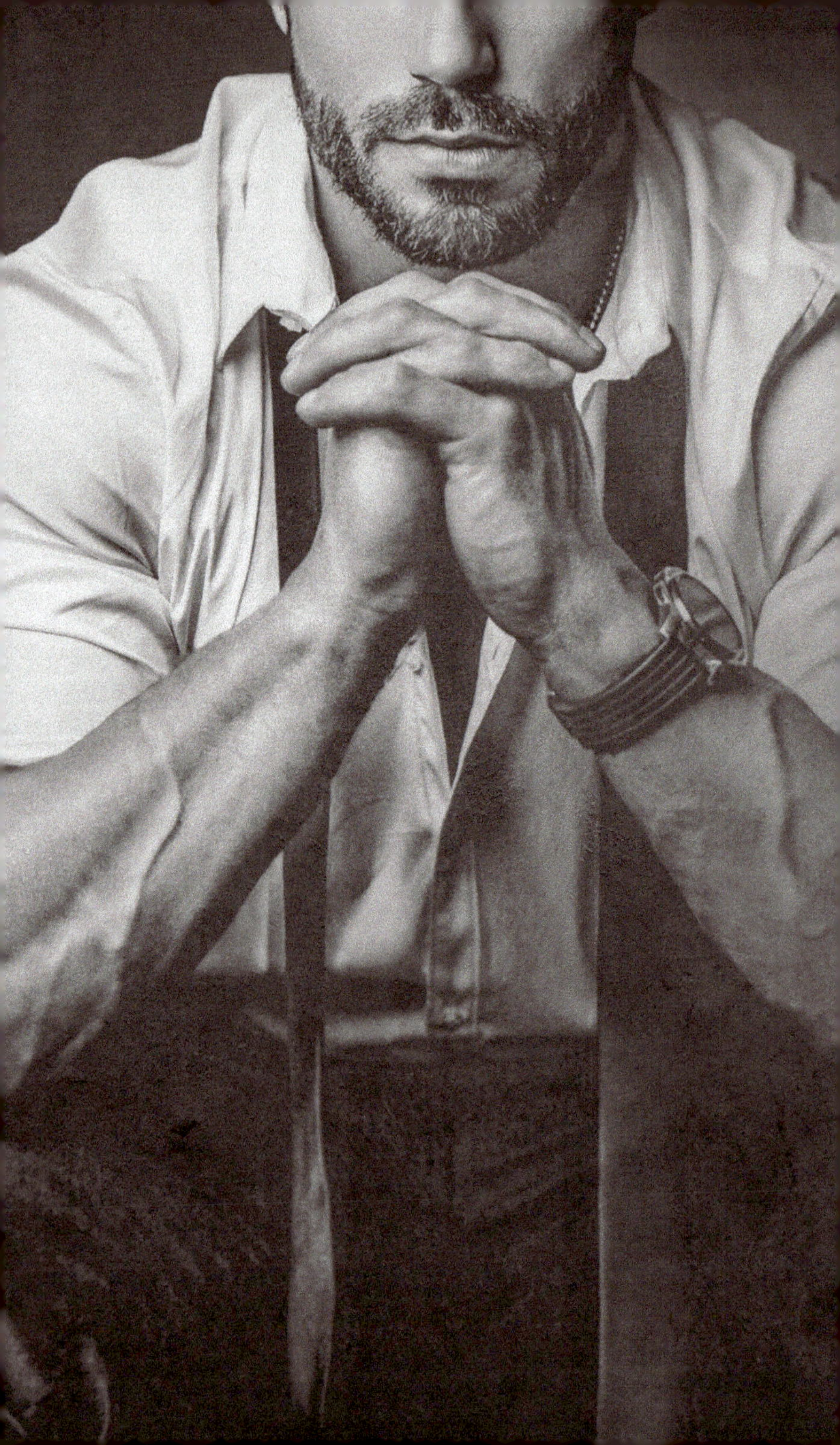

Chapter Twenty-Three

Zac

Present, 5 p.m.

Code Black. Code Purple. Emergency Department. Repeat: Code Black, Code Purple.

Bomb threat. Active threat. Both at once in my department.

I jolt upright, heart slamming against my ribs. I'm still semi-hard from the warmth of Chloe's mouth. Still raw from the emotional purge I unloaded minutes ago. But that moment is gone—ripped away before I can even tie my scrubs.

It's amazing—terrifying, really—how fast your body can go from rest to full-blown crisis mode. Adrenaline hits. I'm already moving before my brain catches up. Out the door. Down the corridor. Didn't get a chance to say what I wanted to Chloe.

We've trained for this. There are drills and protocols. Charts laminated and pinned to the breakroom bulletin board. But drills don't prepare you for the way your throat closes when you realize this isn't a simulation. That the nightmare is reality.

By the time I hit Central, the ER is already transforming. Nurses are rolling beds, staff are shouting across corridors, carts are being shoved into closets, IV lines are yanked from hooks. It's a mess, but it's thankfully somehow organized.

I find Olivia near the nurses' station, phone to her ear, clipboard tucked under her elbow, barking orders at a junior orderly who's clearly about to piss himself.

"Olivia," I call. "Talk to me. What do we know?"

She turns slightly, still with the phone to her ear. "No confirmation yet—security's not answering. We're starting a tunnel evac."

I nod once. "Keep going. Get Clarke and Kensington stationed on the other side. I'll find out what's happening."

Her eyes flick to mine, and for a second, she looks like she wants to argue. But she doesn't. "Be careful."

"Always."

I move toward Triage, pushing through the double doors, and stop cold.

The temperature shifts. It's subtle but unmistakable. Fear.

Patients are crouched in corners, behind chairs, under benches. A mother shields her child with her body. A man presses himself against the wall, trying to vanish into it.

And in the center, a man.

Early twenties. Skinny. Pale. Sweat pouring down his face like rain. In one hand: a kitchen knife stained with rust... or blood. I can't tell, could be both for all I know. The other is gripping the shoulder strap of a black vest with cylinders wired across his chest. The kind of thing you see in movies and hope never to see in person.

Fuck.

My eyes quickly sweep the room. To my right, near the entrance, a security guard, Steve, is standing stock still, taser drawn but not fired. I catch his eye and give a small shake of my head. *Don't engage.*

He bobs his head carefully. He's waiting. Watching. Knowing one twitch could mean a lot of people are dead. I'm guessing that's the only reason he hasn't fired yet. One misstep could take out Triage... or the whole hospital.

I take one step forward, slowly. Deliberate with arms raised, non-threatening.

"Hey." I keep my voice gentle.

The man doesn't react at first. He's pacing in a tight circle, whispering under his breath. Rocking slightly.

"She was just here... she was just here... she was just here..."

The knife wavers as he moves.

I inch closer.

"Who was here?" I ask, quiet.

He pauses. Looks at me like I've just materialized out of thin air.

His eyes are glassy, pupils blown. But I know that look—I'd recognize it anywhere. *Grief.* His expression... It guts me. Eyes red and sunken. Mouth trembling. A man completely broken.

But something's off—more than grief. There's a twist in his posture, a jittery edge to the way his head keeps jerking. He's high. Or crashing. And he's probably having some kind of psychotic episode on top of it.

"Mom," he whispers, barely audible.

"Your mom," I repeat, nodding. "Okay. Is she a patient here?"

His jaw moves, but no sound follows. Just a long, hollow stare, then the smallest chin lift. His hand tightens on the vest strap.

"She was here," he says finally. "And now she's not. She died. And no one told me. I was right here in the hospital, and no one fucking told me."

Grief fires out of him like a gunshot, knocking the breath out of me.

It's not just in his voice—it's in his bones. His shoulders curl in. His knees tremble. He's collapsing from the inside.

"What's your name?"

He blinks slowly. "Alex."

"Hi, Alex. I'm Dr. Zac. I run this department."

I tell him not as an assertion of power but as an offering. A way to say, "I'm here. I see you. You matter."

"I'm sorry about your mom," I apologize. "Truly. But these people"—I gesture around Triage—"they're scared. Let them go, and we can talk. Just you and me."

Suddenly, Alex glances around, as if seeing the cowering crowd for the first time. His lip quivers.

"They don't care," he mumbles. "No one cared. She died alone."

"I care," I say softly. "I care, Alex. Let them go. They're like you. Someone's family."

A long pause.

He nods.

Minutely.

But it's enough.

I motion subtly to Steve. He understands and starts clearing people out. No screams, no abrupt movement. Like pulling a thread from a grenade. A couple of nurses peek out from behind the desk and assist the patients to move in an orderly, quiet procession.

I grab the desk phone and keep my eyes on Alex.

"Olivia," I whisper the moment she picks up.

"Zac? What's happening?"

"He's alone. Homemade vest. Knife. Name's Alex. Mother died here recently. Possible psychotic breakdown. I've cleared Triage. And I'm bringing him inside."

"Jesus."

"Lock it down once I'm through."

"You sure you want him in here?"

"It's a controlled space with fewer people. It's the safest option; I can handle it."

A beat of silence.

"Okay," she says. "We're almost clear. Chloe and I are taking the last two through now."

Chloe.

I can't let myself go there.

Hanging up, I tell him, "You did good, Alex. You let them go. You kept them safe. That matters."

He doesn't answer.

"But let's talk somewhere quieter, yeah? Where no one will interrupt us. Just you and me."

He nods again. Slower this time.

And we move.

I walk backward. Both hands raised. Talking the whole time in a calm and neutral tone. The same voice I use on addicts, and men who want to die without saying it out loud.

He follows.

Each step we take feels like wading through water. Alex's boots scuff quietly, a jagged rhythm to his gait.

I can hear him breathing—shallow, uneven. A choked muttering under his breath. Still clutching the strap with a death grip and the knife by his side.

And still I walk. Backward. Palms out. Voice steady. Pretending this is just another trauma handover. Another Friday night with an agitated relative. Another volatile psych hold.

But it's not.

Because this isn't just a bomb threat. This is grief, raw and unfiltered, dragging its claws through Triage, owning the place and everyone inside.

I recognize it as clear as day.

Casey.

Her name slices across my thoughts like a scalpel. Uninvited and unavoidable.

Five years. Five years, and I still dream about the flatline beep. I still wake up with her name on my lips.

I was supposed to save her. I watched her crash. Watched the life bleed out of her while I stood there, useless. With my hands on her chest, her body going cold under my palms.

It never leaves.

The grief. The helplessness. The rage.

Sometimes, it comes out of nowhere. A voice or a phrase or a scent you haven't smelled in years.

This time, it's Alex. Because his grief is a mirror of my own.

Suddenly, I'm not standing in Triage. I'm not hearing Alex or the codes.

I'm back there—*back with her*. In the kitchen on our last night together.

The conversation I'd do anything to have again.

Tears streak down Casey's face. "It's destroying you," she cries. "And me along with it."

"What am I supposed to do, Case? Pretend it doesn't bother me when my patients die?"

"No. But you need to let them go. I feel like I don't know you anymore. I get your leftovers. You come home and I get a hollow shell."

"That's not fair."

"It's not untrue."

I lean against the counter. "What do you want from me, Case? I'm not drinking. I'm not cheating. I'm just exhausted."

"I'm not asking for perfection," she pleads. "I'm asking for presence. I'm asking to feel like I matter."

"You matter more than anything."

"Then show me."

She steps closer, her body brushing against mine. She rests her forehead against my chest, and I wrap my arms around her.

"I'm sorry," I murmur into her hair. "I know I'm not... I know I haven't been myself."

She lifts her head and looks up at me, eyes shining. "Come away with me. For a weekend. Somewhere quiet. Somewhere we can't be reached."

"I can't. I'm on call—"

Alex's voice cuts through the static. "She was just here."

It echoes in my chest like a goddamn funeral bell.

I want to scream, *Me too. She was just here. My wife. My world. My fucking everything.*

Instead, I say nothing.

Because this isn't about me.

Alex's grief looks like mine. The same fury. The same helpless, hollow ache. The only difference is that I didn't strap my pain to my chest. I didn't leave the house with a knife. But I get it. I get what it means to need someone else to feel the same damn hurt you feel.

This is the longest walk of my life. This is someone carrying pain like a fuse, and I don't know how long I have before he explodes. Literally.

My pulse thuds in my throat.

Stay calm.

I push through the Triage doors. Emergency lighting casts red shadows across white floors. The fire doors are open at the far end—Olivia and Chloe are pushing the last patients toward the tunnels.

Her brows are furrowed; mouth pressed into a hard line. She doesn't look in my direction, but I can tell—she knows we're here. She can feel it. The tension. The presence.

God, I hope she doesn't turn around.

I angle my body, trying to block Alex's view. Keep his attention on me.

Too late.

He stops. Head turning. Knife twitching. Eyes darting.

I keep talking.

"I know it feels like no one listened," I admit. "But I'm listening now."

He looks at me. Dead in the eyes.

"She was left," he tells me flatly. "Alone. For hours."

"I know," I say, watching the rigid set of his shoulders. "And I'm so sorry."

"Sorry doesn't fix it."

"No," I agree. "But it's a place to start."

Ten more steps.

Just ten more.

If I can get him into Trauma One—we have a shot. Give Chloe time to disappear behind those fire doors.

"Almost there." I match his pace. "You're doing great, Alex. Just a little further."

He nods, jaw clenched. His hands are white-knuckled. His breathing's ragged.

We reach the room.

I push open the curtain.

He steps inside.

And I follow, heart pounding, praying to gods I don't believe in.

Because the worst day of his life just met mine. And I don't know if either of us is walking out of this in one piece.

CHAPTER TWENTY-FOUR

Chloe

Present, 5.30 p.m.

I follow Olivia through the double doors leading to the tunnels. A nurse waits at the far end, clipboard in hand, hair frizzed into a halo that screams end of a twelve-hour shift.

Olivia hands over her patient smoothly, rattles off instructions, and signs something on the chart. I step forward to do the same.

Then I stop.

It hits like a second heartbeat in my chest—deep and instinctive.

"I'm not leaving him."

Olivia turns. "What?!"

I swallow. "I'm not leaving. Dr. Zac—" His name catches halfway up my throat. "I can't."

She stares, waiting for the punchline. "There's no choice," she hisses. "Once I hit that trigger, the doors lock. You're sealed in."

I nod.

She shakes her head. "You're out of your mind."

"That's fine," I manage, breathless. "I'm staying."

My mouth is dry. My hands are still trembling—from the rush, from the fear, from everything I haven't said to Zac.

Olivia's eyes search mine—for reason or doubt? She doesn't find either.

She curses under her breath, muttering something about interns, then wheels the bed away without another word.

I turn toward the ER and start running.

But I don't get far. Ten steps into the department, I hear it—a faint, thin voice. A soft clattering. Repeating something over and over in a language I don't understand. Not yelling—*pleading*.

It's coming from behind a curtain.

I stop in my tracks.

No one's around. The corridor is hollow. My legs are moving before I've made a decision. Before I've formulated a plan.

I slip through the curtain.

The bed is a mess of bunched blankets. She's old—eighty-something at a guess—with skin like parchment and eyes wild with fear. Her gown's half off her shoulder, IV cannula pulled nearly sideways, mouth moving fast around a stream of European-sounding syllables.

She was left behind. Missed.

My heart races. There's no time to page anyone. I glance at her wristband.

Name: Elektra Papadopoulos

Age: 88

Language: Greek

Next of kin: Alexis Papadopoulos (Daughter)

"Elektra?" I try. She blinks, eyes watery. Her fingers flutters toward me, birdlike. I take her hand in mine.

"I'm a doctor," I say gently, pointing to my name badge. She probably doesn't understand a word. Doesn't matter. Tone translates.

Her fingers tighten around mine, fragile and freezing. Tears spring into her eyes and she starts repeating something again, quiet and desperate, like a prayer.

I wrap a blood pressure cuff around her arm. HR elevated. BP low. Oxygen at ninety-three percent. Stable enough to move. She's not safe here. Not alone.

"We're moving," I tell her. "Hang on."

There's a wheelchair outside the bay. I drag it in, lock the brakes, and bend to lift her. "One, two, three," I whisper. She's lighter than I expected. All bones and blankets.

She gasps but doesn't fight. I settle her in the chair, wrap the blanket tight around her, and unhook the IV bag, looping it over the chair handle.

"Hold on," I warn her.

Then I run.

The wheelchair jolts and rattles, the IV bag swinging with every bump. Elektra mutters the whole way, a litany of fear. But she doesn't scream or resist. Maybe because I don't stop. I don't hesitate.

All I can think is: *What if I hadn't heard her?*

What if I'd kept moving?

She's not on a monitor. Her chart was missing. She'd have died in that bed. Alone. Forgotten. Confused and scared.

She'd have become a line in the debrief tomorrow. *One patient missed. Timeline unclear.* And that would've been it.

But she has a name. A daughter. A life.

And now, she has me.

I take a breath and push harder. The wheels squeal against the floor, and I see the tunnel doors ahead. They're still open.

Olivia's almost at the end, about to disappear around the bend.

"Olivia!" I yell, breath tearing from my throat. "Wait!"

She whirls around, eyes widening at the sight of the chair.

Running toward me, she doesn't waste time asking questions. "Jesus, Monroe," she mutters, grabbing the handles. "Thought you came to your senses."

"Not a chance."

Her gaze softens as she looks at Elektra—sees the panic, the age, the oversight.

"Good catch."

I'm already backing away.

"I have to go back."

"Chloe—"

"Just lock it."

I sprint.

Behind me, the hydraulics engage. Then hiss. The scrape of metal on metal.

With a heavy, final clang, the fire door locks.

I don't look back.

I've just locked myself in a building with a man wearing a bomb. And for a moment, the reality hits me too fast.

A wave of nausea rolls up from my gut, and the cramp that follows is like being stabbed from the inside. I double over, nearly dropping to my knees, one hand braced against the wall as I fight to breathe through it.

Not now.

Not now, not now.

Pain rips through me—deep, twisting, white-hot. I taste bile. See stars. For one terrifying second, I think I might throw up or pass out—or both.

But I don't.

I close my eyes. Inhale through grit teeth. Drag myself upright.

I've lived with this pain long enough to know it doesn't get the last word.

I do what I always do. I reset.

And I walk.

Because if I let myself unravel, I can't help him. I can't do anything at all.

The ER is unrecognizable. There's no voices or rolling beds. Only a strange, thick stillness and the distant wail of a siren from outside. The overhead lights have switched to red emergency strips, glowing in harsh beats above the exits like open wounds.

I've walked this same corridor dozens of times today. Now it looks like a crime scene. A blood pressure cuff lies in the middle of the floor. Someone's stethoscope dangles from a monitor. Even the hum of the air vents seems louder now.

It's too quiet.

But I've made my choice.

I'm not leaving him.

My sneakers squeak faintly on the floor. Something sticks to the bottom of one—a latex glove, maybe, or tape. I shake it off without looking.

I press my back to the wall. Now it's fear running laps in my chest, cold and precise.

What if he's hurt?

What if he's dead?

What if—?

Stop.

Breathe.

In. One, two, three.

Out. One, two, three.

Confident, capable, and in control.

I move again. Bay four—empty. Bay two—a lone drip bag swinging from the quiet draft of the HVAC system.

Step by step.

Zac wouldn't want me here. He told me to leave. He looked at me, mouth open, about to say something *important* before he bolted out of the on-call room door and disappeared.

What if that's the last time I see him?

What if this all goes wrong, and I never get another moment to say what I should have weeks ago?

I reach Trauma One and hover behind the curtain, staying just outside. But I can't hear anything.

My palms are damp. I wipe them on the thighs of my scrubs and peek slowly around the edge of the curtain.

Zac's gaze snaps to mine.

Crap.

I pull back so fast I nearly eat the floor.

He saw me.

Just for a second, but long enough. His eyes widened.

My heart is thudding hard, trying to pound its way out through my ribs.

Shit. Shit. Shit.

Brilliant, Chloe. Real stealth move. Should've worn the cape. Or maybe a neon sign: INTERN, FIVE FOOT FIVE, TERRIBLE AT ESPIONAGE. But I had to know—with my own eyes—that he was okay.

Now what?

I flatten myself to the wall, listening, straining to hear.

Zac's voice floats through the quiet. It's low and calm. No shouting yet. That's a good sign.

For a moment, I close my eyes.

He's not hurt.

It pisses me off that he walks into danger as if it can't touch him. Like we're all breakable except him. I press my lips together and lean out again, careful not to make a sound.

The man's ten feet from Zac, one hand white-knuckling the vest. The knife is at his side, not raised. Zac's body language hasn't changed—he's open, steady, palms out. Talking. Maintaining eye contact.

I can't hear the words, but the rhythm of Zac's voice is unmistakable. Reassuring and grounded. Like he's talking someone off a ledge. Because that's exactly what he's doing.

And it's working.

I retreat a few steps.

Okay. Breathe. You need to do something. You can't just crouch here like a scared little rabbit. Listen.

Zac's voice, clearer this time, finds me.

"What was your mom's name?" Zac's tone is gentle, coaxing.

The man's response is quieter—almost too quiet. But I catch it.

"Elizabeth. Elizabeth Weston."

Now I have a name.

I drop low and hurry toward Central. At the desk, I duck behind the counter and risk a glance upward.

No movement.

I reach for the mouse and gently nudge it. The screen comes to life. The hospital's patient charting system fills the monitor. I don't know exactly what I'm doing—this isn't part of any protocol—but if Zac's asking about his mother, that must mean she's important. I'm working on a hunch that maybe there's a file. A record. Something I can use.

I pull up the ER admissions and type the name into the search bar.

It doesn't take long. There she is.

Elizabeth R. Weston. Female, 66. COPD. Deceased.

Next of kin: Alexander Weston

She was brought in two nights ago. Admitted via ambulance for shortness of breath. Ongoing history of chronic obstructive pulmonary disease. There's a timestamped update about sudden desaturation in the corridor. Respiratory arrest. Died en route to resus.

And then I see it.

Attending: Dr. Zachery Bennett.

Of course it was Zac.

I stare at the screen like it might rewrite itself. If I blink enough, another name will appear in that attending field—Kensington, maybe. Or Clarke. Anyone else. But it doesn't change.

Zac was her doctor.

And now he's out there talking to her son. The son who doesn't know. The son who wants to blow this whole fucking place sky-high.

I press my forehead to the desk, heart sinking.

My stomach twists—not from fear or Crohn's—but from knowing Zac's out there, trying to fix something that already broke.

He's ten feet from a man ready to explode—literally and figuratively—with nothing to protect him but his voice and open hands and that stupid fake calm expression.

He's playing the hero, because that's what he does—he tries to patch holes in everyone else so he doesn't have to face the one Casey left in him. It's not bravery. It's penance.

I scroll further.

ER notes: Patient was stable when parked in corridor. Condition deteriorated. No beds available. Dr. Bennett started compressions. Called TOD. Family notified: Attempted call. No contact. Son arrived after death confirmed. Escorted by security. Visibly upset.

I close the file.

This wasn't neglect or callousness. It was the system and circumstance.

Alex had arrived too late. He probably didn't even get to say goodbye. No one to explain. Just his mother—dead. A zipped body bag. A system that moved too fast to see him.

I rub the back of my hand across my mouth, trying to focus.

This isn't coming from rage or drugs, but from *grief*—grief that shatters your mind if no one is there to catch you.

Panic flickers through my limbs.

I don't know what to do.

I want to storm in there and drag Zac out. To stand in front of Alex and scream at him that Zac tried to save his mom. That he cared. That he did his best.

But I know I can't do any of that.

Not without making it worse.

I force myself to sit still for a few more seconds, taking shallow breaths through my nose. The pain in my abdomen is sharper now, reminding me that it hasn't magically gone away. But it doesn't matter.

Not compared to this.

I hustle back toward Trauma One, keeping low and close to the wall, every step calculated. My body's heavy and light at the same time. Adrenaline pulling me forward, Crohn's dragging me down. I feel like I'm split into two—the intern who's about to make a dangerous decision, and the girl who used to lie in this same ER, hoping someone would explain what the hell was happening to her.

This isn't about just saving Zac.

It's about providing Alex with something he was never offered two nights ago.

Truth. Closure. A reason not to destroy everything.

And I'm the only one who can offer him that.

Once I'm outside Trauma One, I press my palm to the floor and push up—

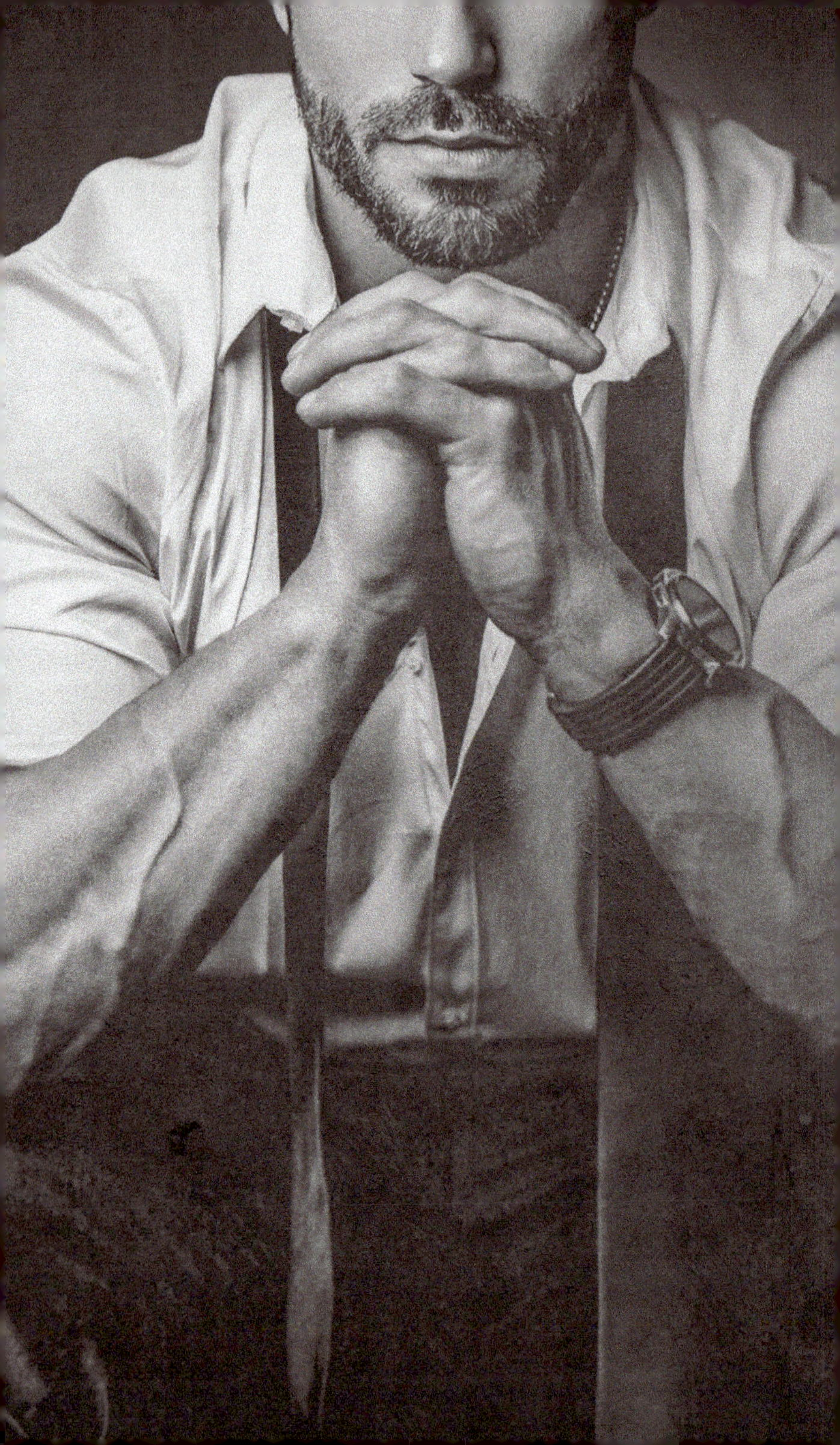

Chapter Twenty-Five

Zac

When he said that name, Elizabeth Weston, I knew this wasn't going to end well.

"I thought we could sit," I offer, gesturing to the two plastic chairs near the sink.

No response. His eyes dart across the room, memorizing it. Every corner. Every shadow. Almost as if he's waiting for someone to jump out at him.

"Just sit and talk. No pressure. No judgment."

Still nothing. Just more pacing, tighter now, he's stuck within a memory and doesn't know how to step out of it.

I keep my hands visible. I'm not holding anything. And I'm not trying anything. I'm just here. With him.

"I get that you're angry, Alex," I say. "And you have every right to be. Losing someone—especially suddenly—rips something out of you. It changes how you see the world. How you see people."

His shoulders tense. His fingers flex around the vest strap.

"She was all I had," he croaks.

I nod slowly.

"She raised me by herself," he adds. "Two jobs. No help. Everything she had, she gave to me. And I—I left her."

"You were there for her," I reassure him. "You called an ambulance. You stayed with her."

"I *left* to get coffee," he snaps, voice cracking. "I was gone for five minutes."

"And that doesn't make it your fault."

The knife wobbles in his grip. He paces a short arc, back and forth, like a dog on a chain, wearing a trench into the linoleum.

"She was fine when I left." His voice rises, uneven. "They said she was stable. I asked the nurse at the desk, and she *smiled* at me. Said she was fine."

His eyes meet mine briefly. It's not only grief, but shame and fury, too. He doesn't know what to do with it all, so he's turned it into this—*this* moment, with wires and a knife and the weight of what-ifs stitched into his skin.

I let the silence stretch between us.

"She was scared," he mutters. "She said she couldn't breathe, and they left her in a fucking corridor."

I don't move.

"She died alone," he cries.

I remember. *I remember her.* Elizabeth was short of breath, stable at first, but spiraled fast. I started compressions. Felt her ribs break under the pressure of my hands. Knew, even as I tried to save her, that we were too late.

"I remember her. She was brave. She didn't want to be here, but she came anyway. For you."

He stares. A long beat.

"Don't try to make her sound noble. You don't get to change the story."

"I'm not," I urge, drawing in a slow breath through my nose, willing him to hear me. "I'm telling you what I saw and what we briefly talked about."

Alex's head drops.

I take a cautious step toward one of the chairs.

"We can sit," I offer again. "You've been on your feet a long time. You look exhausted."

He doesn't move.

"Just a seat," I add. "Not surrender. A chance to rest. I want to hear about her."

He walks toward the chair—two slow steps—and then stops.

"Why?" he mumbles.

"Because you matter," I say. "I want to hear everything. I want to hear what you loved about her. What you miss. What you're angry about. All of it."

His lips part like he might respond—but then his face shifts. He starts pacing again. Faster. The knife taps his thigh. Each turn sharper. Tighter.

"She loved lavender," he tells me. "Planted them on the balcony, even though the building manager complained about the smell. She said the world didn't need more rules, it needed beauty."

I nod, heart thudding. This is the grief cracking open. The raw center.

"Last week, she told me she was tired," he goes on. "I didn't listen."

He's not really talking to me anymore. He's talking to the empty space beside him.

"I should've made her come in sooner."

"You did what you could," I say.

He ignores that. "You ever watch someone disappear right in front of you?"

Every goddamn night.

"Yeah," I whisper. "I have."

He stops moving again. His face is pale, drawn tight over bone.

"She was all I had," he breathes. "And now she's gone. And no one cared."

"I care."

He flinches like I struck him.

His pain is spilling out in fragments now, and I let it. I don't interrupt. I've learned that logic doesn't work in moments like this. You can't throw reason at someone whose world has shattered. It won't stick.

You have to meet them inside the collapse.

I step a little closer. "You're right to miss her. That kind of pain doesn't just disappear."

And I feel it again. My own grief, rising like a phantom in the room.

The heartbreak in his voice sounds exactly like mine did that night in the OR.

And I get it.

The fury. The helplessness. The desperation to *blame someone*, because if you don't, the grief will swallow you whole.

I don't want to be the person he blames. But I understand why he needs someone.

"She couldn't stand hospitals. Said they made her feel like she was already dead."

Another turn. Another pass of the room.

"She was scared to come in. I told her it'd be quick. That they'd fix her up and she'd be back home by morning." His voice breaks on the last word.

"That's not your fault," I say, firmly. "None of this is your fault."

He spins to face me suddenly, eyes wide.

"Then whose is it?!"

He's breathing rapidly now, his whole body tight with energy. He doesn't raise the knife, but his fingers tremble around the handle.

"Someone let her die," he cries. "They said she was fine. And then they left her."

I keep my voice even, but I don't take a step closer this time. "She wasn't left."

"She *was*. No one called me. They bagged her up and rolled her out like trash."

"I'm sorry. *Truly*. We tried to contact you, but it wasn't quick enough. It never is. No one should lose someone like that."

He takes a step back, rattled, like he doesn't know what to do with the information.

And then I see it again.

Movement at the edge of the curtain. Subtle. Peripheral. But unmistakable.

Chloe.

I clench my jaw so hard my teeth ache.

The first time I saw her, I nearly barked her name across the room. Came this close to blowing everything. But I swallowed it down. Let it slide. Told myself she got the message.

Clearly, I was wrong.

She stayed.

Goddammit, she stayed.

I told her to leave in the on-call room. Begged her to. And now she's feet away from a man with a knife and probably enough explosives to level the department.

I don't react. Not visibly. But my heart stumbles like a misfiring valve.

I'm not failing someone I care about again. I won't.

I want to yell. I want to lunge across the room and pull her out by her scrubs.

But I can't.

What if Alex sees her? What if he thinks she's hiding something? What if he panics and lashes out?

My mind starts racing.

She's not behind a wall or behind glass. There's no shield. Just a flimsy curtain and a whole lot of good intentions.

She's going to get herself killed, and I won't be able to stop it.

And worse—I should have known.

Because this is *exactly* who Chloe is.

She's brilliant, but stubborn. She's probably trying to find a way to help. Or worse—try to *be* the help. She'll wait for a break in the tension and then jump in. I can feel it, like static in the air.

Which is why I can't let her stay in the shadows and pretend she's invisible. I know what she's thinking. I know she's creeping closer, waiting for a moment—any moment—to *do something*.

Something brave.

And probably something *catastrophically stupid*.

Alex is still pacing, trapped in his spiral of grief—he hasn't noticed her yet.

That's the only thing keeping this room from detonating.

I can't afford to be distracted.

I can't afford for *her* to become the distraction.

If I don't control the narrative now—if I let Alex discover Chloe—it could all fall apart.

"Dr. Monroe," I announce, loudly enough to cut through the air.

The pacing stops. Alex tenses. "Is there someone else here?"

I pivot slightly, placing myself between him and the curtain where I saw her move. "She's not a threat," I inform him. "She stayed because she was worried. That's all."

He doesn't answer, but his breathing picks up again.

"Dr. Monroe," I repeat, "please come out."

A heartbeat of silence.

Then, soft footsteps.

She emerges slowly, chin high, eyes focused. Her scrubs are wrinkled, hair unraveling, skin pale as bone. Defiant. Brave. Stupidly brave.

And I could kill her. I could take her into my arms and shake her. I could yell at her. Because the second she stepped back through those ER doors, she put herself in the blast zone.

She stops just behind me. One pace back, not quite beside me.

"Chloe," I grit. "What the hell are you doing?"

"I'm not leaving you," she states simply. And that's it. No argument or bravado.

Only stating a fact.

Jesus Christ, this woman.

Alex eyes her, wary. "You a doctor?"

She nods. "Intern."

"You stayed?"

"You're not the only one who's lost someone." She shrugs.

His eyes flicker. "What do you mean?"

But she doesn't answer. Just glances at me. Broken and blistering honesty in her face.

I turn to Alex again.

"I didn't want her here," I tell him. "But she came anyway. Because that's who she is."

He doesn't respond.

I push forward.

"Alex, if you could get the truth about what happened to your mom—no bullshit, no spin—would you want it?"

Alex swallows. He doesn't say yes, but his posture shifts. His grip on the knife loosens a fraction.

"She was stable when she came," I report. "She deteriorated faster than anyone expected. We tried to reach you after she passed, but... obviously we didn't try hard enough. And for that, I'm truly sorry."

He remains silent.

"I accessed your mom's file. I can confirm that," Chloe adds.

Alex's eyes narrow. "You want me to trust *you*?"

"I want you to trust yourself. To hear the truth. To choose what you do with it," she tells him.

Chloe steps forward. Voice clear and clinical.

"Your mother's name was Elizabeth R. Weston. Admitted two nights ago at 10.15 p.m. for COPD exacerbation. She was triaged as stable but decompensated suddenly in the corridor. Resuscitation was attempted. Time of death recorded at 10.42 p.m. Attempted call was made to the next of kin, Alexander Weston."

He's frozen.

Then his voice drops. "Who was her doctor?"

She swallows hard. "Attending physician..." Her voice trails for a beat before she finishes, quieter now, "Dr. Zachery Bennett."

He stares at me. And for a second, I think this is it.

The tipping point.

Every second that ticks by might be the one that snaps whatever thread he's holding on to.

I don't move.

Neither does Chloe.

The words hang in the air between us like smoke.

"You?" he asks. His voice is soft, *dangerous* in its stillness.

I nod.

"She died alone, because of you?"

"I was with her. She wasn't alone."

"You didn't save her."

"I know."

He backs away a step. Then another.

My hands stay raised. I don't chase the silence. I hold still. Say nothing. There's nothing I can say that won't be a spark.

Behind me, Chloe is deathly still.

Alex's eyes flicker between us.

A vein throbs in his neck. Sweat beads above his brow.

Then he mutters something I barely catch. "Of course it was you."

And I brace.

Because I can't tell if what's coming next is a breakdown... or a bang.

CHAPTER TWENTY-SIX

Chloe

Present, 5.50 p.m.

I can't believe he called me out.

I was doing fine—hidden behind that damn curtain, staying still, keeping quiet, trying to help. I wasn't planning some grand rescue.

Okay, maybe I was.

But now?

I'm standing here, exposed and shaking, because *Zac* lit a spotlight straight to me.

The heat is rolling off him. That furious kind of silence that says, "you're smarter than this. What the hell are you doing?"

But screw that. I wasn't being reckless—I was being careful. I was *listening.* I was trying to find a way to de-escalate the situation. And now I can't. Now I'm a liability. The one thing I didn't want to be. I've lost my shot at helping.

Zac moves subtly, stepping slightly between us. Protective without making it obvious.

Alex notices, though. "You think I'm going to hurt her."

Zac doesn't answer.

"Alex," I say gently, "I don't think you *want* to hurt anyone."

His fingers twitch on the knife handle. "Doesn't mean I won't."

He raises it—not to swing, just to point.

At me.

"Come here."

Zac reacts instantly. "No, Chloe."

But I'm already moving.

I have to.

Slow steps. Every muscle in my body is screaming at me to stop—but I don't.

Because I saw the hesitation when he lifted that knife. I saw the crack in his armor. The thread of humanity still hanging on.

If I can hold on to that thread... we still have a chance.

"Chloe," Zac warns in a deep voice.

"I know," I whisper.

Alex watches every step I take like I'm the one who might detonate.

I stop in front of him, barely a foot apart. The knife's still pointed at my chest.

"Wh-who'd you lose?" he asks. "You said you lost someone."

I could tell him about Casey—but that's Zac's grief, not mine. I could bring up poor Borris. But instead, I go with something real. Mine.

"Myself," I confess.

He frowns. He was expecting a name.

"I've spent half my life in the hospital, with my mom by my side. I've spent *hours* with doctors who didn't believe me. Who gaslit me. Who didn't care enough to listen."

He tilts his head.

"But I also remember the ones who stayed. The ones who looked me in the eye and said, 'I believe you.'" I glance back at Zac. "Some of them care more than others."

Alex's gaze cuts to him, then back to me. "He let my mom die."

Zac doesn't flinch. "I tried to save her."

"It wasn't enough." Alex's mouth trembles.

"No," Zac agrees. "It wasn't. But it's the truth."

The silence that follows pulls the thread too tight.

And up close, I see it.

The vest. The wires. The crude metal plate. The blinking red light, steady and slow; a mechanical heartbeat.

One wrong breath away from disaster.

My voice comes out softer than I mean it to. "Alex, do you think she'd want this?"

He blinks. "What?"

"This. You. Right now. Knife in hand. Bomb strapped to your chest."

Alex's throat bobs as he swallows.

His mouth opens. And for a moment, the anger breaks. Not into calm, but into sorrow. A grief wide and wild.

Then—

Bang!

A crash in the corridor. Loud and piercing. Metal on linoleum. A dropped tray, maybe. A cart falling over? Doesn't matter. Because in here, it might as well be a gunshot.

Alex jerks so violently I feel it in my chest—like we're tethered, and his fear yanks me forward. His arm flies up, knife flashing, wide and fast and unthinking. Not at me, but in *defense*. Or reflex.

Zac moves fast, holding his palms up.

"Alex." His voice is firm but low. "It was just a sound."

Alex's eyes dart. His face gray with sweat. Pupils huge.

The light on his chest keeps blinking.

Red.

Red.

Red.

Zac is still talking. Reeling him back in.

And me?

I'm frozen.

Everything inside me is screaming: *Don't move. Don't breathe. Don't become the reason this explodes.*

Alex's eyes are wild. He's not here. His body is in Trauma One with us, but his mind is somewhere darker—somewhere collapsing. Bleeding grief and panic in equal measure.

The recognition drains from his face. And I realize he's not looking *at* us anymore. He's looking *through* us.

"Alex..." I whisper.

His gaze snaps to mine—and for a second, I think maybe it worked. Maybe I've reached him.

But there's nothing in his eyes except confusion. He doesn't know where—or *who*—he is.

He's caught between the world that broke him and the one trying to hold him still. And he doesn't know where to land.

The room narrows to a single point: this breath, this second, this choice.

I need to say something.

Do something.

Be something.

But my mouth won't move.

The fear isn't in my brain—it's embedded in my bones.

Because if I say the wrong thing, he might snap. If I say nothing, he might snap anyway. And if Zac moves again, if someone coughs in the corridor, or if a door slams—

We'll all be statistics.

This is it.

The break.

Zac's voice drops even lower. "Alex, I need you to listen to me."

He's drenched in sweat. Beneath his vest, his shirt clings to his chest. His eyes keep flicking.

The red light flashes.

I want to move. I want to *reach him*. But if I shift now, he might think it's a threat. He might react.

I glance at Zac. His eyes cut toward me briefly. I see everything in that look.

Don't. Move.

So I don't. I stay still, chest clenched on a breath, legs locked, fingers curled into the fabric of my scrubs to keep them from trembling.

Alex exhales, long and shaky.

His eyes flick to me again.

His lips tremble.

But then—

Another sound. Softer this time.

A scuffle of shoes. More than one pair.

Police? Security?

It doesn't matter. Because it's enough.

Alex jolts, and the moment ruptures.

His body coils. His hand twitches.

Zac surges forward. He yells something—Alex's name, perhaps. Or mine.

But I can't hear it.

Because the sound flooding my ears is *too loud*.

The rush of blood.

The pulse of terror.

The light still blinking.

Red.

Red.

Red.

And the moment we were desperately holding together—thread by thread—just blew apart in our hands.

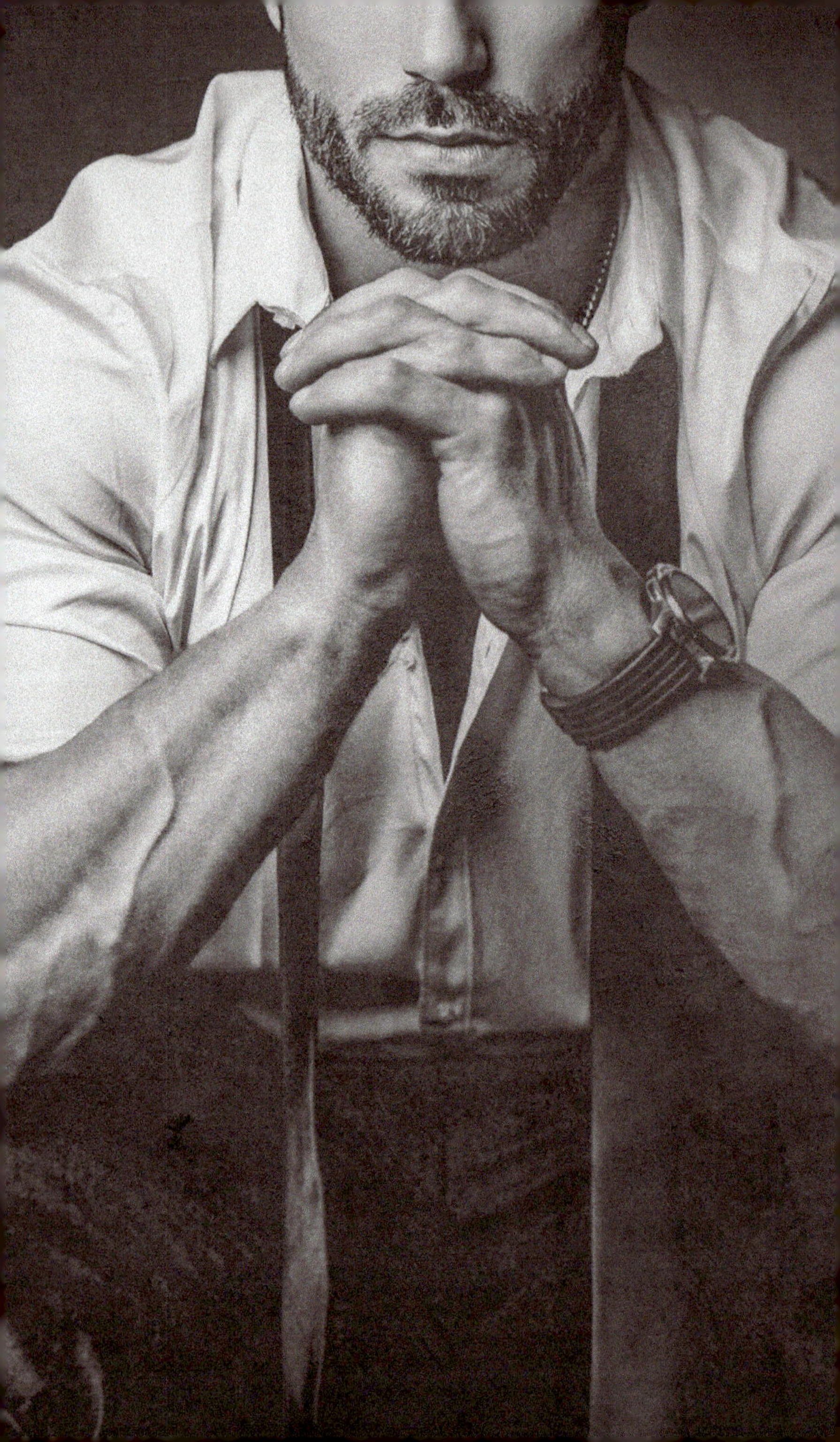

Chapter Twenty-Seven

Zac

Present, 6 p.m.

It doesn't register at first—it's a blur of motion.

His body jerks. Eyes wide. Blade arcing toward Chloe.

No. Not toward her. *Into* her.

The movement is a reflex. There's no precision, no intent. Only panic—lashing out like a cornered animal.

And Chloe's too close.

I shout.

Her name tears out of me, but the chaos swallows it.

The blade cuts the air.

Then—flesh.

A gasp, sharp and stunned.

It's not a scream. But rather a noise I've heard a thousand times in trauma rooms—a body choosing shock over voice.

She stumbles, clutching her shoulder. Blood spills between her fingers in fast streaks.

My vision narrows.

The vest. The knife. Her face.

I move without thinking.

Time collapses. There's no strategy. No plan.

Just *go*.

I lunge straight into Alex.

We crash to the floor in a tangle of limbs and breath. We're not fighting, it's a scramble. I wedge a knee in, slam my forearm across his throat, but he bucks under me, stronger than I expected.

The knife—

I don't know where it is. I didn't see it leave his hand.

God, please let it have slid out of reach.

His elbow slams into my jaw. Bright white pain blooms across my face. I taste blood—my lip, maybe. Or tongue.

Doesn't matter.

I drive my palm into his chest, pinning him. My other hand claws at the strap of the vest. It's thick. Duct-taped. There's the hard edge of a toggle switch beneath the layers. One wrong move, one pulled wire—and it's all over.

"Don't," I hiss. "Don't move."

He lashes out again, catching me across the temple. My vision spins. He's not trained or skilled. But panic makes people powerful.

And he's drowning.

"You hurt her," I snarl. "You *hurt her*."

"I didn't mean... She moved—"

My voice is hoarse, raw. I want to hit him. But I don't. I clamp his arm under my knee, press the vest with one hand, and rest the other over the trigger site. I'm not fighting a killer. I'm fighting an unraveling man.

And Chloe—

God.

Chloe.

I glance over. Her scrubs are soaked. She's on the ground, one hand compressing her shoulder, blood leaking in thick rivers. Still conscious but barely.

I didn't get there fast enough.

I didn't stop him in time.

Alex thrashes beneath me, gasping, clawing, trying to break free. He's wild and disoriented.

"I didn't mean to—" he chokes. "I didn't want to—"

"Then stop."

"I can't—"

"You can."

He bucks again. His arms strain, pulling on the wires across his chest. I slam my hand over the vest's center, holding everything in place.

"Chloe," I rasp. "Get out. Now."

She doesn't move.

Her face is white, but her eyes are locked on me.

"I'm not leaving you," she argues, voice frayed but sure.

Goddammit.

She has to move. *Now.*

"Go," I bark. "He could still—*Go!*"

She doesn't.

Instead, she hauls herself upright and stumbles toward the trolley, bracing herself against it with a death grip. She grabs the trauma shears and throws them to me. "Cut it off." Her body shakes, but her aim is steady.

She's not running.

She's standing with me.

Alex groans beneath my hold.

"Let me up," he pleads. "Please, I need—"

"You're done," I snap.

Then I feel it.

Warmth. Blood seeping into my side.

Is it mine?

A quick mental check. No pain. No wound.

It must be Chloe's.

Finally, Alex sags, sobbing now, deep, guttural.

Chloe's leaning hard against the trolley, her face pale as paper, blood running in claret lines down her arm. She's clutching her shoulder, and I can see it in her posture: she's seconds from going down.

I want to go to her. I want to pull away from Alex, run to her side, get pressure on the wound, elevate the arm, and keep her *awake—*

But not yet.

"Don't move," I growl, tightening my grip across his chest.

He's not struggling anymore. He's quivering.

"She didn't deserve it," he whispers, almost to himself.

"I know," I say. "I know, Alex."

He shakes his head.

"You need to stay still."

"I just... wanted it all to stop."

He didn't come here to destroy. Only to bleed in a place someone might notice.

I shift, slowly, keeping one hand pressed on the vest and using the other to check the wiring—enough to find the toggle switch and battery casing. The LED light is still blinking, steady and slow.

Not a countdown.

"Alex," I coax gently. "We need to get this off you."

He flinches. "No. No, if you touch it—"

He's curling in on himself now. Shrinking under me, trying to disappear into the floor.

"Alex, listen to me. You don't have to die today."

His eyes flick to Chloe. "She's bleeding."

"She's alive," I tell him.

"Because you tackled me."

I say nothing. The truth is, I don't know. Another half-second and the knife might have gone somewhere else—her chest, her neck.

The wound doesn't look deep, certainly not fatal.

Still, she's pale. And her breaths come in shallow pulls.

I have to finish this.

"Let me take it off," I repeat.

He stares at me. "You think I can go on after this?"

"You're not the only one carrying pain. Carrying grief."

His face crumples.

And for a terrifying second, I think he's going to reach for something else.

But he doesn't.

He exhales deeply.

Then nods.

If he lets me undo the main strap—

If I can keep tension off the trigger—

I might be able to slide it free.

I reach carefully. Unfasten the Velcro with one hand, then use the shears to cut through the duct tape layer by layer, working meticulously.

"Don't move," I whisper. "Just relax."

"I'm sorry," he mutters. "I didn't want this. I just wanted someone to know how it felt."

I know.

I *know*.

I ease the vest up, off one arm, then the other. The wires are still taped to the battery pack. I shift back, carefully moving off Alex, then hold my breath as I lower the whole thing to the floor, laying it like a newborn out of his reach.

And then—

I let go.

No bang. No final flash. Only the sound of Alex sobbing into the floor.

I crawl to Chloe. She's on her knees, arm limp, blood soaking through her scrubs, smeared across the floor, her hand slick and trembling in her lap.

"Hey," I whisper, cradling her face in my palms.

Her lips twitch. "Hey, Z."

I ease her onto the floor. She doesn't resist.

Her skin is cold. Her heartrate fast.

"I don't think it's deep," she murmurs.

"I know."

I grab gauze from the nearby trolley and press hard.

She sucks in a sharp breath.

"Shit—"

"Sorry. I've got to stop the bleeding."

"It's okayyy..." Her eyes flutter.

"Chloe." I grip her jaw lightly, guiding her gaze back to mine. "Eyes on me."

She half-laughs. "You're mad at me."

"I'm furious."

"Worth it."

Her eyelids droop.

"Do not close your eyes."

"I'm not." But her voice is slurring now.

The blood's slowing. I don't think the knife hit an artery. But it's enough to knock her out if I don't get pressure applied and fluids in fast.

"I need to lift your legs," I warn her. "You'll feel dizzy for a second."

She nods once.

I prop her feet up on a bin and keep my hands over the wound. Her blood's covering me—warm, slick, painting my scrubs in long red smears.

But she's alive.

That's the only thing I care about right now.

I glance back toward Alex.

He hasn't moved.

He's curled on the floor like a child, the vest lying in the corner like a shed skin. He looks... *small*.

And that's when I see it.

Blood.

Not Chloe's.

His.

Pooling under his shirt.

A single, deep red bloom just under his ribs.

I look around, then spot it. The knife.

Still on the floor.

Still bloody.

When I tackled him—when he flailed, when we fell—he must've landed on it. Drove it into himself by accident.

I crawl toward him, half-panicked. I check the wound, trying to assess, but I already know.

The blood's coming too fast. He's going into hypovolemic shock.

"Alex—" I grab his wrist, feel for a pulse.

Faint.

Thready.

He looks up at me, his face slack, tears still drying on his cheeks.

"I didn't mean to," he whispers.

I squeeze his hand.

And then—

He's gone.

His eyes stay open.

His chest stills.

No dramatic gasp. No final scream.

Just gone.

I sit back, hands slick with his blood. My own pulse thunders in my ears.

And then Chloe coughs quietly behind me.

I snap back.

She's still here.

Still bleeding.

Still fighting.

"Zac?" she wonders, dazed.

"I've got you." My voice cracks. "I've got you, Chloe."

I lift my head, throat raw. "We're clear! Need some help in here. Now!"

A swarm of people flood into the room: police, security, and others I don't recognize. Then I see Olivia, cutting through the crowd. Her eyes widen when she sees us, and she drops to the ground beside me, already pulling gloves on, barking orders.

"Get the vest secured," I shout to the nearest responder.

They move fast with practiced urgency. I don't move from Chloe. Not an inch. Someone tries to take over applying pressure on her shoulder, but I wave them off.

I've got her," I snap.

"Zac—"

"I SAID I've got her."

They all back off.

Chloe stirs. "You're such an ass."

I laugh, broken and breathless. "I know."

They lift her to a gurney. Call out vitals and start fluids.

"Give her to me," Olivia instructs.

If it were anyone else, I'd refuse. But it's *Olivia*. So I let go. Only because she's in good hands.

I turn and look at Alex.

He remains still.

I lower myself to the floor, kneel in the blood.

His.

Hers.

Mine, maybe. I can't even tell anymore.

But I don't get up. I can't. Not until I've stopped shaking.

Because this was never a hostage situation.

It was two people with broken hearts, trying not to detonate.

And only one of us made it out.

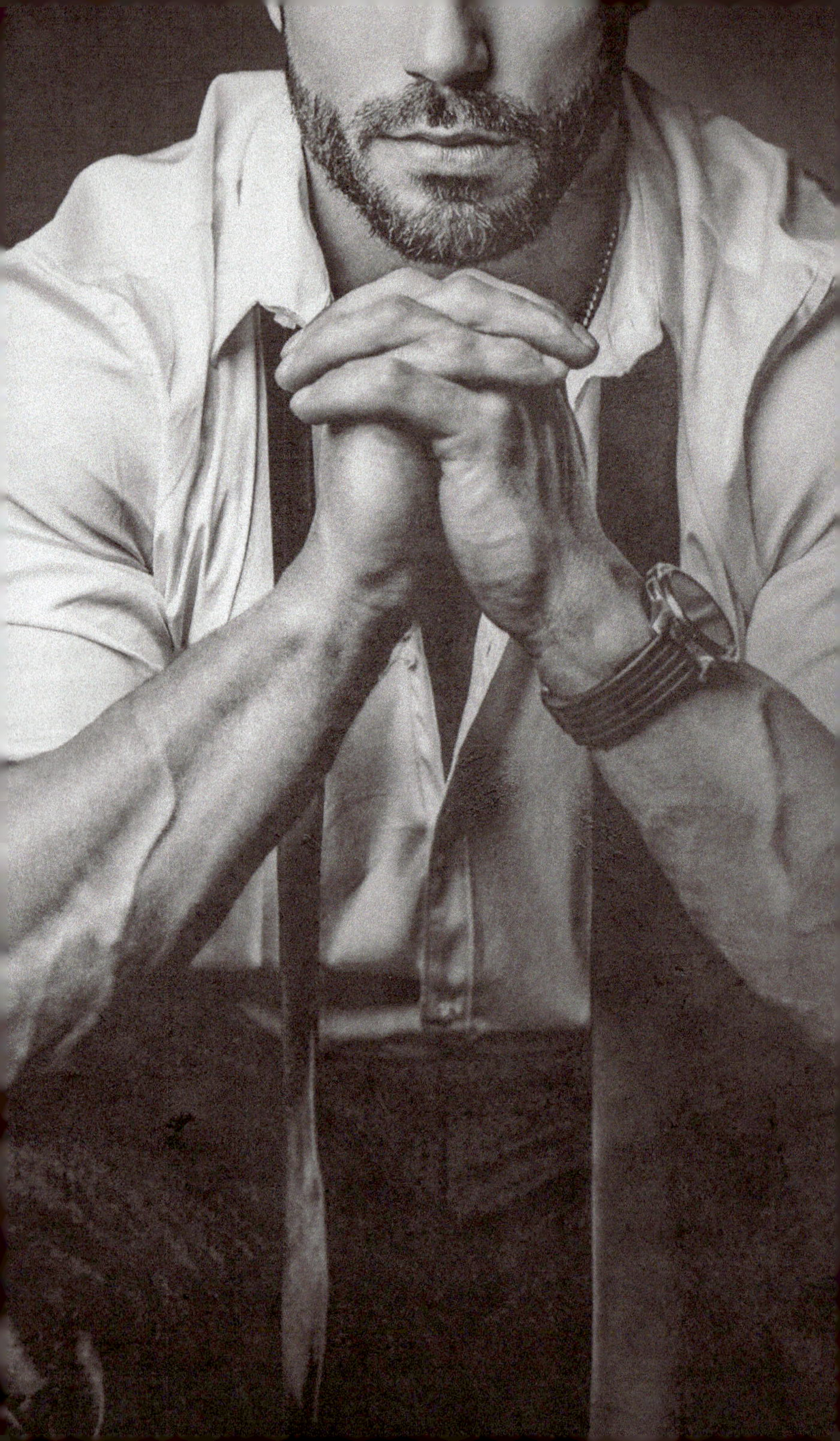

Chapter Twenty-Eight

Zac

Present, 6.15 p.m.

Death doesn't leave silence.

It leaves static. It buzzes in your ears and crawls under your skin. Your breath is deafening, your heart beats too slow, and your body can't remember what comes next now that the thing you were fighting to stop is... over.

Alex is still on the ground.

Slack.

Gone.

And I keep staring at his chest, thinking it might rise again—as if I imagined his final exhale, or somehow misread the moment his pulse went still beneath my fingertips. But I didn't. I felt it. The warmth vanished. The life left him like a flame pinched between fingers.

And yet I stare anyway. If I stop looking at him, reality will sink in.

The ER lights are back to full brightness. Everything feels exposed. I have to squint against the illumination of the fluorescents bouncing off the walls and linoleum.

Somewhere nearby, Chloe is in a bay as a patient. Where she shouldn't be. And around us, the hospital resumes its chaotic life.

Nurses appear in the hallway, sleeves rolled up, hair re-tied. Orderlies straighten equipment and pull cleaning supplies from the closet. Someone huffs a laugh that's quiet and stunned. The brittle, hollow sound of disbelief you make when adrenaline starts to leave the body.

The air is starting to smell like antiseptic again. Chaos is being wiped away with a lemon-scented cloth and the right brand of floor polish. To me, it smells like erasure. And I hate it. Chloe's still bleeding, and they're already prepping for the next patient.

I push myself off the floor and step into the corridor. Heads turn—police, security, nurses, the team I've worked with for years—and I don't blame them. I must look like a ghost emerging from the wreckage, scrubs soaked in blood that isn't mine. I keep moving. Drifting past open bays and whispered voices, searching for Chloe.

She's perched on the edge of the bed in bay five, and Kara—one of my night shift nurses—is already peeling back her torn top to reveal the wound beneath. It's not as bad as I let myself imagine. Four inches across, jagged and angry, a weeping red canyon carved into skin that never should've been torn.

Chloe sucks in a breath through her teeth, her fingers clutching the bed frame tight enough to blanch the knuckles. She doesn't make a sound beyond that.

I can't take my eyes off the wound.

"You need to sit," Olivia directs from behind me, but I don't. I move closer instead.

Closer to Chloe.

Closer to the damage *I* caused.

She doesn't meet my eyes or speak. But she doesn't stop me, either.

Kara presses fresh gauze onto the wound, and Chloe flinches. Her breathing stutters, her jaw tightens. But she swallows the pain whole.

It makes me feel worse.

Because she's hurting, and she thinks she has to hide it. Because she thinks I've earned so much guilt, I can't carry hers, too.

She shouldn't have been in that room in the first place. She shouldn't have had to stand between me and a man with a knife. She shouldn't have bled for me.

I should have stopped it.

"Zac." Olivia's voice is softer this time. "You're covered in blood. You need to get checked out."

I shake my head once.

She doesn't argue again. Just walks away.

Kara works quickly, disinfecting and taping a pressure dressing in place. Chloe winces again.

"Do you think he wanted to die?"

It's a simple, terrible question, said in a voice gone distant around the edges.

I think for a long moment before answering. "I don't think he knew how to move past it."

She nods slowly.

"He looked so young," she murmurs.

"I know."

Another moment of quiet. She flexes the hand of her uninjured arm, as if testing what her body still remembers how to do.

Kara finishes bandaging and slips out of the bay, leaving us alone.

"You look like hell." She catches me off guard.

I let out something between a laugh and a groan. "Thanks."

The adrenaline has crusted into salt at my temples, and sticky residue behind my neck. I smell like sweat and old blood.

"I mean it." Her warm gaze meets mine, unwavering. "You're pale. Your hands are shaking. Your pupils are blown. When was the last time you had something to drink?"

"I don't know," I reply honestly.

She exhales breathily, and it sounds like it hurts her to do it. She shouldn't be worrying about me. I wasn't the one who got stabbed. I was the one who let it happen. And now all I can do is stand here with blood on my hands and nothing to offer but regret.

I move to the edge of the bed.

My knees fold slowly, and I sit beside her without touching, careful not to shift the dressing.

The silence between us isn't empty. It's thick. Full of things neither of us knows how to say.

I think she's waiting for me to speak. Or maybe she's giving me the opportunity to fall apart.

I don't want to. But I'm not sure I can hold it back, either. I rest my hands on my thighs and stare at them. My hands are covered in scrapes and scratches.

"You saved me," she says.

I blink.

"I didn't—"

"You did."

Her voice doesn't allow room for argument. It silences every protest inside me, cutting through every half-truth I've been hiding behind since we left Trauma One. She doesn't let me minimize it. Or shift the credit elsewhere.

She's giving it to me—and I don't know what to do with it.

"I didn't get to him in time," I whisper. "I couldn't stop it."

"No one could," she replies, and there's no softness in it, only truth. "But you stopped it from getting worse."

I look at her—and God, she's wrecked. Her lips are dry and cracked, lashes clumped with the remnants of tears she didn't let fall. Her hair's come loose from its bun, tangled with dried blood. And her eyes... they aren't angry. They're tired. Bone-deep and soul-weary, holding everything together until it's safe to let go.

"You shouldn't have been in that room," I state.

"I know."

"I should've made you leave."

"You tried."

I let out a bitter breath. "Obviously not hard enough."

Kara returns, quickly checking Chloe's vitals. Her numbers are good, but her blood pressure is still low.

She needs rest. More fluids. And time.

Kara inserts an IV, hanging the saline bag before connecting a line of antibiotics. She tells Chloe that a surgeon will be down soon to assess the wound. Then she slips away again.

"Still hurting?"

"Not the worst pain I've had," she remarks.

"That doesn't mean it's okay."

"No," she says softly. "But it means I can bear it." Then, quietly. "Are you okay?"

I should lie. Should nod and say, "Yeah, of course, I'm fine", shift the focus back to her.

But instead, I admit, "I don't know."

Her eyes flick to mine and I don't look away. I let her see everything.

The exhaustion. The guilt. The fury. The ghost of Casey's name still lodged in my throat. The moment Alex went still beneath my hands. The blood crusted under my nails. The memory of it slick on my palms.

All of it.

"I didn't want to remember her," I whisper. "Not today. Not with him."

His pain echoed like a shadow of my own—different in shape but made of the same never-ending dark spiral. And I hate how familiar it felt.

We were more alike than I wanted to admit. He carried his grief like a fuse, burning slow and quiet until it finally reached the charge. I carry mine like a lockbox—sealed tight, buried deep, hidden under a thousand ER shifts. I didn't fall apart, I... stopped showing up. For the people I cared about, for my patients. Even for myself.

I stopped feeling.

I cauterized the wound.

Called it control.

But that's not living. That's survival. That's a life where you keep breathing but forget what it means to feel *anything*.

And I saw where that path leads. I saw it in Alex.

He didn't want to die, not really. He just didn't know how to keep living with that kind of weight. And somewhere along the way, I started walking the same road, only quieter. Slower. But still heading toward the same destination.

I couldn't save him.

I couldn't save his mother.

And I couldn't save Casey.

Because I don't get to control the ending. I never have been able to. All I can do is show up. Keep the wound open, even when it bleeds. Because feeling it, that's the part that means I'm still here. And I want to stay here.

Chloe watches me carefully.

"I miss her," I admit.

"I know," she whispers, reaching for my hand.

"I thought I buried it," I say. "But it's still there. All of it. Hiding under the surface."

"That's where grief lives," she replies. "It's not something you put away... it's something you carry."

It shouldn't feel comforting. But it does.

We sit together in the stillness. Outside, the ER keeps moving. Phones ring. Monitors beep. Footsteps pass behind the curtain. I want to stay in our little bubble before the rest of the world catches up. Before someone pulls me away to fill out Alex's cause of death notice and file an incident report. Or before I have to explain what happened to the hospital administrator and police.

Chloe shifts slightly and winces.

I reach for her, instinct flaring. "Hey—easy."

"I'm okay," she breathes. "Just... sore."

"Try to rest."

"I'm not tired."

"Doesn't matter."

She opens her mouth to argue, but instead the fight ebbs out of her. I help her recline gently, careful not to jostle her shoulder.

She lets me.

"I'm staying," I say, pulling the blanket higher over her legs.

"You don't have to." Her eyes meet mine.

"I know." I sink into the chair beside the bed anyway, elbows on my knees.

But I have to.

Because I can't walk away from her. Not after everything we faced, everything we said, everything we nearly lost. Not when she saw the grief, the cracks, the pieces I never meant to show—and stayed.

So I remain by her side. And this time, I don't try to close the wound. I let it breathe.

Chapter Twenty-Nine

Chloe

Present, 8 p.m.

The moment the knife went in, I didn't feel it.

There was pressure, sure. It felt sudden and wrong, but I didn't feel the pain. Then the world tilted sideways, Zac's voice broke through the cacophony, and everything fractured into panic.

The pain came later.

Fire bloomed under my skin, starting in my shoulder and spilling down my ribcage. Sharp, hot, swallowing everything. I remember thinking: *That's a lot of blood*. But instinct told me it wasn't fatal, that no artery had been hit.

Now, I'm lying on the bed because Zac told me to. Everything in me still buzzes—mind wired, thoughts racing—but my body is too wrung out to argue. And if I'm honest, he's right. I need to rest, whether I want it or not.

My shoulder throbs—a deep pulsing ache—and with the adrenaline slowly ebbing away, it leaves my limbs heavy.

The curtain rustles, and a tall man in navy scrubs steps inside. Late fifties, looking fresh. No doubt just started his shift. He gives me a quick nod, then glances at the chart in his hand.

"Dr. Chloe Monroe, our hero intern. I'm Dr. Baird, ortho. Stab wound to the left deltoid region. Still conscious, yes?"

I blink. "Barely. But give me five minutes."

He smiles faintly. "Good. If sarcasm is intact, then you're not circling the drain."

He helps me sit up, propped at an angle against the pillows, then moves closer. With clinical detachment, he peels back the dressing Kara applied and inspects the wound. "You hated your first day in the ER that much, huh? Decided to take on a mad man." He prods lightly at the edges. "It's superficial in terms of depth—no obvious damage to major vessels, tendons, or bone. You're lucky. Another inch and you'd be meeting the ortho team under much grimmer circumstances."

"So, no surgery?"

"Nope," he responds. "You're stable. This isn't life-threatening, but we need to keep the antibiotics going, and keep it clean."

He glances at Zac, who's standing to the side, tense and silent, bloodstained hands resting on his hips. The surgeon raises an eyebrow.

"You want to do the superficial layers?" he asks Zac like he's a second-year resident instead of the department head. "You've got the hands. Unless you've forgotten how to suture, it's not exactly heart surgery."

Zac doesn't answer—just levels him with a glare that says, "fuck you" louder than words ever could.

I bite back a smile. This guy's hilarious. Either he's messing with us, or he somehow missed that Zac's not only the head of the ER—he's a world-class cardiothoracic surgeon, too.

Dr. Baird turns back to me with a smirk. "You trust him?"

I look at Zac.

More than anyone.

"Yeah," I say softly. "I do." My smile breaks free.

"I'll leave you to it, then. Go home, get some rest—at least a full week to recover before you're back on duty."

He gives us one more glance, then disappears behind the curtain.

And just like that, it's quiet again.

Zac steps to the sink, scrubbing with a focus that feels more like penance than hygiene.

"If I ever turn into a smug, smartass surgeon like him, you have full permission to slap me. Hard and preferably in public. What an absolute cockhead."

I burst out laughing.

He disinfects the wound with quiet precision. Palpates the skin with gloved fingers that shake just enough for me to notice. His eyes stay on my shoulder, not on me. But I'm watching him.

The tension in his neck. The strain in his eyes. The way he won't look at my face while he's doing this.

"Local," he informs me, lifting a syringe. "You'll feel a sting."

Understatement of the year.

He injects it before I can steel myself, and the burn makes me hiss.

"Sorry," he murmurs, and he means it.

But he still doesn't look up. He keeps his gaze on the wound, on the instruments, on anything but my face.

He threads the needle slowly. His gloved hands are practiced but not steady. The tremble in his grip isn't surgical—it's personal. His brows are drawn. There's blood dried along the curve of his jaw, and I want to reach for a cloth and clean it, but I don't move.

"Hold still," he commands. But I think it's more for him than me.

I don't move.

He doesn't, either.

His fingers hover a half-second longer than necessary before he touches me. When he finally begins, it's with the reverence of someone touching something precious.

The thread pulls tight. The silence pulls tighter.

And somehow, it's more intimate than our time together at Eden. This is devotion.

He works quietly and carefully.

"You're doing fine," he praises softly.

"Are you?" It slips out before I can stop it.

He doesn't answer right away. He pauses mid-stitch, shoulders tight, head bowed.

"Not really."

I nod.

Fair.

"Your hands are shaking," I add.

"I know."

"How many more?"

"I've done four. Four more to go."

"Want me to count them with you?"

That gets me a faint exhale—might've been a laugh. "I'm good."

"All right." I close my eyes. "But I'm counting in my head anyway. For morale."

The next few seconds pass with only the sound of thread through skin and Zac's breathing.

"How long were you together?" I ask suddenly, blinking my eyes open, fixing them on the ceiling.

"Since we were kids," he answers. "We met in high school. In the band. She played the flute and hated the brass section. Said we were too loud."

I smile faintly. "What did you play?"

"Trumpet," he admits. "Badly."

"Figures." I let out a short, dry laugh.

"She used to make me mix tapes. Labeled them by mood. One said, 'For when you forget what the sky looks like.' I still have it."

I swallow.

"She sounds wonderful."

"She was."

I look down, and he's finished the fifth stitch.

"I wasn't ready to lose her. I think part of me still isn't."

I nod slowly, still not looking at him. "That's okay."

"It doesn't feel okay."

"It's not supposed to."

The skin pulls together as I feel the tug of him placing the sixth suture. Then the seventh.

"She didn't want kids," he continues softly. "We were going to adopt. She wanted the kind of family you choose."

Finally, I dare to look at his face.

"I think she would've liked you," he adds.

"Then I wish I'd met her."

The last stitch goes in.

He snips the end and cleans the site once more. After applying a clean bandage, he tapes it gently in place.

"Done."

His hands are finally steady, but only because they've finished the job. He strips off the gloves and scrubs his hands raw at the sink. Water splashes over the basin, trails across the floor. When he looks back, he's wearing the same expression I've seen on people who survived the worst day of someone else's life.

Guilt dressed as composure.

"I should've made you leave," he says.

"We've been over this."

"I know. But—" He shakes his head.

"There's nothing you could have said or done that would have made me leave," I say with conviction carved into bone. Because I mean it. I'm not going anywhere.

He sinks into the chair beside the bed.

"It wasn't just that," he explains.

I tilt my head. "Then what?"

He looks at me. His eyes are bloodshot, the rims red, irises glassy.

"I was terrified."

"Of the bomb?"

He shakes his head. "Of you dying."

Oh.

He looks down at his hands again.

"I could survive everything else. But not that."

I reach over, brush my fingers against his.

"I didn't," I remind him. "I'm still here."

"But I watched you bleed."

"And you stopped it."

"I watched him stab you."

"And I didn't break."

That gets his attention, and he looks at me again.

"You didn't," he echoes.

I nod. "Because I wasn't alone."

And for the first time since we left Trauma One, I see my Zac returning. He exhales like it's the first breath he's let himself take in hours. Shoulders down. Head bowed.

"I've watched a lot of people die," he tells me.

His gaze is distant, aimed somewhere past the curtain, past the present.

"I've called TOD on strangers, on kids whose names I never learned. I've coded and zipped up people I trained beside. I once wrote a discharge note for a man who died on the toilet while I was arguing with radiology."

A breath escapes him—almost a laugh. But it's hollow. Empty.

"None of it touched me the way this did." His voice is quieter now. "The thought of losing you. I couldn't bear it, not again."

My throat tightens. I don't speak. I tighten my grip, linking our fingers more firmly.

He doesn't flinch. Doesn't resist. He lets me be there for him.

"I assumed I was already broken," he explains. "That there wasn't anything left to lose. But then you stayed. And I realized—I've been lying to myself since the day I lost her."

He squeezes my fingers.

"I've been scared of this." His words come out shakily. "Of you. Of how much space you take up in my chest. It's not adrenaline talking. It's you."

He leans forward, and I meet him halfway, resting my head on his shoulder. He exhales, a tremor splitting it.

"You were the first thing that felt real after everything," he says. "What if I had lost you?"

I tilt my face toward his. "You didn't," I remind him. "You didn't lose me."

"I want you," he states. "Not just at Eden. Not just when we're bleeding or barely holding it together. I want the version of us that exists outside all of this. When it's only... us."

I meet his eyes.

"You were right to be scared," I say.

He flinches. "Don't."

"I was scared, too."

He holds my gaze.

"Not just of the bomb," I explain. "Or the knife. Or what could've gone wrong. I was scared because I realized how much I wanted to live. And how much of that..." I pause. "How much of that is because of you."

He goes still.

"I was in that room because I chose to be," I say. "And I'd choose it again."

"Even if it killed you?"

"Yes." I don't hesitate. "Because I'd rather bleed next to you than be safe without you."

"Jesus, Chloe…"

"I mean it."

"I know." His voice is hoarse. "That's what terrifies me."

"I think that's what love is."

That stops him cold.

I don't say it for effect. I say it because it's time.

It's been circling within me for weeks now, tightening like a noose every time I tried to deny it. It's not some dramatic realization or some spontaneous confession brought on by trauma. It's the truth. And I'm done pretending.

He leans forward again, elbows on his knees.

"You can't love me," he tells me softly.

"You don't get to decide that."

"I'm broken."

"So am I."

"I carry ghosts, Chloe."

"So do I."

"I couldn't save her. I couldn't—" He cuts himself off and runs a hand over his face. "I can't lose someone again."

"I know," I soothe. "But you didn't lose me."

"I almost did."

"But you didn't," I repeat firmly. "You didn't."

He looks at me, eyes glassy. His fingers drag over the stubble on his jaw, down to the back of his neck. He closes his eyes, pained.

"I don't know how to do this," he whispers. "I was fine being alone. I'd gotten used to it. And then *you* happened."

"Then we figure it out," I reply. "Together."

He opens his eyes and stares like he's still waiting for the catch.

"Are you sure?"

I nod. "More sure than I've ever been."

Zac leans forward. Slowly. His fingers ghost over my cheek before they settle, warm and trembling. I swear his touch makes me ache in a different way.

When his lips meet mine, it isn't with the heat we've known before. It's not desperate or hungry.

It's reverent. With the care you'd whisper into the dark.

He pulls away, his forehead rests against mine, and we stay like that—breath mingling, hearts slowing, no words spoken because none are needed.

I close my eyes and let the moment anchor me. In my heart. In my bones. In the part of me I used to keep closed off. The part I protected like it was a fortress because I thought needing someone made me weak.

Now I understand—letting someone in isn't a sign of fragility. It's choosing to feel, even when that terrifies you. Love doesn't stop the bleeding. It means you don't have to bleed alone.

His breath fans warm against my skin.

"Still scared?" I whisper.

He nods, his voice a low rasp. "Yeah. But I'm done running from it."

I reach for his hand. Link our fingers.

"Me too," I agree. And I mean it with everything I am.

Chapter Thirty

Chloe

Present, 10 p.m.

The weirdest part isn't that I almost died. It's how fast the hospital forgets it happened.

By the time I swing my legs off the bed, the shift change has already started. Someone's already disinfected the floor I bled on. A junior doctor strolls past eating a granola bar, scrolling through his phone. No one would guess this place was evacuated just hours ago.

That's the ER for you. Crisis cleaned up before the coffee brews.

When I ease upright, every part of me protests. My shoulder throbs in slow, mean waves. My joints creak. My eyelids feel sandpapered. But I'm standing. I'm not dead and that's got to count for something.

Zac's hand reaches out, palm up.

I slide mine into his.

And we fit.

I stare at our joined hands. His fingers laced through mine is something stupidly normal. Strangely domestic. We could be heading to brunch; instead, we're shuffling away, battered and bruised.

"You ready?" he asks.

"God, yes," I exhale.

We step into the corridor together, fingers still linked, and my stomach somersaults. He hasn't let me go. Not even with everyone watching.

Fresh-faced staff move past us—scrubs still crisp, ponytails high, sneakers still white.

A few people glance our way. One nurse gives a quick nod—half sympathy, half *glad it wasn't me.*

I probably look like hell.

Hair wild, dried blood streaks down my arm, scrubs torn at the shoulder and soaked through in patches.

Zac doesn't look much better. He's still in the same stained scrubs. His jaw's tight, his neck mottled from stress. But he walks beside me, not afraid of showing everyone he's with me.

We pass Central, where Olivia's aggressively shaking cinnamon into her coffee.

"You two finally heading out?"

Zac nods. "Trying to."

Her eyes flick to our joined hands. "Hydrate. Sleep. Maybe try therapy. Or tequila. Either one."

"Why not both?" I mutter.

"I like the way you think." She winks.

I manage a small smile.

Then Olivia smirks, eyes gleaming. "Now, tell lover boy to bring you back in one piece. I'm not pulling a double shift because you two thought near-death was foreplay."

Zac coughs a laugh. I squeeze his hand tighter.

We're almost at the exit when I spot Jax by the vending machines, squinting at the choices.

"Give me a second." I look up at Zac.

He nods and hangs back.

I approach Jax, and he glances over, raising a brow. "You're still upright. Impressive."

"Barely." I ease myself onto the bench beside the machine. "Trying not to leak out of my bandage."

He chuckles and crouches to retrieve two water bottles from the slot at the bottom, then joins me on the bench.

"Hydration," he says, handing one over. "Doctor's orders."

I accept it and twist off the cap, the cool condensation making my fingers slippery. "Thanks." I take a long sip and exhale. The corridor's quieter now.

"You all right?" he asks casually, but he's watching me closely. He already knows the answer, but he wants to see if I'll say it out loud.

"I will be," I share after a pause.

He bobs his head and looks away, tapping his fingers against his thigh. "That was a shitty day."

"That's one word for it."

"Not exactly how I pictured our first shift going."

"Same," I say. "I was hoping for a celebratory muffin."

He chuckles, then sobers up. "You scared the shit out of us, you know."

"Yeah. I scared the shit out of me, too."

Another long pause stretches. Then he turns slightly toward me.

"You and Zac," he begins. "You're a thing now?"

I glance down at the water bottle in my hands, turning it over once. "We're figuring it out."

"You know how it's gonna look, right?" he asks gently. "Intern with the head of department? People are gonna talk."

I look up at him. "I didn't plan on this. I didn't even know he worked here. But..." I exhale and reach up to smooth the frizz in my hair. "We'll find a way."

Jax studies me a moment longer, then shrugs. "As long as they've stopped talking about me face-planting in Trauma, I'm good."

I snort. "Please. I'm happy to take the heat. Consider it a public service."

Then he grins. "Sienna's gonna have a field day with this."

"Oh, *I know*," I groan. "She's gonna make us a group chat. And memes. Probably merch."

"She's already designing a logo."

I shake my head, but the smile won't leave my face.

He nudges me lightly, avoiding my shoulder. "Just... be careful, okay?"

"I will."

We sit there for a moment in the quietness of the corridor. Then I rise, slow and stiff, my shoulder protesting. Jax stands with me, offering a quiet nod.

"Rest up. Catch you next week?"

"I'll be here."

I turn to the exit with Zac by my side, the hospital doors sliding open with a soft sigh.

Outside, the sky is ink black, the moon and stars smothered in clouds.

The parking lot is empty, and we cross in silence. Zac's thumb brushes over mine as we walk. He hasn't said much since we left the bay, but his presence is louder than words.

As we reach the edge of the lot, he stops.

"You okay?" I wait, brows drawing together.

He shifts to face me, our hands still linked. His mouth twitches, trying to fight a smile.

"Wanna go on a date?"

I blink. "Sorry—what?"

He smiles—a little. That lazy, sideways thing he does. "Let's go on a date. Right now."

I stare at him. "Is this a joke? After the day we just had?"

His voice drops low. "Why not? Life's too fucking short, and I've been waiting months for you to make the first move, and it turns out"—he squeezes my hand—"you're too chicken shit. So. Here we are."

My mouth drops open. "I am not—"

He lifts a finger to gently press it against my lips. "Shhh. You're adorable when you lie."

I laugh despite myself. Exhausted and aching, but laughing somehow.

He grins. "My place. I'll make you a late dinner—a gourmet, medically approved purée."

"If you serve me soup with a straw, I'm walking into traffic," I warn.

He chuckles. "Then we'll crash. No phones. No pagers. No alarms. Only you and me, passed out in my Californian king, drifting off into oblivion."

That. Sounds. Fucking. Amazing.

"Is it weird that I think that's the sexiest thing you've ever said?"

He leans in, mouth brushing my ear. "And when we wake up... I'm gonna fuck you like you've never been fucked before. I'll show you *exactly* what it feels like to fuck when you're in love."

My brain short-circuits.

Did he—

Was that—

He pulls back, eyes locked on mine.

"I love you, Chloe. So fucking much."

My heart lurches. I don't breathe.

He said it. He actually said it.

Zac surges forward, tugging me by my good arm, his grin breaking wide and real across his face.

"Let's get the hell out of here."

And we do.

Hand in hand.

Bruised and bandaged, but moving forward—with every scar out in the open.

CHAPTER THIRTY-ONE

Chloe

Twelve Weeks Later

We should be getting ready.

Our clothes are still folded at the edge of the bed—my top borrowed from Zac's drawer, his pants draped over the chair, belt looped through, button undone, forgotten.

But instead of dressing, I'm face-down in the sheets, knees tucked under me, arms stretched out to the headboard. Zac's hand anchors my hip; the other's tangled in my hair, keeping me where he wants me as he drives into me hard and fast and entirely without mercy.

I'm *moaning* for it.

"Zac," I gasp. "We're gonna be late—"

"I said, five more minutes," he growls. His tone—dark silk and gravel—slides down my spine. "You can take it, little one."

He pulls back slow, cruelly slow, until I whimper—then slams in again, harder, sending the headboard into the wall. Again. And again.

"You're always saying we don't have time," he mutters, lips grazing my ear. "But your cunt's calling bullshit."

"Zac—" My voice breaks on a sob.

He stills just long enough to hiss, "Try again."

Right. Rules.

"Zaddy," I rasp, wrecked and breathless.

His groan rips through him. "That's more like it."

He grabs my wrists and presses them to the mattress beside my head, fucking me like it's the only language we speak. Deep, ruthless strokes that pull me apart and rebuild me in the shape of this—*of us.*

"Fuck," he hisses, pace faltering. "You're dripping. Want me to fill you up before we go?"

The words are primal, and I soak them up, my body caving toward his.

"Yes," I pant. "Please."

I'm trembling—shaking beneath him, desperate for release. And when it comes, it's not a climax. It's a full-body collapse. A surrender.

Seconds later, he follows, cursing, hips jerking, teeth grazing my shoulder as he spills into me. He lowers himself over me, his body molding to mine. The only sounds are our breaths—ragged, uneven—and the thump of his heart against my back.

I smile into the sheets.

He presses a kiss to my shoulder, then another to my spine.

"Now," he whispers, "we're really late."

I roll onto my side, grinning. "I'm telling her it was your fault."

He wipes the sweat from his brow with the back of his hand, mouth curling. "Worth it."

I stretch, lazy and content, and feel him dripping down my thighs. He sees it too and smirks, smug and satisfied.

Totally worth it.

We pull into the cemetery, tires crunching over the gravel. Zac kills the engine, but neither of us moves. Through the windshield, the morning light filters across the rows of headstones, making them glow a little. It's still in a deliberate way. Even the wind knows not to be loud here.

I rest my hand on the door handle, but don't open it. Zac's staring straight ahead, unreadable. I give him a moment.

And in the quiet, my mind drifts—twelve weeks back, to the shift from hell.

To the blood, the blade, the bomb.

I made it through my ER rotation. I don't know if emergency medicine is where I'll end up, but I got through it. Took the hits, logged the hours, figured out how to build boundaries and keep myself intact. I'll need those skills on Monday when I start pediatrics with Jax. Thankfully, Sienna got shuffled into a different rotation.

Some nights, I think about Borris. My first loss. He came in with abdominal pain and left zipped up in a bag. It wasn't only gallstones. It was his heart giving out quietly, without warning. But knowing that doesn't make it sting any less.

I went to a Russian restaurant last week. Ordered pelmeni in his honor. I knew it wouldn't taste the way it would if he'd made it—but it felt right. A quiet toast to someone I only knew for a few minutes and still think about more than I should.

Zac found his way back to surgery. Back to the OR where he belongs. He needed the ER first—to fall apart, to remember who he is when the noise dies down and to put him back together again. But above all, to be the surgeon he used to be—only better. He's not the same man who walked into that trauma room months ago. He's more... whole.

I take a breath, push the door open, and step out into the morning air.

The grass is damp under our shoes, the air crisp with eucalyptus, cut lawn, and wet earth. Kind of peaceful, actually.

We walk between rows of marble, hand in hand. Zac carries the bouquet—jasmine, deep pink gardenias, and a stem of freesia I tucked in before we left. They're not traditional. But they feel right.

We stop in front of her grave. He doesn't speak—just hands me the flowers.

I crouch.

CASEY LYNN BENNETT

BELOVED WIFE, DAUGHTER, AND FRIEND.

LOVE FIERCELY. LOVE WELL.

The lettering is simple. Elegant. True to what I imagine of her, if Zac's stories are anything to go by.

I brush a brittle leaf off the edge of the stone.

"Hi, Casey. It's good to finally meet you."

Zac stands behind me. His warm hand settles on my shoulder.

"I didn't know you," I say, "but I've gotten to know your husband. And I wanted to say thank you. For loving him. For shaping him. For holding a space in his heart until he was ready again."

Zac makes a quiet sound behind me. I glance back—his eyes are glassy. He crouches beside me, and together we place the flowers on her grave.

We don't speak. The silence says enough.

Zac reaches for my hand, his fingers wrapping around mine. His thumb moves in slow, thoughtful circles over my skin.

"I don't feel bad," I murmur.

He glances at me. "For what?"

"For showing up like this... with your cum soaked into my panties."

Zac blinks.

Then he laughs—startled and helpless. It breaks across him like light.

"She'd have loved that," he says eventually.

"She'd better," I reply, lips twitching. "Because I'm not sorry."

"No," he sobers. "You shouldn't be."

She's not a ghost between us. She is a part of him. And I don't fear that.

I'm grateful.

Because without Casey, I wouldn't have *this* Zac. *My* Zac. The one who walked through hell and came out the other side. The one who chose life again—who chose me.

I run my fingertips over the carved letters. Not as an intrusion. As a thank you.

"For giving me him," I whisper.

Zac hears it. I feel it in his grip.

He leans forward, kisses his fingers, and presses them to her stone.

"Thank you, Case," he says softly. "For letting me go."

We rise together, fingers still locked, and move forward. We're not leaving the past behind, but bringing it with us.

EPILOGUE

Chloe

Six Weeks Later

Somewhere nearby, a phone blares "Baby Shark." I can't help myself; I start doing the motions. A couple of nurses pass me, chuckling. I shimmy in response. *No shame.*

Pediatrics is fun. Way more colorful than the ER—and way more brutal. There's a cartoon tiger grinning above the nurses' station, a stash of coloring books by the sink, and a rainbow of plastic chairs.

"You're a natural," Olivia had said when I told her about the rotation. "Smart, empathetic, and unfazed by bodily fluids. Perfect fit."

Turns out, she was right. In six weeks, I've witnessed more tantrums, tickle fights, and weaponized snot than I ever thought possible. One toddler swallowed a LEGO because his sister promised it would turn him into a Transformer. I can confirm, it didn't.

I find Jax in the playroom, paper crown askew, stuffed animals fanned around him like a plush royal court.

"Queen Chloe," he booms. "Come to dethrone me at last?"

A six-year-old girl with a nasal cannula giggles.

I curtsy. "Your reign of juice-box tyranny ends today."

Jax springs to his feet. "Your patient is waiting to obliterate you at Connect Four."

"I was born ready."

We make our rounds. I check vitals; Jax distracts the children with dance moves so ridiculous they should be illegal. Somehow, it works. We're a well-balanced team.

It's just past noon when I step out for lunch. I'm halfway to the cafeteria when I hear his voice.

"Dr. Monroe."

I turn, already smiling.

Zac's standing there, coffee cup in one hand, brown paper bag in the other, sunglasses tucked into the open collar of his button-down. He's stupidly attractive.

"Fancy seeing you here," I joke.

"I heard pediatrics had a goddess on staff. Had to see for myself."

I roll my eyes, but my smile's stuck. "Lunch?"

He holds up the bag. "Luna's Pizza."

My heart actually flutters. "Extra thin crust?"

"Half cheese. Half pineapple."

I gasp. "Have I told you that I love you lately?"

"Not nearly enough." He leans in, gives me a quick, familiar kiss that still makes my knees weak.

We snag a spot at a tiny garden table under a hibiscus bush, which is valiantly pretending it's not dying, and dig in. I'm halfway through my cheese slice when I instinctively go for the pineapple on the other slice.

Zac raises an eyebrow. "Really?"

"What?"

He leans over and plucks it from my fingers, popping it into his mouth.

"Why did you order pineapple, then?"

"For me. Not for you to eat, you shameless food thief."

I blink. *Okay. Rude.* Also, fair. The promise of pineapple sweetness completely distracted me.

Zac sighs, exasperated. "You're a menace."

I grin, licking a smudge of sauce off my thumb. "Yeah, but I'm your menace."

The sun's warm. My stomach's full. And I'm feeling great.

Even if I flirted with death by pineapple. Again.

Some girls never learn.

Good thing I've got a doctor who makes house calls.

Craving more Chloe & Zac?

Sign up for Jade May's newsletter and get instant access to an exclusive 5K bonus story—featuring Chloe's birthday dinner, a private jet, strip poker at 30,000 feet, and a romantic escape to Italy with Zac.

And yes... *that* romantic Italian escape? You'll see it again in Book 4, *Unleashed by Eden*—Carter & Violet's story.

Simply scan the QR code below.

Also by Jade May

Eden Series

Tempted by Eden

Seduced by Eden

Devoured by Eden

Unleashed by Eden

About The Author

Jade May is an international bestselling author of angst-filled, high-heat romances laced with kink—where the tension runs deep, the chemistry runs hot, and happily ever after is always guaranteed.

Jade is also a passionate advocate for people with disabilities and those suffering from chronic illnesses. She has been featured in several major Australian media outlets speaking about the power of romance fiction to help people with disabilities awaken their sexuality and cope with chronic pain. Inspiring others to embrace their desires and live their best lives through her fiction is a dream come true for Jade.

She lives in sunny Sydney with her two favorite humans: her husband and son.

Connect with Jade

Sign up to Jade's newsletter for the latest news on releases, giveaways and previews of covers and exclusive book art!

www.authorjademay.com

@authorjademay